Praise for Sharon Ward

Sharon Ward's IN DEEP is a stellar, pulse-pounding debut novel featuring a female underwater photographer. A heady mix of underwater adventure, mystery, and romance.

— Hallie Ephron, New York Times bestselling author

Pack your SCUBA fins for a wild trip to the Cayman Islands. *In Deep* delivers on twists and turns while introducing a phenomenal new protagonist in underwater photographer Fin Fleming, tough, perceptive and fearless.

— Edwin Hill, author of *The Secrets We Share*

How much did I love In Deep? Let me count the ways. Fin Fleming, underwater photographer, is a courageous yet vulnerable protagonist I want to sip Margaritas with. The Cayman Islands are exotic and alluring, yet tinged with danger. The underwater scenes and SCUBA diving details are rendered in stunning detail. Wrap that all into a thrilling mystery and you'll be left as breathless as - well, no spoilers here. You must read it to find out!

— C. Michele Dorsey, Author of the Sabrina Salter Mysteries: No Virgin Island, Permanent Sunset, and Tropical Depression

Breathtaking on two levels, Sharon Ward's debut novel IN DEEP will captivate experienced divers as well as those who've only dreamed of exploring the beauty beneath the sea. The underwater world off the Cayman Islands is stunningly rendered, and the complex mystery involving underwater photographer Fin Fleming, especially the electrifying dive scenes, will have readers holding their breath. Brava!

— Brenda Buchanan Author of the Joe Gale Mystery Series

In Deep is a smart and original story that sucks you in from page one. Edge-of-your-seat suspense, a hauntingly realistic villain, and a jaw-dropping twist make this pacy read unputdownable until the very last word.

— Stephanie Scott-Snyder, Author of When Women Offend: Crime and the Female Perpetrator

Killer Storm

Killer Storm

The Fin Fleming Scuba Diving Series

Sharon Ward

 PENSTER PRESS

Covers by Milagraphicartist.com

ISBN eBook: 978-1-958478-01-1

ISBN Trade Paper: 978-1-958478-02-8

ISBN Hard Cover: 978-1-958478-03-5

Printed in USA

First Edition

For Jack, World's Best Husband

Milan, welcome to the family

Erin L, Scott, Taylor, Cameron, Erin R, Colin, Josh, Jen, Ryleigh/Parker &
Isaac—Love you all

Molly, world's best dachshund

Contents

Foreword

Thank you to everyone who has followed Fin's adventures. She and I both appreciate it.

For those of you who have pointed out that an Atlantic Pygmy octopus like Rosie would only have a twelve to eighteen month life span—thank you. I already knew this, but because so many people were upset about the death of Harry the stingray, I decreed Rosie to be immortal.

If that's too far-fetched, think of her like the dog owned by Robert B. Parker's Spenser. Pearl has been with Spenser since the beginning. Once she reaches the end of her days, Spenser gets another dog just like her and names her Pearl. Not Pearl Two. Just Pearl.

Assume Fin has done the same thing with Rosie.

Also, please remember Fin is a professional diver, certified in all kinds of technical diving categories well beyond the training and experience of recreational divers. If you're a diver, don't do what Fin does. Stay within the bounds of your training.

Foreword

Always plan your dive and dive your plan. Don't dive alone. Don't dive too deep. Don't use mixed gases unless you've been trained. But have fun. Diving is a blast!

Chapter 1
8 hours ago

S TORM ADVISORY BULLETIN
HURRICANE WILLARD ADVISORY NUMBER 38

NWS TPC/NATIONAL HURRICANE CENTER MIAMI FL

DANGEROUS HURRICANE WILLARD THREATENS THE CAYMAN ISLANDS. PREPARATIONS TO PROTECT LIFE AND PROPERTY SHOULD BE RUSHED TO COMPLETION. MAXIMUM SUSTAINED WINDS HAVE INCREASED TO MORE THAN 135/156 KM/HR WITH HIGHER GUSTS. THIS IS CATEGORY FIVE ON THE SAFFIR-SIMPSON HURRICANE SCALE. SOME FLUCTUATIONS IN INTENSITY ARE LIKELY DURING THE NEXT 24 HOURS.

HURRICANE FORCE WINDS EXTEND OUTWARD UP TO 90 MILES /150 KM FROM THE CENTER AND TROPICAL STORM FORCE WINDS EXTEND OUTWARD UP TO 175 MILES /280 KM.

STORM SURGE FLOODING OF 8 TO 25 FEET ABOVE NORMAL TIDE LEVELS ALONG WITH LARGE AND DANGEROUS BATTERING WAVES CAN BE EXPECTED THROUGHOUT THE CAYMAN ISLANDS DEPENDING ON THE EXACT TRACK OF WILLARD.

RAINFALL AMOUNTS OF 12 TO 30 INCHES POSSIBLY CAUSING LIFE-THREATENING FLASH FLOODS AND MUD SLIDES CAN BE EXPECTED ALONG THE PATH OF WILLARD

Chapter 2
6:30 AM

I tossed the storm advisory aside. It was ominous, but our preparations were well underway at this point.

Just to confirm that in my own mind, I looked out my open office window at the increasingly angry sea, watching Stewie, RIO's director of dive operations, supervising the removal of all our boats to send them to drydock. The ocean swells had grown overnight, and whitecaps were licking at the top of RIO's dock. The sky was a looming grey, and there was a bite to the breeze unusual for Grand Cayman.

The smell of hot coffee made me turn around.

"Dr. Fleming, you're in early," Benjamin Brooks, RIO's CFO, said, sliding a steaming cup onto my desk. He smiled, and I realized again how lucky I was to have him as a friend and sort of boyfriend. He was more than a friend although less than a soulmate. I enjoyed his company, but I always held him at arm's length even though he'd made it clear he wanted more. Not for the first time, I wished my best friend Theresa was around so we could talk about my confused feelings. Unfortunately, she and her husband Gus were traveling in Europe on Fleming Environmental Investments business.

I returned Benjamin's smile. "More like I stayed late. I've been here all night," I replied as I popped the lid off the coffee. "Thanks for this. You can't imagine how much I need it."

"Finola Fleming, you can't keep burning the candle at both ends. It's time to tell Maddy you need an assistant."

The 'Maddy' he referred to is my mother, Madelyn Anderson Russo, the founder of the Russo Institute of Oceanography, which we called RIO for short. I'd spent my childhood in the corridors at RIO or on the research vessel *Omega*, and since everyone around me called her Maddy, I'd always called her that too.

I'd been working long hours at RIO covering for Maddy, its absent director and a world famous oceanographer on the order of one of the Cousteau clan or Sylvia Earle. I was so tired the thought of breakfast and some quiet time in my cozy home on Rum Point on the North Side of Grand Cayman made me sigh with longing.

Benjamin was always thoughtful, and he immediately recognized the depths of my exhaustion. "But right now, you need a break. C'mon. Let's get some breakfast and then I'll drive you home before the storm hits."

My official job at RIO was supposed to be VP of marketing and chief underwater photographer, but with Maddy away working with the folks at the Woods Hole Oceanography Institute on a joint project, my workload had increased exponentially. I'd been struggling to keep my head above water, and that had never happened to me before.

I already held down several jobs, each with a demanding load of details, but usually I handled my varied workload with ease. Now I was feeling overwhelmed, which was even more galling because the mountain of desk work had kept me from diving for the last several days. I was feeling the stress of being away from the ocean in addition to the work overload.

I sighed. "Sorry, Benjamin. I can't take time for breakfast. I've got to finish this spreadsheet today. And thanks for the offer, but I won't need a ride home. I'll be staying here through the storm. I have to make sure the research labs are okay."

"Fin, you've turned into a drone. You used to be fun." His words were said lightly, but I could hear the concern behind his teasing.

I looked at him over the tops of my new glasses. I'd been spending so much time on my computer lately that my eyes were feeling the strain. Then I looked back at my screen where I'd been working on finalizing RIO's budget for next year. It's a well-known fact that I hate spreadsheets. And numbers. "I have to finish RIO's budget for the next fiscal year. We need to have it ready for the board of directors meeting."

Benjamin cleared his throat. "Too bad RIO doesn't have an accomplished and highly experienced CFO on the staff to do those budgets for you."

Benjamin was RIO's CFO, and he was definitely accomplished and highly experienced. But my fatal flaw—or at least one of them—is assuming everything is my responsibility, and because of that assumption, I tend to take on too much. I realized I should have delegated this project to him weeks ago.

When he saw the realization hit me, he laughed. "And I believe I'm supposed to be the chief number cruncher around here. You're the creative genius. Don't waste your time messing around with spreadsheets instead of doing what you do best. You should be in the ocean, taking beautiful photographs, not sitting inside crunching numbers."

He walked around my desk to peer at my screen. "Departmental budgets? Piece of cake. Let me handle them." His fingers hovered a half inch above the keyboard of my Mac. "May I?"

I shrugged and swiveled the computer toward him. His fingers flew across the keys as he emailed the much-despised spreadsheets to himself. "I'll have them back to you by end of the day. Now let's go. Time for breakfast."

I'd always loved my job at RIO, mainly because it required me to dive every day, but lately, I'd felt chained to my desk. My mother had turned most of the day-to-day operation of RIO over to me last year while she'd been living in New York City. And now this new project with Woods Hole was taking up all her time, and she'd hardly set foot on Grand Cayman in almost a year.

Plus, my father, Newton Fleming, had asked me to keep an eye on the operations of his business, Fleming Environmental Investments, while he too spent time in the states. At least his assistant, Justin Nash, handled most of Newton's company's routine decisions, and my brother Oliver was working there part time when he wasn't at school in New York. That meant I only had to get involved in the really big issues. But the ocean is my happy place and sitting out my life on dry land had never been part of my plan.

Still, I had responsibilities. "There's a storm coming," I said. "It could be dangerous. I need to stay here."

"The latest predictions say the storm will miss us. And anyway, danger is your middle name," said Benjamin.

"Not so," I said, flipping the paper with the latest advisory his way. "Hurricane Willard is coming on with a vengeance."

Benjamin read the storm warning. "Yikes. Okay, I stand corrected. But anyway, I stopped by the dive shop on the way in. Stewie is already supervising the removal of all RIO's boats to drydock to wait out the storm. He's closed up the shop and put on the storm shutters. Eugene is buttoning up the main building, and per your orders, Vincent has taken the *Omega* out to deep water to ride out the storm. And since you're crazy busy here, I was afraid you'd forget about your own house. I sent a couple of the maintenance guys over to your place to put up the hurricane shutters and stow all your outdoor stuff in the cabana. You can relax. Even your home is safe. Everything is as ready as it can be. Let's go. You'll be able to relax once you get home."

"Thanks, Benjamin. I did forget about the outdoor furniture at home," I said. Now I was worried about what else I might have forgotten.

"Forgetting things isn't like you, Fin, You're usually on top of every detail. You have to get some help around here," Benjamin said. "You'll drive yourself into the ground."

"Okay, you're right." I held up my hands to stop any further arguments. "Let's get some breakfast from the café and then I'll go home." I dropped my blue-light glasses on my desk and slid my feet into the flipflops I'd kicked underneath.

When we reached the café, there was a sign on the door saying it was closed because of the storm. I'd given the order for RIO's café, gift shop, and aquarium to stay closed today when the storm seemed imminent. Another thing I should have remembered. Another oops. I rubbed my forehead in frustration.

I pulled the café's keys out of the pocket of my cargo shorts. "I guess, we'll have to make our own breakfast."

We settled for toast and another cup of coffee, then we donned the traditional sailor's yellow rain gear and walked out the back door of the RIO building onto the crushed shell paths leading to the onsite dive shop, the picnic area, and RIO's marina. I nodded approvingly when I noticed Stewie had already stowed away the picnic tables from the lawn and closed the storm shutters on the dive shop.

The team of contractors from the drydock boat storage facility was busy hauling all RIO's boats out of the water, but they paused a minute to don their own raingear before going back to work loading the boats on the carrier. It looked like they'd have all our boats out of the water in plenty of time to beat the full fury of the gathering storm.

The first drops of rain were beginning to fall, and according to the weather reports, it would be a deluge before long. The early raindrops were already big and hard and felt like angry pellets smashing into my skin. If this was any indication of the fury of the coming storm, we were in for a bad day. Despite the rain, Benjamin and I continued across the lawn to check in with Stewie, who had recently taken over dive shop operations.

Stewie's return from rehab several months ago had been a piece of unexpected good luck. He was a huge help to me now that he was clean and sober, and I hoped he could stay that way for good.

He turned and smiled at me when I entered. As I did whenever I saw him, I discreetly checked him out for any signs of a relapse, but his weathered face looked lean and healthy under the brim of the hood of his yellow rain slicker.

He pulled the last knot tight around the tarp he'd used to cover the tank compressor. "That's done," he said dusting his palms on his T-shirt. "I think the shop is ready. I'll just go check with the boat handlers to make sure they're on schedule, and then we'll be all set to ride out the storm."

"Why don't you take off now, Stewie. You've been working all night and I want to be sure you get home before the storm hits," I said. "I can take care of anything else that comes up."

Stewie looked at the lowering sky and assessed the rising wind. "If you're sure it's okay, I wouldn't mind leaving now. It's been a long night."

"Go home and stay safe. Thank you for all your hard work coordinating the storm prep. I appreciate it."

He looked pleased at my words. "Fin, you be careful out here. This storm is a monster of a hurricane. Keep inside, out of the foul weather. And with a storm like this, conditions can change fast. Make sure you stay alert."

"Will do, Stewie."

Stewie had been one of my stepfather Ray Russo's closest friends, and he'd known me since I was a little girl. Sometimes he felt he had the right to remind me of safety rules even though I was his boss now. And I was a licensed technical diver, a certified PADI dive instructor, and a master boat captain. I do know my stuff.

But I don't mind his worrying. We've been through a lot together.

I took a deep breath of the ozone laden air. "You should go home too, Benjamin. It'll be much safer for you. You've never been through a tropical hurricane, and it can get pretty intense."

"All the more reason I should stay with you," he said. "I'm not leaving you here alone. No way. No how. Can't let anything happen to my best girl." He reached out to brush a raindrop off my cheek.

"Your car would be safer in your garage at home," I told him. "And you'd be safer there too. Since you haven't been through a storm like this, you may not realize how bad it can get."

"I do know how bad it can get, which is why I'm not leaving you here alone." Benjamin crossed his arms stubbornly. He had a habit of being a bit controlling and high-handed, reminding me unpleasantly of my ex-husband, Alec Stone. It was the reason I'd never let myself fall in love with him despite his efforts.

Or at least, it was one of the reasons. The other was Liam Lawton, but I try not to think about Liam too much.

After managing to evade the high collar of my rain slicker, an unpleasantly cold, fat raindrop slid down my neck and along my spine, making me shiver. I didn't want to waste time arguing about where Benjamin stayed during the storm, nor did I want to give in and let him stay with me.

I had no intention of going home and leaving RIO unattended, but I told him what he wanted to hear. "I'll go home if you'll go home," I said.

"Good. I'm ready." He pulled his car keys from a pocket in his shorts.

"You go on ahead. I need a minute to see Rosie and make sure everything is okay in the lab." Rosie is an Atlantic Pygmy octopus.

She'd been the subject of my doctoral thesis, but she later became more of a pet than a lab animal. I liked to think Rosie and I were friends as well as lab partners.

Benjamin looked suspicious at my change of heart, but he nodded. He and Stewie headed out to the parking lot and their cars. I watched them drive away before I went back inside, even though the rain was intensifying by the minute. On my way to the lab, I picked up my computer and rounded up a couple of flashlights from the supply closet in case of a power outage, although between the emergency generator and the massive battery backups for the lab and the infirmary, I was confident I wouldn't need the flashlights.

As I crossed the lobby, I noticed Ralph, our new security guard, biting his lip and watching the storm through the huge panes of glass that defined RIO's atrium.

"Ralph," I called to him. "Why don't you go home before the storm gets really bad? Nobody will be out in this weather. The building will be safe, and you should be with your family. I hear your new baby is due any day now, and your wife will want you with her."

"I don't know, Doctor Fleming. I don't want to leave you here all alone during the storm. Like you say, it could get bad."

"It's okay. What if your family needs you? If the baby comes, I'd rather you were at home with your wife than stranded here. You can go. And by the way, call me Fin." I smiled at him.

"Thanks" he said. "I think I will leave then if you're sure it's okay. My wife does get nervous in a storm, and now with the baby coming...." He crossed the lobby back to the guard room to grab his raincoat. "I'll see you later. And thanks for this."

I locked the front door behind him and continued heading for the research labs, a suite of windowless rooms located in the center of the building. As soon as I entered, I could tell that most of the sea creatures in the lab were edgy. They could sense the storm coming. Even Rosie didn't pop out of her shell when I approached.

Killer Storm

I sat down at one of the lab tables and since Benjamin had volunteered to do the budget spreadsheets, I decided to do something fun. I started working on a photo collage I'd wanted to put together for a new poster to sell in the gift shop.

After about ten minutes, I realized I needed some sketches I'd left in my office, so I left the lab to pick them up. When I glanced through the slats in the hurricane shutters that covered the huge windows in my office, I noticed the team from the drydock had left the marina.

I was still watching the gathering storm when a solitary figure in yellow rain ran down the dock and across the lawn toward the parking lot. I couldn't see the person's face or discern anything about them under the bulky slicker and baggy rain pants. I hoped whoever it was got home safely.

It took a moment before I realized a big problem—one boat had been left behind by the boat handlers. I raced to the back door between Maddy and Benjamin's offices to see if I could catch the team before they left, but they were long gone by the time I reached the door.

Peering through the raindrops, I noticed the storm surge had gotten worse just in the short time I'd been inside. Waves were crashing over the dock, and the solitary boat was straining at its lines. With a shock, I recognized it as my brother Oliver's new boat. I wondered why the boat handlers hadn't taken it along with all the others on the list I'd given them.

With a sinking feeling, I realized why this boat had been left behind. I had forgotten to add Oliver's boat to the list. He'd just bought it from a boatyard in New York, near where he attended college, a few days ago and had it delivered so it would be here waiting when his semester ended. He'd worked hard and saved up to buy it. If I didn't get it to safety, it would be smashed to bits against the dock or the nearby ironshore. If that disaster happened, it would be my fault. Another fine example of me screwing up by taking on too much.

Without thinking about the danger, I ran through the door and across the lawn. Waves crashed up onto the grass and washed across the wooden boards of the dock. The storm was getting worse, but I kept going. I was sure I'd be able to get the boat to deeper water and still get back to shore safely. I wasn't thinking of the danger to me, only of how hard Oliver had worked to buy the boat.

I jumped aboard and raced below to start the engines. I untied the mooring lines and backed out of the slip. The ocean tossed the boat like it was made of paper, and I had to grip the wheel hard to stay in control, but I was determined to save this boat because Oliver loved it.

Gunning the engine, I headed out to sea until I knew I was over deep water and with any luck, far enough from shore to keep the boat safe during the storm. I threw the anchor overboard and let out a long line to allow the boat to ride the swells, which were already about fifteen feet high, and getting higher by the minute.

My pulse pounded when I looked back at the dock. Knowing I'm a strong swimmer, I'd assumed I'd be able to make it back to land easily, but I hadn't realized how quickly the storm was intensifying. The shoreline was only a few hundred feet away, but it might as well have been miles. Yet the only way for me to get back to safety was to swim through the mounting turbulence.

In addition to being a strong swimmer, I'm a lucky one. My brother's dive gear was all set up in one of the tank racks near the swim platform in the back.

I threw on Oliver's buoyancy control device—his BCD—slid his mask over my face and stuck my feet into his full foot fins. I checked the tank's pressure gauge, and the tank was full, but because the storm was escalating so rapidly, I probably wouldn't have stopped to change it even if it had only held a breath or two of air. I was relieved to have the full tank, but even a partial fill would normally be enough to get me to shore. I stepped off the boat, knowing I'd have to drop below the surface as quickly as possible before I became disoriented by the wild sea.

Killer Storm

The water, normally warm and placid here in the Caymans, was like ice. As I'd expected, the waves were almost irresistible on the surface, and I was tossed around like a beach ball in the windstorm. As good a swimmer as I am, if I stayed on the surface, I knew I'd never make any headway against the ocean's might, even though the tide was coming in. My best hope was that the water was calmer at depth.

I dropped down to the bottom as quickly as I could. The tidal surge was almost as intense as the storm surge, moving me forward and backward at least fifteen or twenty feet with each pulse. Luckily, since the tide was heading in, my forward motion slightly exceeded the backward pull. I made slow but steady headway toward shore.

I held on to submerged rocks with all my strength to avoid losing ground to the ocean's pull when the waves receded, and I scurried toward shore as fast as I could when the tide surged ahead. The perilous journey was short in distance, but it seemed to take forever until at last, a wave broke over my head and I felt air against my skin. I was in the shallows.

I heaved my body up onto the dock, digging my fingers into the rough wood so the ocean couldn't pull me back. It took everything I had to stand up against the wind and the waves, but I did it. I tore off my borrowed dive gear, leaving it to the mercy of the ocean. I'd buy my brother a new rig when this storm was over, but the tank and BCD were too heavy and awkward to wear while fighting against the powerful wind. I'd need every ounce of strength I had to make it safely back to the building as it was.

If I made it back to the building.

I ran along the remains of the dock, sloshing through the rushing water sluicing over the boards. Waves crashed over the wood, pulling my feet out from under me with each step, the water trying to suck me back into its clutches. It was disorienting and made me dizzy, but to falter now meant certain death. I ran, bulling my way through buffeting winds so strong they felt like hitting a solid wall.

One more step. Another.

I felt grass under my bare feet, but my ordeal wasn't over. The waves had followed me across the dock, and they reached out with grasping fingers of cold water. My feet were frozen and numb. I pushed ahead, my bare feet sinking into sucking mud with each step. I crouched low, to make myself a smaller target for the wind and pushed ahead.

I was running as fast and as hard as I could but making very little progress. I couldn't —wouldn't—give up. I couldn't lift my head to check my position, but I knew I was less than fifty yards from the door to RIO and safety. It might as well have been miles. Each step felt like my last, but after every tortured footfall I sucked in a breath and mustered the resolve to take one more.

The visibility was terrible through the driving rain. I couldn't see even a few inches ahead of me. I stretched my arms out in front to prevent me from bumping into the building. It seemed like ages before my fingers touched the heavy, solid steel door, and I pulled it open. The wind took it from me and slammed it back against the concrete wall, knocking out a large chunk of cinderblock that must have weighed at least a pound or two. The furious wind picked up the mass of cement and carried it away before I could react. There was nothing I could do about the flying boulder except hope it didn't do any property damage or hurt anyone. I stepped inside and tried to shut the door.

The wind followed me in, pushing me back, the gusts making it almost impossible to pull the heavy door shut. After what felt like a lifetime, still shivering with fear and cold, inch by inch, I managed to get the door shut and locked.

Chapter 3
Killer Storm

I dragged my weary body down the corridor to my office to call Oliver and let him know what was going on with his boat. I could feel the window glass bowing under the force of the wind, even though the windows in my office were storm certified and sheltered behind clear hurricane shutters. It was only mid-morning, but it was almost as dark as night outside. The storm's noise was deafening, like the howling of ten thousand banshees.

The noise was so loud it would have been impossible to make a phone call. The windowless research labs, located in the center of the building, are connected to an uninterruptible power supply to keep the tank filters and aerators going in any weather. I could be assured of lights and electricity in there as well as a quiet place to make my call. I grabbed my phone and hurried down the dim hallway to call my brother and let him know about the danger to his boat. I wanted to reassure him that I'd take care of any damages since it was my fault the boat had been left to the ravages of the storm.

I didn't quite know what to say to Oliver when he answered the call, sounding muffled and sleepy.

"I'm sorry," I said. "This is all my fault."

"What is?" he said, still not sounding fully alert.

"I was in a hurry to get the list of boats to the dry dock manager. I accidentally used an old one without realizing your new boat wasn't on it. They took all the other boats but left yours on the dock."

"Get them back. That shouldn't be a problem."

"I can try, but I doubt they'll come back. The storm is getting really bad now."

Oliver swore. "I love that boat. I worked hard to earn the money to buy it. Nothing better happen to it. You're in charge of the marina and all the boats. You should have seen to it." His voice was low and angry, and the threatening tone was unlike my brother's usual sunny disposition. He must be tired.

"I'll do my best to take care of it," I said before I hung up. Next, I tried calling the boat storage facility, but as I'd expected, there was no answer. They must have finished stowing all the boats and gone home.

I didn't want to go back out in the storm—and it was too dangerous now anyway—but I wanted to see if Oliver's boat was still intact. I headed back to my office with its clear view of our dock and cove.

It was a shock when I stepped out of the lab area. The power was now out throughout the RIO building, but I could tell the auxiliary generator was running because the emergency lights were on in the halls. I saw through the windows that the emergency lights were also on outside, but the storm clouds made the night darker than usual. Between the cloud cover and the heavy rain, the lights were barely lighting up the nearby dive shop and the marina.

I walked to my office to get a better view of what was happening on the ocean side of the campus, and I was horrified at what I saw. The roof of the dive shop was lifting in the wind, and I knew it wouldn't be long before it succumbed to the force of the storm.

While I watched, one of the dock posts was torn away. The wind hurled it through the air, and the beam struck the roof of the dive shop. It went right through, leaving a craterous hole in its path. I wasn't sure if Stewie had finished moving all the inventory into the main building before I'd sent him home. If he hadn't, everything left in the shop would be ruined.

I couldn't see Oliver's boat through the driving rain, falling as thick as though the universe had drawn a curtain between me and the ocean. All I could see in that direction was froth and foam breaking over the dock.

Reaching into the bottom drawer of my desk, I pulled out an old pair of binoculars I used occasionally to identify birds or distant boats. I panned across the area beyond the marina, looking into the distance where I'd anchored my brother's boat for safe keeping.

At first, I saw nothing but furious waves, beating out their frustration against the dock and the beach. Then I dialed in the focus and saw Oliver's boat floating upside down, borne on the crest of a particularly angry wave.

Although the boat had capsized, it appeared to be intact and still tethered to the anchor. All her electronics would be ruined, but the boat itself might still be salvageable if the storm didn't last too long.

While I watched, another of the dock posts began to quiver and thrash under the wind's assault. It would only be a matter of minutes before this post was also airborne. It was time for me to head back to the safety of the windowless research lab in the center of the building. I grabbed a small, battery operated NOAA weather radio off my bookcase to bring with me. The frequent updates they broadcasted would help me keep abreast of the storm's progress.

NOAA—the National Oceanic and Atmospheric Administration— is a part of the United States Department of Commerce, and it provides weather and navigational reports for the Caribbean region as well as the US lands and water. NOAA would be broadcasting weather advisories frequently during the storm. At least with the radio I wouldn't need to go near the windows to keep abreast of the storm. I would know what was happening outside the RIO building without having to leave my isolated sanctuary.

I made a detour by the café to grab a few of our famous chocolate chip cookies before I went back to the lab to continue my work. I was looking forward to making a cup of coffee to go with the cookies using the pod machine in the lab.

My father's company, Fleming Environmental Investments, sometimes called FEI, had funded a solar tech startup company. Newton had equipped all our homes with solar power as well as conventional electricity, and the RIO building had also been equipped with a solar wall— a large backup battery capable of storing enough power to keep essential operations like the research lab and the infirmary running for several days. The power never goes out in the lab or the infirmary no matter what the weather, but the backup batteries are too bulky and expensive for us to run the entire operation that way. But as long as a power outage doesn't last more than ten sunless days or so, we have electricity to run the filters and aerators in the lab and medical equipment in the infirmary—plus a small microwave and a coffee maker in each location. I was grateful for Newton's foresight in ensuring that in the absence of conventional electricity, the research team would still have access to hot food and fresh coffee.

I pushed the button to start my coffee brewing and nibbled on a cookie. When the coffee was ready, I got down to work. Since Benjamin had taken on the dreaded budget, I was free to work on my photography projects. I took another bite of my cookie and then opened a video I had been editing, part of this year's RIO documentary. RIO's annual television specials and media sales brought in most of the money to keep RIO operational, ensuring the documentaries and specials were all compelling was a big part of my job.

The clip I was working on was a short segment featuring Maddy, Doc, and me. We'd been beta testing a new concept in 'portable' diving bells. We'd used the untested version of the devices last year to help us through some unplanned decompression stops during a rescue operation, but that operation had been too desperate and uncertain to be filmed.

But Doc had received an updated set of the diving bells from the manufacturer a few months before we began filming the documentary. The three of us had put the units through their paces. I had done most of the videography myself, but Stewie and Oliver had both taken some turns as well enabling me to be in the finished film.

I'd practically grown up in front of the camera since Maddy and her late husband Ray Russo had always made sure I'd been featured in the documentaries, making me a "famous" diver. Not famous like Maddy, who was acclaimed the world over as an oceanography pioneer and an expert diver, but famous enough that I was often recognized as I went about my life.

I disliked seeing myself on film though. That made it hard for me to edit clips I was in without getting self-conscious. I often walked a fine line between including enough of me to satisfy my fans and making myself happy by eliminating my image completely. I chewed slowly on a bite of cookie while I concentrated on cutting a few extraneous frames.

Every few minutes, the NOAA radio crackled and sent out a weather update. The storm had settled in over the Caymans and it showed no sign of either moving on or dying down. By dinner time, it was still going strong.

The RIO building had large windows along all the outside walls. The front entry and the roof of the lobby atrium were glass. I knew it wasn't safe to leave the lab in the building's interior as long as the storm was raging, but I was getting antsy stuck in the dim, window-less research area. And I was starving.

I decided to grab something from the café's freezer and have an early dinner while watching a movie on the comfy couch in the infirmary's waiting room. I knew everything I needed would be running because the infirmary shared the research lab's backup power supply to keep any patients safe.

The windowless infirmary was also in the center of the building, and it had a small waiting room for friends and family members of our patients. In addition to the couch, the room was furnished with a big screen television set mounted on the wall, a small microwave, and a pod-style coffee maker.

The infirmary's waiting room was just a few feet away on the same inside corridor the lab was on, but I took the other turn leading to the rear entrance between the executive offices. I wanted to pick up something for dinner from the café and then see what was going on outside.

Except for the dim emergency lighting over the exits, everything was dark as I approached my office. It didn't matter. I knew these hallways like I knew my own home. I stepped into my office to check out the view from my windows.

The sky was dark and forbidding, black clouds scudding across the horizon. The constant flickers of lightning through the clear hurricane shutters only accentuated the darkness. As I'd predicted, the dive shop roof had collapsed completely, and the walls had been penetrated by what looked like pieces of the dock's railings, sticking out from the cement like porcupine quills.

I made a mental note to increase the fundraising goal for next year by the cost of rebuilding the dive shop as I continued staring out at nature's might.

Good. Oliver's boat was still there, riding the giant waves, upside down. It may have capsized, but at least it hadn't been shattered on the iron shore or pushed out to sea. I could only hope it continued to ride out the storm more or less safely.

An especially loud clap of thunder made me jump, and a fallen palm tree battered the clear storm shutters protecting my window. Even though the shutters were made from the same materials as ballistic body armor, it was definitely time to get out of there. I retraced my steps to head back to the center of the building where it was safer.

The corridors were eerie in the barely adequate illumination of the emergency lighting. Spooky shadows skittered in the lightning flashes that showed through the clear hurricane shutters protecting the windows along the hall. Once, when I looked up, I would have sworn one of the shadows was a person, hunched over and running away from me. But it must have been my imagination because nobody in their right mind would be out in this weather, and all RIO's doors were locked anyway. I shrugged and picked up my pace as I walked toward the infirmary. Still nervous, I locked the door behind me.

The waiting room was warm and inviting, with soothing art on the sand-colored walls and comfortable furniture. There was a small refrigerator that held soft drinks and a pod-style coffee maker on a low table against a side wall. The pale blue couch was plump and cozy. I sat down and started poking through the movies in RIO's video library, since I was pretty sure no streaming services would be operational long enough for me to stream an entire movie tonight. Service could be iffy when the weather was bad.

I homed in on a heist movie—a recent release staring two of Hollywood's most bankable stars. I queued up the movie, but I was exhausted. The nearby beds looked snug and relaxing. It wouldn't hurt anything if I just closed my eyes for a moment to catch my breath. I changed into some scrubs, crawled into the nearest infirmary bed, and went to sleep.

When I woke up, I listened for the sounds of wind and rain, but the silence seemed almost deafening. The overhead lights were off. The stand-by generators had shut down, dousing the emergency lights, and the building was in total darkness. Even the battery backup seemed to be offline because there were no lights on in the infirmary at all, even at the nurse's station. A quick glance at my luminous dive watch told me that while I'd slept, most of the night had passed. Although it was still pitch dark, it was almost morning.

To my surprise, I'd slept soundly. The new day was still in its wee hours and the sun hadn't even thought about coming up yet, but the roar of the winds and waves was gone. Despite the end of the storm, neither the emergency lighting nor the regular lights had come back on. That made no sense to me. There should still be plenty of power in the battery backup panels. No matter what the outside world was going through, the uninterruptible power setup for the lab and infirmary should still have been operational.

I felt my way to the supply closet and pulled the door open to grab a couple of fresh flashlights. I flipped one on and stuck another into one of the capacious pockets of my scrubs for a backup. Following the beam of my flashlight, I headed toward RIO's basement, to see what was wrong with the generators.

Because of the high water table on the island, the basement was really more of a crawlspace. The ceiling height was only four feet, making it spooky at the best of times, but with only the feeble beam of a flashlight to brighten the gloom, it was downright scary.

The ceilings were too low to allow me to stand upright. I had to crouch as I walked, and I kept a wary eye open for the low-hanging pipes that crisscrossed in all directions. Large spider webs festooned the corners and the spaces between the pipes. The basement was damp, musty, and smelled like low tide.

Muck and debris had flowed in through the flood vents, and several inches of slimy water covered the cement floor, making walking treacherous as well as disgusting. Some of the flood water had already receded, but the mud was still deep enough that it sluiced over my thin flip flops and slathered itself on my toes. I suppressed a shudder and kept moving toward the utility area in the far corner, where the breaker box, the battery backup apparatus, and the emergency generator were.

Somehow, the battery backup had become disconnected. I assumed some of the storm debris that had flooded the basement had bumped it and dislodged the connection. I plugged it back in. I pushed the reset button on the silent main generator, and it sprang to life. The emergency lights flickered on, and immediately, the basement was much less eerie.

I felt better until I noticed the door to the nearby breaker box was ajar. Eugene, our head of maintenance, would never have been that sloppy.

I flicked the door all the way open and saw the main breaker was in the off position. I pushed the switch back to on, and the regular lights came on. The generator sputtered to a halt again; its services no longer needed.

I was puzzled about how the emergency generator, the battery backup, and the breakers had all been switched off, but I'd get Eugene to look into it when he reported for work. When I turned to leave the basement, I noticed a flash of bright yellow fabric peeking out from behind the generator. When I pulled the bundle out, I realized it was a complete set of yellow oilskin foul weather gear.

The garments couldn't have been there long because the jacket and overalls were still wet from rain, but neither muddy nor stained from the flood waters. Their presence meant someone must be in the building, and I was supposed to be alone.

I picked up the raingear and carried the bundle with me as I returned to the main floor. Again, I locked the infirmary's entry door behind me. In the supply closet, I stuffed the garments into a plastic bag and stowed the bag on a shelf. I rinsed the slime off my feet in the infirmary shower and changed back into my cargo shorts, t-shirt, and a zippered hoodie I'd found hanging on a chair at the nurse's station. Of course, everything went on over a bathing suit— so I was dressed in my usual garb.

I was toweling my feet dry when my phone rang, the noise startling in the stillness. It was barely four A.M., but Caller ID said it was Maddy—my mother, Madelyn Anderson Russo.

As usual, she jumped right in without any preliminary chitchat. "Newton and I are worried about you. Are you okay?"

"I'm fine here. How are you, Newton, and Oliver?"

"Newton and I are fine, but Oliver returned to Grand Cayman a couple of days ago. Don't tell me you haven't seen him?" She sounded alarmed.

My own heart thudded at the news that Oliver was on the island. It wasn't like him not to check in. And if he'd been here on Grand Cayman, why hadn't he seen to his boat himself before the storm? Why hadn't he said anything about being nearby when I'd called? What if he'd come to RIO after my call last night and tried to save his boat?

Now the boat was overturned, and if he'd been aboard, my brother could be dead. No way anyone could have survived if they'd been on the boat during the hurricane. I'd barely made it out myself, and the storm hadn't even reached its full power at that point. My hands started to shake.

I didn't want to worry Maddy, so I tried to laugh it off. "Oh, you know Oliver. He's probably holed up somewhere with Genevra and forgot to check in. I'll track him down later today when things calm down a little more."

"Okay. Let me know when you touch base with him, please. Now, how are things in the lab? Any damage?" Maddy knew me well enough to know I wouldn't have left the research lab unattended during a storm.

"The lab is fine," I said, hoping I was telling the truth since I hadn't been in to check on it yet this morning. "The dive shop got hit hard. We might have lost some of the inventory."

"Well, as long as no one was hurt, it's all good," she said.

Now that she knew there was nothing urgent here, I sensed she was eager to get back to her research. I said goodbye and let her go.

Before I could do anything else, the phone rang again. This time, it was Doc. I answered on speaker. I didn't even have time to say hello before she started talking.

"The *Omega* took some storm damage. We won't be back today. Is anyone there hurt?"

"Not that I know of," I told her. "I sent everyone home before the storm got too wild."

"Good. Well since you're okay there, and I've got a few injured sailors here, I'll hang up now."

I laughed. Nothing came between Doc and a patient, except another patient who needed her more.

Chapter 4
A New Day Dawns

I walked through the building, assessing the damages, but I had to pick my way carefully because RIO's outer corridors were awash with mud, broken glass, and assorted debris. The rain had poured in through the broken windows, and flood waters had seeped in under the doors. It was slow going in my flop flops. I made a detour to my office to swap them out for an old pair of running shoes to protect my toes from the slime.

After changing my shoes, I peered through the storm shutters covering my office window into the dimness outside. The early morning sun was struggling to break through the lingering clouds. It was hard to see much this early, but I decided to call Oliver while I was there. I needed to make sure he was all right. He hadn't been himself when we'd talked last night.

He sounded sleepy when he answered. "Hey, Fin. Everything okay over there?"

"Yeah, we're good. It's a mess but nothing that can't be fixed. How are you?"

"Good. If you're okay, then I'm going back to sleep. I was up all night watching the storm." He gave a huge yawn.

"Sure thing. Just I need to tell you about your boat…"

His voice was sharper now, and he groaned. "Again? What about my boat?"

"I forgot to put it on the list for the crew moving our boats to drydock. By the time I realized it had been left behind, the storm was already raging. I took it out away from the dock and anchored it on a long line, even though the storm was bad enough by then I barely made it back. Overnight, it capsized." I paused a moment and took a deep breath.

"Don't worry about it. I'll come over to check it out when I get a chance. Catch you later." He disconnected the call.

Not only was this totally unlike my usual chatty and cheerful brother, but it was also a complete turnaround in his mood from when we'd spoken last night. I wondered if he was having problems at work or at school, or even in his budding relationship with Genevra Blackthorne. His personality was all over the place. Well, I wasn't going to pry. He'd tell me what was going on when he was ready.

I walked down the filthy halls to the rear door and stepped outside. My feet squelched into the soggy ground as I slogged along the path that was usually delineated by pristine white crushed shells.

Today, the paths were just muddy tracks. The crushed shells—what was left of them—were strewn around the lawn, brown and filthy. Downed branches and debris dotted the lawn, and most of the shrubbery had been uprooted. The gardens were bare, all the flowers, trees, and ornamental grasses gone.

I walked around the building to RIO's rear campus to get to our storage building. It was in a sheltered area well away from the ocean and buffered from the wind by the RIO building itself, so I hoped it would be okay. As I walked, I assessed the damage to the main

28

building. Despite the hurricane shutters, many of the windows had been shattered by flying debris. All the shrubbery and plants were gone. The low-lying parking lot was under at least six inches of water, and the sign that once hung over the main entrance lay in pieces in the mud. I sighed. We had a big job ahead of us.

I opened the door of the storage building and noted the windowless structure was in perfect order. The sturdy cinder block building seemed to have escaped unscathed, probably because it was on a small rise and set back from the ocean where it was sheltered from the wind and above the flooding. I grabbed one of the kayaks from the stack against the wall and hoisted it to my shoulder to take to the water. It was slow going with the awkward burden of the kayak on my shoulder.

Due to the storm, the entire lawn had become more of a swamp than a grassy expanse, and my feet sank in the soggy ground up to my ankles. It was a huge effort to make any progress because the mud tried to suck my running shoes off my feet with each step.

I stopped halfway across the front lawn to catch my breath and decided to rest there a minute and call the boat storage facility to see about getting Oliver's capsized boat upright. I wanted to get started on repairs as quickly as I could.

It was early for any business to be open. I'd planned on leaving a message, but someone picked up on the first ring.

Surprised, I stammered out a hello. Then I explained what had happened and asked if they could help.

The man who'd answered said, "Yes, we can handle it. We'll be right over,"

I'd been certain the boat storage company would be inundated with work after the storm. I was surprised at the promise of quick service. "Are you sure?" I asked. "You must have a million customers asking for help."

"Your stepfather and I were friends. You need my help. Of course, I'll come. It's no problem. I'd have done the same for him. And besides, you're actually the first call of the day." He chuckled. "Nobody else is up this early."

Even though he'd passed away several years ago, once again my stepfather Ray Russo had come through for me. I felt a stab of longing for Ray as I said a silent 'thank you' to him along with my audible 'thank you' to the man on the phone.

My heart nearly broke when I crossed back to the rear of the building and saw the devastation up close. The marina's dock had vanished, just a few timbers floating on the waves to show it had ever been there. The tiny sand beach was gone too, nothing left but gravel and rocks. The ocean water looked dirty, filled with dirt, bits of seaweed, and broken coral. The only thing back here that seemed to have survived the storm unscathed was the ironshore—the calcified shells of long-dead sea creatures that makes up much of the Cayman Islands' uppermost surface.

I wanted to check out the damage to the dive shop, because from where I stood, it looked extensive. The door was hanging open, attached to the jamb with just one hinge. Up close, the dive shop looked even worse than it had from the window in my office. The entire roof was gone, and an uprooted palm tree had impaled itself through one wall. The tree's roots were hanging in mid-air a few feet above the mud.

I poked my head inside and groaned. It was a mess. The floors were covered with mud and silt. The roof was gone, and most of the walls had been pierced by flying debris. Water dripped down the walls, adding to the mess on the floor. The shop would have to be completely rebuilt.

The only ray of light was that it looked like Stewie had removed all the inventory before I'd sent him home. He'd also covered the tank fill compressor with multiple layers of waterproof tarps and tied each layer separately for extra security. The storm hadn't managed to strip all the layers away, largely thanks to a piece of the roof that had fallen in front of it, acting as a protective windbreak holding back the gusts. We'd been lucky.

It was still early morning, and after the storm, I didn't expect to see anyone here yet. I jumped a mile when Stewie stood up behind the compressor.

He grimaced when he saw me. "Pretty bad," he said. "Lucky, I got all the inventory into the storage building before the storm hit. We may want to put everything on sale anyway. Or add it to the rental stock. Up to you." He looked down at the clipboard in his hand. "I have the list of what was here."

I nodded. "If there was any clothing, send it out to be cleaned and then donate it to the homeless shelter. Probably a good idea to add all the remaining inventory to the rental stock. We didn't have a lot of inventory coming into hurricane season anyway, and it's always good to have the latest stuff available for rent." Then I had a thought. "We'd better call Chaun though. The dock has been destroyed. All his RFID sensors must have been lost."

"Nope," Stewie said. "I pulled them all off the slips yesterday before the storm, just in case. They're in the maintenance storage closet in the main building with the computer and the inventory. We'll be good to go as soon as we have a dock to put them on. And as soon as we get the front door of the dive shop rehung, I'll put a reader on it. That way we can still keep track of the tanks coming and going, even if we can't track them to individual slips."

"Good job," I said, marveling again at how mature and competent Stewie had become after his last stint in rehab. There was a time when I might have found him here, lying drenched and drunk in a pile of spoiled goods instead of working on the cleanup before the sun had even risen.

I gave him a high five and went back outside. I was picking up trash from the back lawn a few minutes later when the distant grumble of chains unspooling broke the early morning stillness.

Looking up, I saw two barges from the boatyard near Oliver's capsized boat.

Divers were already in the water, affixing chains attached to cranes mounted on the barges to opposite ends of the boat. I marveled at the quick response.

Once the chains were in place, the barges pulled away from Oliver's boat, causing it to roll over and turn upright again. Most modern boats are self-righting, but older designs and large boats like Oliver's don't have this advantage. They can be hard to recover if they capsize. I breathed a short-lived sigh of relief that the dreaded task had been accomplished relatively easily.

One of the divers from the barge emerged from the water, and I walked forward to meet him. "Thanks for coming quickly. I appreciate it."

He smiled and looked out at the boat. "What do you want us to do with it? We can tow it to drydock, or…"

"Just anchor it here for now. I can bring it over later after I check it out."

"No anchorage…" the man started to say.

Just then Stewie came out of the shop with a length of anchor chain in one hand and a spool of rope in the other. Stewie had already attached one end of the rope to the chain.

Stewie and the man from the barge shook hands. "Glad to see you made it through the storm okay, old friend," said the man.

Stewie laughed. "Who you calling old, Alan? As I recall, we're the same age."

Alan grinned at him. "We are indeed. But even though we're old friends, I can't let you anchor a boat without a permit."

Stewie nodded. "I get that, but it's not a problem. We can anchor it to one of the footings for the missing dock. They should still be sturdy enough to hold her." Even though the wooden dock had been destroyed, the heavy steel and cement footings had remained in place.

"Good idea," I said. "I'll swim out and attach the line for you." I kicked off my sneakers and took the spool of rope from Stewie. "While I'm out there, I'm going to check the boat out. See how bad the damage is. Maybe if it's not too bad Oliver will forgive me for forgetting about it," I said.

Then I stripped down to my bathing suit and waded into the water. The ocean was still cold and turbid from the storm, but the boat wasn't far away. I dove and swam out, letting the line float off the spool behind me as I went.

I climbed aboard Oliver's boat and attached the line to a cleat on her bow. When I had made the line fast, I waved an arm overhead to let Stewie and Alan know I was all set. While I'd been swimming, they'd connected the length of chain to an iron ring on one of the ruined dock's footings. Now Oliver's boat was securely anchored just beyond the breaking waves.

Stewie and Alan stared across the water at the boat, now floating serenely on the waves. Stewie went into the dive shop to continue his cleanup. Alan waded into the water and began the swim back to his barge.

Chapter 5
Discovery

I surveyed the damage to Oliver's boat. The deck and many other surfaces had already dried off in the early morning wind, but there was mud and dead sea grass everywhere I looked. All the maps and charts were gone, and the cabinet doors in the main cabin and the galley swung open, revealing the emptiness inside. The smell was horrible, with an underlying hint of rot unlike the usual fresh scent of the ocean.

I ignored the smell and spent a few minutes disconnecting all the instrumentation on the helm and putting everything in a pile near the transom. Maybe Chaun, my friend and the local tech genius who had installed our RFID inventory system, would be able to find a way to save it. If not, I'd just buy everything new.

I climbed the ladder to check out the duplicate instruments on the flying bridge. I disconnected the GPS, fish finder, and sonar here, although I was pretty sure I'd have to replace all of these for Oliver too unless Chaun could work some magic. I was just about ready to climb down the ladder when I saw Dane Scott, Detective Sergeant of the Royal Cayman Islands Police, tying a kayak up to the boat.

I jumped down to greet him. "Welcome aboard, Dane," I said.

Dane climbed awkwardly up on the boat's transom. He was nowhere near as comfortable around water and boats as I was, but he tried gamely to keep up whenever I was around. He was barefoot, and he walked across the deck to take the electronic equipment from me.

I kissed his cheek. "Dane! What brings you out here?"

Dane and my mother had been having a relationship when she threw a wrench in the works by remarrying Newton Fleming, my father. Even though both my parents swore the marriage was just for convenience while they were in the process of adopting Oliver, Dane had refused to continue his relationship with Maddy as long as she was married to someone else. But the adoption had been final for months now, and my parents had made no move to get another divorce. We hadn't seen much of Dane Scott around RIO recently.

"Hey, Fin. I just wanted to check on you, make sure you're okay. That was quite a storm yesterday, and Maddy called to let me know you were all alone out here. She asked me to check and make sure you were okay." He added the instruments he'd taken from me to the pile I'd made. He looked around at the mess on Oliver's boat. "It's gonna be tough to bring this boat back up to your standards. What happened, anyway?"

I sat on the ladder's bottom rung while we talked. "Oliver and I had a miscommunication about who was making the arrangements for his boat to be taken to drydock. Bottom line, we both overlooked it. At the last minute, I swam out and put it on a long line, but the storm was too much for it and it capsized. I barely made it back to shore myself."

He shuddered. Despite having grown up on the island, he'd never been a big fan of the ocean until he started his relationship with Maddy. However, his newfound interest in boats and water seemed to have died along with their love affair. He'd started, but never finished, his scuba diving certification.

He put his hands in his pockets and went into the cabin, and in a few seconds, I heard a muffled curse. "Ow! What the heck is that for?" he said.

He was standing near the hatch to the engine compartment. Although I'd been too intent on assessing the instrumentation earlier to notice it, now I realized the compartment had been locked shut with a large brass padlock, and a slim steel rod had also been passed through the latches, preventing the hatch door from being lifted.

"Wow. That's weird," I said.

"Maybe somebody locked it because the latch is broken," Dane said. "But it sure is a tripping hazard."

"Rat's. I'll need to open it up to assess the engine for necessary repairs. I wonder if the key is around here anywhere?" I looked at the mess around me with a sinking feeling.

"Not likely it's still on board if the boat capsized. Who knows where it is by now." He shrugged. "But maybe I can help."

He bent down and slid the steel rod out of the latch, then pulled a small packet from his pocket. He turned his back was to me, and I couldn't see what he was doing. After a few minutes, he rose and faced me, the open padlock in his hand. "Ta Da," he said.

I thought we would both be more comfortable if I didn't acknowledge his lock picking skills. I simply lifted the hatch to the engine compartment.

It was dark and dank down there, and I could see a couple of inches of water sloshing around.

"Allow me," Dane said with a smile. He took the heavy flashlight from his belt and shone it around the compartment below. As the beam hit the back corner, we both froze.

It took a second for me to recognize what I was seeing. I almost thought it was a woman dancing, facing away from us, hands in the air and body twisting slowly with the rhythm of the ocean. The dancer was petite, with short brown hair still wet from the sea, and she seemed to pivot around her hands. After a second, I realized her hands had been chained to an overhead pipe.

With the next surge of waves, the body spun slowly to face us, a ghastly expression on her face that seemed a parody of her once beautiful smile. But even the most stunning bone structure couldn't make up for the bruises around her throat and the marks nibbling sea creatures had left on her face. I screamed.

Chapter 6
An Accident Happens

"Oh my God. It's Cara Flores. It's Oliver's birth mother. Oh God, we have to help her." I reached for the ladder to go to her aid, but Dane held me back.

"You can't help her, and you can't go down there. This is now a crime scene," He put a sheltering arm over my shoulder and led me away from the open hatch up to the deck.

I was shivering and my teeth were chattering. You'd think after all the dead and nearly dead bodies I'd seen in the last few years I'd be used to the sight of death, but it doesn't work that way. Each time was a shock that filled me with horror and sorrow.

Dane held me until my trembling ceased, then he took a step back. "You good?"

I nodded. "Cara…"

"Yes, it's Cara. But I need you to stay strong. I want you to take the kayak back to shore. Get Stewie, and the two of you go wait for me in the infirmary." He rubbed his chin. "You'll have to be the one that holds your group together. Make sure nobody leaves the infirmary, and nobody goes anywhere alone. And as soon as you get inside, call Roland. You remember Roland?"

"Yes. Stanley's twin brother. He's one of your investigators." I'd worked with Stanley and Dane on a kidnapping case a little over a year ago.

"Right. Tell him what's happened, and I want him here with the team. He'll know what to do. And then you keep everybody together inside until Roland or I say it's okay to leave. Don't tell anyone about what's happened. Got it?"

I nodded. "What about Oliver? Shouldn't I let him know? She's his birth mother..."

"No." Dane shook his head. "Let me see if I can figure out what happened here first. Then I'll tell him." His face looked bleak. "Believe me, you don't want to be the one who has to tell anyone about something like this."

I bent to pick up the electronic equipment I had removed from the helm, but Dane put out a hand to stop me. "Leave all that here, please. There might be some evidence on it." He grimaced. "Although after being underwater overnight, it's pretty unlikely."

I nodded and stepped into the kayak Dane had used to reach the boat. I untied it and pushed myself away before paddling to shore.

I stopped by the dive shop to pick up Stewie and my sweatshirt. I was freezing, even though the air was warm. "We need to go inside. Dane will be along in a few minutes to explain things." I said.

His smile faded. "Uhoh. It's never good when DS Scott wants to explain something. What's going on?"

"I can't say. We'll find out more soon." I said.

Stewie brandished his clipboard with the list he'd been making of required repairs and replacement parts. "I have work to do. Can't I stay here and finish up?"

"Nope. C'mon. We're supposed to wait in the infirmary."

"I'll meet you there in a few minutes," he said. "I want to get a look at some of the additional damage. "I'll go in the back way and check out the pool."

"I'm going in the front way. I can use a coffee," I said. "Want me to bring you one?"

"No thanks," he said. "I had coffee on the way in this morning. I really want to see how the pool fared. I can start on a repair plan to get the pool operational as soon as possible so it doesn't interrupt the dive class schedules."

RIO had an Olympic sized saltwater pool where we conducted our scuba training classes. It was almost as key to our operations as was our research vessel, the *Omega*. Stewie's concern was well warranted.

"Don't be long. Dane wants us all together in the infirmary." I picked my way along the walk to the front door and pulled out my keys to open it before realizing the door was ajar.

I knew I had locked the door yesterday when I sent Ralph, the security guard home. It was possible the wind had pushed the door open during the night, but it seemed extremely unlikely.

I shivered, remembering the figure I thought I'd seen running through the hall, and the wet raingear in the basement.

I'd slept here all night.

Alone.

Maybe.

I hurried inside because I wanted to get to the infirmary. I was picking my way through the trash on the atrium floor when my heart nearly stopped with terror. Benjamin lay sprawled unmoving on the floor in a mess of blood and spilled food. A large tree branch was on the floor nearby. The glass roof of the atrium had been breached, and rain had poured in. The whole floor was awash, and Benjamin's face, resting on an overturned tray from the café, was barely above the water level.

I raced over to Benjamin and took his pulse. It was there, faint and slightly thready. I passed my hands along his limbs, checking for injuries. He groaned but didn't wake up when I touched his right leg. There was a large gash on the side of his head, and it was bleeding profusely, the dark blood mixing with the dirty floodwater.

I tried to call emergency services, but the lines were down again. I knew I'd have to handle this myself. I needed to get him to the infirmary, but even before that, I needed to stabilize him to be able to move him safely.

"Hang on, Benjamin. I'll be right back. I'm gonna take care of you." I didn't want to move him without a doctor present, but it wasn't safe to leave him in the lobby with several inches of water covering the floor and all the glass and mud. I covered him with my sweatshirt and then rose from my crouch beside his body and ran to the infirmary. I looked for Stewie to help me, but he wasn't there yet.

I debated running to the pool to try to find him but remembering how bad Benjamin looked and how deep the flood water was, I couldn't take the time. I grabbed a gurney and a body board from the triage area and pushed the gurney as fast as I could back to the lobby. It seemed to take forever as the wheels stuck in the mud or caught in debris hidden in the slimy water. Finally, I managed to reach the lobby. Benjamin hadn't moved.

I'm no doctor, but I've been trained in medic first aid, and although much of my experience is in diving-related accidents, I know my way around most injuries. I knew I would need to stabilize Benjamin's spinal column before I attempted to move him because he'd been hit in the head and fallen, and I didn't know the extent of his injuries.

I snapped a cervical collar around his neck and taped his injured right leg from the hip to the ankle to a board. I didn't have the expertise or equipment to take an x-ray. More permanent repairs would have to wait for a pro. In the meantime, this would keep his leg stable until I could get him professional help.

Killer Storm

Taking the body board off the gurney, I slid it under him, then slowly and gently rolled him onto it. I tried to ensure his entire body moved in unison, to prevent possible damage to his spinal column or internal organs, but with only one person on the task, it wasn't easy. I wrapped him in the board's stabilizing straps for transport, hoping I hadn't caused him any irreversible damage when I moved him.

I positioned the gurney at its lowest setting, very near the floor. I tried lifting the board onto the gurney, but it was too large for one person to maneuver safely, at least without potentially injuring the patient. I tilted the stiff body board at an angle. Now Benjamin was lying sideways, held in place against gravity by the body board's straps, and pushed the board the few inches necessary to rest it against the gurney's edge.

Then I raced around to the other side and grabbed the board by the lift handles and pulled it toward me. The body board moved, pivoting on the gurney's edge, and the far side rose off the floor as it did. When the opposite edge was nearly at the level of the stretcher's mattress pad, I started gently lowering the side I was holding, and the board settled onto the gurney. A few tugs and a lot of pulling, and it was centered on the stretcher and ready for transport. I raised the rolling stretcher to normal height, put up the siderails, and race walked to the infirmary, cursing the muddy water with every step.

I wheeled the gurney into the first of the curtained cubicles and set the brakes. I grabbed my phone and dialed emergency services again. I got a message from the phone company telling me all circuits were busy due to the weather. I tried calling Doc but got the same result. I'd have to continue to handle this on my own.

After gathering alcohol swabs, a couple of sterile instrument packs, gloves, and some bandages from the supply closet, I returned to Benjamin's side. He looked ghastly—pale and sickly. He hadn't moved at all, and his eyes were closed.

I didn't have a pulse oximeter to test his blood oxygen, and I didn't know if it would help, but I figured it couldn't hurt. I stuck an oxygen cannula in his nose and turned on the flow of gas. Then I set about cleaning his wounds.

There was a deep gash on the side of his head, and blood had flowed down across his face and neck. I pulled on a pair of gloves, and gently cleaned the blood off. He flinched when I touched the wound itself, although he didn't wake up.

I remembered seeing a high-intensity lamp with a magnifying lens in the supply closet. I ran to get it. When the light shone on his face, I saw several slivers of wood and small pieces of broken glass embedded in the wound and the skin of his face.

After changing my gloves, I tore opening an instrument pack and used the medical tweezers to remove the visible splinters and glass shards. It had to have hurt, but Benjamin didn't stir. I covered the wounds with gauze.

I used a small squeeze bulb of sterile water to clean off his closed eyes and mouth in case there were tiny bits of glass dust on him, then I lifted his eyelids to make sure there was no glass in his eyes. I couldn't see very well, even with the high-intensity lamp, so I decided it would be a good move to flush his eyes with sterile water.

I covered his upper body with an absorbent pad, then I irrigated his eyes with sterile eye wash. In case I had missed some glass, I folded a few of the gauze pads and put them over his eye sockets to prevent him from rubbing them if they itched or irritated him. His shirt was wet and stained. I slipped his arms out of it, then pulled it over his head, careful not to touch his wounds or his eyes. I put his arms into the sleeves of a clean scrub shirt, gently pulled the wide neck over his head and then covered him with a soft blanket.

I'd done everything I could think of. I pulled over a chair and sat beside him, holding his hand to let him know I was there if he woke up. I felt a rush of affection for this sweet, gentle man.

I knew I didn't love Benjamin the way he loved me. Not like Newton loves Maddy, or the way Maddy had loved Ray. Or even the way I still love Liam.

Killer Storm

Benjamin and I were more than friends.

Less than soul mates.

I cared deeply for him, and there was no other word for it but love. It just wasn't the kind of love I knew he wanted and deserved. But the threat of losing him was causing me to reevaluate my emotions. Once again, I wished my best friend Theresa was around to help me make sense of all this.

I tried calling both emergency services and Doc again, but the circuits were all busy. It would probably be days before phone service was back to normal. In the meantime, it would be hit or miss. I was wracking my brain trying to think of something else to do for Benjamin when it occurred to me that I might be able to reach Doc with a text. I pulled out my phone and began typing.

Benjamin hurt. Can u come?

I watched the three dots that meant she was replying, but it felt like hours before her answer came through.

At sea on *Omega*. Send picture & list what u did

I stepped back a few feet and snapped a picture of Benjamin's torso, then a close up shot of his face. I sent those off, then began typing a list of all the treatments I had given Benjamin. It took forever for the message to go through, probably because of the size of the picture files as well as the storm damage to the cell networks.

She sent a thumbs up emoji.

All good. Nothing else 2 do. Bland food. Tylenol. No coffee. I'll come soon

I hadn't expected her to come. Not really.

I sighed and sat on the bed beside Benjamin, holding his hand.

My phone rang and I answered quickly without looking at caller ID because I didn't want the noise to disturb Benjamin.

"Are you okay? Do you need anything?" said Liam. "I've been trying to get through to you for hours now."

My heart thudded. Liam, my onetime boyfriend. Onetime fiancé. And my sometimes boss. I didn't want to let him know what was going on at RIO, because I knew he'd try to move heaven and earth to make things better. And Dane had told me not to talk to anyone about finding Cara's body, so I said, "I'm good, Liam, although the place is a mess. Benjamin was injured, but he'll be fine. Thanks for asking. How are you? Everything okay over at Quokka Media headquarters?"

Liam and I had broken up quite a while ago, and now we were friends. Or more than friends. Or maybe not. We were still trying to figure all that out. I was scared of being hurt again. And then there was Benjamin in the mix. Maybe if Liam wasn't around, I could love Benjamin the way he should be loved.

Meanwhile, Liam, who is an Australian high-tech millionaire, had founded a media company when my slimeball ex-husband, Alec Stone, managed to get himself installed as Editor-in-Chief at *Your World* magazine, where I'd once been a contributing editor.

It had taken some persuasion, but Liam had eventually convinced me to switch my monthly photo montage column to Quokka's flagship periodical, *Ecosphere*, where I was now nominally the managing editor. Since *Ecosphere* was my third job after RIO and Fleming Environmental Investments, in reality Genevra Blackthorne, who was Liam's assistant as well as my newly-adopted brother Oliver's girlfriend, did most of the work while I focused on the photography. It was a sweet deal for me. And working at Quokka meant I crossed paths with Liam frequently, which was a major benefit as far as I was concerned.

Quokka's headquarters were in the business district of Georgetown here on Grand Cayman, and Liam lived in a sumptuous apartment that took up the entire top floor of the building. Genevra had a smaller apartment on a different floor, and unless he was staying in

Maddy's penthouse condo, Oliver spent much of his time there when he was in town.

"Great news about Benjamin. All good here too, Luv," he said. "We're far enough inland that we missed the brunt of the destruction. A few broken windows. Power out for a while, although the generators worked fine. And now we're back. What can I do to help you get RIO back up and running?"

"We're not in too bad shape, but we're just getting started on the assessment. I don't think we'll need anything, but I'll let you know if I think of something." It was hard not to talk to Liam about Cara, but I knew he'd come racing over. That would annoy the police.

"How did Oliver's new boat make out in the storm? I don't see it in the boatyard." Liam's penthouse home's wall of windows looked out over much of the island, and he had a clear view of the boatyard.

I felt even worse now for not telling him about Cara. "Capsized," I said ruefully. "I forgot to put it on the pull list."

"Maybe I can help with that," he said. Luckily, he hung up before I could tell him I'd already handled it. Or blurt out that I'd found Cara's body aboard.

I slipped my phone into my pocket and sat down in the chair next to Benjamin's bed.

A few minutes later, Stewie walked into the infirmary. He did a double take when he saw Benjamin lying there unconscious. "What happened to him?"

"I'm not sure, but I think he got whacked with a flying palm tree. I texted with Doc. She said he should be okay for now, but she won't be back for a while." I smiled at him. "But then, you probably already knew that." Doc and Stewie were in a relationship, and I think that was a huge part of why he'd stayed sober this time.

I heard Oliver's furious voice snarling from behind me. "Now you're running the infirmary too? Is there no end to your talents? But you did get the recovery crew here fast. At least you got something right."

I'd never heard Oliver sound this angry. I couldn't imagine what had gotten into him. Last night he'd been angry. This morning he'd been his usual mellow self. Now here he was, enraged again for no discernible reason. My parents had recently adopted Oliver, even though he was already an adult by the time they'd met him. They felt so strongly he needed to become a part of our family that even though they'd been divorced for nearly twenty-five years, they'd remarried to facilitate the adoption process.

Oliver had always been sweet and helpful, but now my head was spinning from his mood swings. Everybody loved him—so much so that despite him being an adult, my parents had adopted him to be sure he'd have family to turn to in an emergency. But he was different today—almost unrecognizable.

I tried to keep my voice calm. "Stewie, would you stay with Benjamin, please? Let me know if he wakes up?" I bit back my annoyance at Oliver's attitude as I pulled the cubicle curtains closed. "I told you I'll pay for the repairs." My voice was cold as I tried to hold back my annoyance at Oliver's attitude.

"It's not about the money or even the damage to the boat. You're supposed to be in charge here while Maddy's away, but you are so busy with all your other activities you let this happen. Lucky it was only your stepbrother's boat you forgot about. What if it had belonged to a paying customer?"

This tirade was so unlike my sweet brother that for a minute, I was shocked into silence. I stared at him with my mouth open.

Wiping his hands on his shorts, a sheepish-looking Stewie stepped out of Benjamin's cubicle to respond. "If that boat had belonged to a paying customer, they'd have to take it up with their own insurance company. RIO's not responsible for moving any boats except their own. Read your mooring contract. You should be thanking your sister. She risked her life to save your boat because you were too lazy or too stupid to take care of it yourself. And it was my fault, not hers, for not double-checking the list of boats to move to drydock."

Oliver glared at Stewie but said nothing. He turned and strode away, anger apparent in every step he took.

I took a deep breath to regain some semblance of calm. "It's not your fault, Stewie. It was my responsibility. Oliver will be happy when he goes outside and sees his boat upright, and we'll get it fixed good as new. Maybe better. At least, we can do that when Dane releases it." I stood up. "And there was no need for you to get involved. I can fight my own battles. But something else must be bothering Oliver. This isn't like him at all."

"It is kinda like his crazy mother and that looney twin sister of his though," said Stewie. He too turned and stalked out of the infirmary.

I started to go after him to remind him that Dane wanted us all in here, but my phone buzzed again. It was a busy day for phone calls, especially considering how early it still was and with the ongoing intermittent problems with the cell system. The screen said it was Newton. I answered quickly. I loved talking to my newfound father.

"Hi, Sweetie," he said. "Did you make it through the storm okay? Everybody all in one piece?"

"Pretty much. Benjamin got conked on the head by a flying tree limb, and Oliver's boat capsized. The building is a mess, full of mud and debris, and the dive shop is probably a goner. Other than that, everything is good." I bit my lip. I wanted to tell him about Cara. At one time, they'd been very close. But I'd promised to let Dane tell people first. I bit my lip and kept quiet.

"Well, when you're ready, let me know what you need to get everything back in order, and I'll transfer the funds to cover the cost of repairs."

"Thanks, Newton. You're like our own guardian angel. Should I work with Justin on the request?" Justin Nash was my father's assistant at Fleming Environmental Investments, and we often worked closely on joint projects. And since I was my father's second in command at Fleming Environmental, whenever Newton was out of town, I also had the final okay on Justin's work.

Newton was silent for a moment. "Why don't you work with Oliver on this one? I'd like to get him more involved in day-to-day operations, and he's done with school for a while. He should have plenty of time. And include his boat repairs in the funding request, please."

"But it was my fault his boat capsized. I should pay for it."

"Nope. Not even if I was down to my last billion," Newton said with a laugh. "Oh, and if you wouldn't mind, please don't mention to Justin you're working on this project with Oliver. He's got plenty of his own work to do, and I don't want him looking over Oliver's shoulder on this."

I was surprised by this request because Justin really had been Newton's right hand for years, but Newton knew what he was doing. "Got it." I said. "My lips are sealed." Newton laughed and clicked off.

I looked up to see Benjamin sitting up in bed. His eyes were still covered with gauze

"Welcome back," I said.

He groaned. "What happened?"

"You went a few rounds with a flying tree limb. Tree limb won, but to be fair, I think you were punching outside of your weight class. How do you feel?"

He grinned. "Like I was smacked in the head by a flying tree limb.' He lifted a hand to point at the gauze. "Can you take this off?'

"No problem, but you have to let me know if you feel any pain in your eyes. There was a lot of broken glass. I think I got it all out, but I want to give your eyes another rinse anyway, just in case. Okay?"

He nodded. I gently removed the bandages that held his eyes shut and rinsed each eye thoroughly, wincing at the deep purple bruising on his face. "How does that feel?"

He blinked. "No problem. Eyes seem fine, although I have a major headache."

"I'm not surprised. I think you may have a concussion. Doc said you could eat though. Are you hungry?"

"Yeah. I'd love some bacon and scrambled eggs."

"Sadly, not on the menu yet. For now, you get dry toast and apple juice. Maybe later you can have some eggs. Sorry. Doc's orders."

"Coffee?" he said wistfully.

"Apple juice. I'll be right back."

I left the infirmary and headed for RIO's café to gather some food.

Despite the storm shutters, most of the windows in the café itself were broken or cracked. The kitchen had no external walls, so it was still intact. I pulled a couple of slices of bread from the bin and popped them into the toaster. While I waited for the toast to pop, I poured a glass of apple juice into a reusable insulated mug with the RIO logo on it. When the toast was ready, I put the plate and mug on a tray and picked my way through the mess back to the infirmary.

Benjamin looked better than he had when I'd left him just a few minutes ago. His skin was no longer ashen, and his eyes weren't as glazed and vacant. If he did have a concussion, it didn't seem like there'd been permanent damage. I placed the tray on the mobile table beside his bed and maneuvered it into position over his lap. He pushed the button to move the bed into an upright sitting position and picked up a slice of the dry toast. "Nothing for you?"

"I'm getting myself a coffee as soon as I know you're all set."

"Can I have a coffee too?" he said even more wistfully than the first time he'd asked.

"Maybe later you can have some. I'll check with Doc when she calls in." I went into the next room where there was a small pod-style coffee machine and made myself a cup. I sat on the couch in the waiting area to drink my coffee, but I kept an eye on Benjamin while he nibbled his toast.

He fell asleep as soon as he finished his juice. I removed the tray and left a note letting him know where I was. Then, forgetting Dane had said to stay in the infirmary, I went off to start the necessary cleanup. I took a shower in the locker room in the pool house, and by the time I was out, Eugene, RIO's head of maintenance, was on site. He was standing in the center of the lobby, writing on a clip-board. I assumed he was listing and prioritizing assignments for his crew.

As soon as I saw him, I remembered I'd told Dane I'd call Eugene's brother Roland about the body we'd found on Oliver's boat. With a guilty start, I pulled my phone from one of the pockets in my shorts and dialed police headquarters. Once again, I was stymied by the message from the cellphone carrier that communications were still down due to the storm's effects.

I didn't have Roland's direct cell number, so I couldn't text him, but I had the next best thing right in front of me. I walked over to Eugene and asked him to text his twin that Dane wanted him to come to RIO ASAP and that I would take him to Dane as soon as he arrived. "Oh, and Dane said to ask him to bring the team."

Eugene looked at me with curiosity, but he knew better than to ask what was going on if Dane wanted Roland involved. He pulled his phone from the breast pocket of his shirt and sent the text.

A few minutes later, his phone dinged with Roland's reply.

"He's on his way," he said.

Stanley Simmons, Eugene's assistant, was in the atrium area too, pushing a mop around the lobby floor to corral all the debris in one spot and trying hard not to make it obvious he was listening to my conversation with Eugene.

Stanley had been in a terrible car accident last year, and he still walked with a limp. He'd only recently returned to work, and he was supposed to be taking it easy for the first few weeks. I walked over and reminded him not to overdo it. "We have all the time in the world to finish the cleanup and repairs."

Eugene nodded. "Exactly what I told him you'd say. He's a stubborn one though."

"How about this. Why don't you go to the infirmary and check in on Benjamin? He got hit with some flying debris last night, and I think he's got a concussion. He needs someone to stay with him, but I can't be there full time. Can you fill in for me? You can sit at the nurse's station there, and then you can start working on a list of all the projects we have to finish to get RIO back up and running. When you're done, work with Eugene on prioritizing them, and he'll give you the cost estimates as they come in. If you can, keep a running total of the estimates. I need to pull all that together to get the additional funding we need. Anything you can do to get the information all in one place really fast will be a big help."

Eugene nodded approvingly. "Good idea. Stanley, we've got lots of people who can mop floors, but no one else knows how this place runs the way you and I do."

Stanley nodded. "But I can carry my weight…"

"Yes, you can. And right now, this is the best way for you to do that. You're the only person who can stay with Benjamin and track the repairs at the same time without letting something else drop. I need you on this." I smiled at Stanley.

He nodded. "Okay. Is there anything I should do for Benjamin?"

"Wake him up every couple of hours if he doesn't wake up on his own. Give him a couple of the pills I left on the desk in the nurse's station if he complains about pain. Don't let him leave the infirmary, and no coffee or caffeine until Doc can get here to check him out. Got it?"

Stanley nodded. "I'm on it." He leaned his broom against the wall and walked across the lobby to the corridor that led to the infirmary.

"I'll be in the lab. Will you send Roland there when he arrives, please?"

Eugene agreed. I left to check on the lab fish—our research subjects. Even though they were away from any sight of the weather, the storm had unnerved them. I needed to make sure they were all doing well now that the hurricane was over.

Chapter 7
Checking in at the Lab

I t was quiet and dim in the lab, although some of the occupants seemed a little edgy, probably still sensing the aftermath of the storm even in here, although the temperature and lighting in the lab were always the same.

I'd sent all the research staff home to ride out the storm, and I was sure they were all still cleaning up the damage to their homes. That meant I was still on the hook to manage the lab and to feed the specimens. I picked up a clipboard and went tank to tank, recording the water temperature in every one of them and adding observations about each of the fish and other inhabitants. Luckily the short period when the battery backup had been disconnected hadn't been long enough to affect the water temperature too much. I checked the feeding schedules and fed those specimens due for a meal. It didn't take long to complete all the tasks I'd assigned myself. Now I could do what I'd really come for. I wanted to spend a few minutes with Rosie.

Rosie is an Atlantic Pygmy octopus, and although she was originally the subject of my doctoral thesis, she's now more like a pet. She's a tiny thing—less than the size of my palm even with her tentacles unfurled—and she's incredibly smart.

But before I reached Rosie's tank, there was a knock at the door. Roland popped his head in. I could see his partner Morey behind him. "C'mon in, gentleman. We can talk while I finish up here, then I'll run you out to the boat where Dane is."

"Good idea," said Roland. "I hoped I'd get a chance to see Rosie while I was here." The big man grinned at me as he crossed the lab, Morey trailing behind him.

I washed my hands at the big sink in the back of the lab, and then walked over to Rosie's aquarium. As usual when I approached her tank, she peeped shyly out of the shell where she spends most of her time. She always checked to see who was heading for her haven. Once she was certain it was me, she quickly oozed over to the glass wall and propelled herself to the top of the tank. She stuck one of her tiny tentacles out of the water, showing she wanted to hold hands. I put a finger in the tank, and she wrapped herself around it, turning a blissful coral color as soon as we touched.

Roland and Morey stood off to the side. Morey's eyes grew wide when Rosie held my hand, and he broke into a grin. Roland was smiling too.

"No matter how many times I see this, I can't believe it. I swear she feels real affection for you," Roland said.

I nodded. "I like to think she does. And she seems to enjoy learning new behaviors to make me happy. She's a sentient being with real feelings and emotions." I let Rosie cling to me for a few moments before I gently pried my hand away.

Showing her displeasure at the loss of contact, she turned a dull sandy color and drifted to the bottom of the tank. She hovered there, watching me until I relented and pulled out the cards I'd used while training her. There was little doubt she wanted to play.

I held up a card, and Rosie retrieved the matching marble and dropped it to the bottom of the tank in front of me. I repeated the process through the entire deck of pictures, marveling, as always, at Rosie's brilliance.

She can discern colors and shapes, and she never makes a mistake when retrieving objects. Although all octopuses are smart, I felt an almost maternal pride in Rosie's achievements. In my opinion, Rosie is exceptional.

When we'd finished our game, I dropped a small piece of clam in the tank. Rosie flashed her special pink thank you color and took her prize back to her shell home to enjoy in privacy.

Morey and Roland stood behind me watching Rosie's performance in obvious amazement. Even though I'd introduced Roland to Rosie a year ago while we worked together on a kidnapping, he was still as astonished at her talent as he'd been the first time. Morey had never seen her in action before today, and he was stunned. "When you talked about this, I always thought you were pulling my leg," he said to Roland.

"Would I do that?" Roland said, with an exaggerated look of innocence on his face. "But now, if you can spare a minute, Fin, can we ask a few questions about what's going on? If we're any slower reaching DS Scott, he'll blow a gasket."

"Sorry. You can tell him it's all my fault. Everything's a mess here from the storm, and then Benjamin was hurt. It took me a while to call you."

Roland's eyebrows rose. "How did Benjamin get hurt?"

"I'm not sure what he was doing here, because he was supposed to have gone home before the storm got heavy. But somehow, he was hit by a flying log in the lobby. He might have a concussion, but I think he'll be okay."

Roland nodded but his expression seemed dubious. "We'll want to talk to him before we join Dane. Now, why don't you tell us what happened. Start from the moment you woke up this morning."

I started reeling off the events of my day, but almost immediately, Roland homed in on the bundle of raingear I'd found in the basement.

"Where are the clothes now?" he asked.

"I put them in a bag. They're in the infirmary. I'll get them for you." I stood up to go, but Roland put out a hand.

"Let's all go." He and Morey exchanged glances, but I couldn't tell if there was any significance to the looks.

We walked through the halls, and I marveled at how much cleaner the floors were already. Eugene's team had been working hard, but Roland frowned when he saw the floors had been swept clean.

He whipped out his phone and speed dialed his brother. He and Stanley must both have had their phones set to use RIO's network and WIFI calling because the call went right through. "Hey, Eugene. I hate to do this to you because I know how much you hate a mess, but I have to ask you to hold off on any cleanup or repairs until we finish our investigation."

He paused a moment, listening. "Yeah, I'm serious. Murder. Maybe an attempted murder along with it. Hold off."

He listened again. "She's standing right beside me." He thrust his phone at me, but to be honest, I hardly noticed because I was fixated on the words "attempted murder." Did Roland think someone had tried to kill Benjamin?

Roland held the phone up to my ear, and I heard Eugene speaking. "Whatever Roland wants is fine," I mumbled.

Eugene audibly sucked in a breath. "Are you okay?"

"Why don't you have your team meet us in the infirmary? That way everybody will be in one place if Roland needs to talk to them. I was supposed to tell you earlier, but I was distraught about Benjamin's injuries, and I forgot."

Roland pulled his phone away from me. "See you there, Bro."

We'd been walking toward the infirmary while talking to Eugene. By this time, we were right outside the door. "Benjamin might be sleeping. Let's be quiet if we can."

My concerns were unnecessary. When we entered, Stanley was at the desk working quietly. Benjamin was sitting up in bed, playing cribbage with Stewie. He looked up and smiled when he saw me.

"Good idea, Stewie. Mental stimulation is good for the patient. How are his math skills after his injury? Still bad, or did getting bonked on the head improve him?"

Benjamin laughed at my teasing, but his smiles faded when he saw Roland and Morey standing behind me. "Uhoh. What's wrong?"

Stewie's phone buzzed. He put down his cards and stepped outside to take the call. Morey watched him go, then he took out his own phone and started his recording app.

Roland approached the hospital bed. "What happened to you, Benjamin? How'd you hurt your head?"

Benjamin became serious fast. "I came back to make sure Fin was okay. I knew she wasn't really going to go home, even though she promised she would." He shot me a look I pretended not to notice. "While I was crossing the lobby, I must have been hit on the head by a flying branch. Knocked me unconscious for quite a while."

"Did you see anything suspicious or was anyone around before you were hit?" Roland asked.

Benjamin screwed up his face and thought. "It's pretty hazy, but I don't remember seeing anyone or anything out of the ordinary."

"Okay. Can you remember if the glass roof of the atrium was intact when you came in? And the windows?

"I think they were both intact. I remember being impressed at how well everything had held up to the storm." Benjamin looked at me quizzically. "What's going on?"

Instead of answering, Eugene asked another question. "May I look at your injury?"

"Uh, sure," said Benjamin. "It's not that bad. Fin did a good job patching me up."

I went over to the bed and removed the gauze covering the head wound. Morey moved in and took some pictures.

Roland turned to me. "This looks like the blow came from behind, from the left. If I recall the lobby layout, the path to your office, the research lab, and the infirmary would all require the use of the corridor on the right of the lobby, correct?"

I nodded. "Yes. The other corridor leads to the gift shop, the café, and the aquarium. The pool, the gym, and the locker rooms are that way too."

"There's no glass on that side of the lobby, right?"

I saw what he was driving at, and I could have kicked myself for missing it. If Benjamin had been hit on the left side of his head, his injury couldn't have been from flying storm debris because the storm was blowing from the other side. Someone must have hit him.

I hoped my conclusion was wrong. "But he was covered in broken glass when I found him," I said.

"The roof and windows may have been broken by the storm, but whatever broke them wasn't responsible for this wound," Roland said, gesturing to Benjamin. "Now, where's that bag of raingear you found?"

I went to the supply cabinet and returned with the bag full of yellow oilskins. "I didn't mention this before, but I thought I saw someone running through the halls last night. I decided it was my imagination—just shadows. But then the emergency generators and the main power were both turned off this morning."

Eugene walked in just in time to hear my last sentence. "That's impossible. Everything was running fine when I left yesterday. And when I arrived this morning"

I nodded. "I turned the generators and the battery backup back on when I woke up. That's when I found the oilskins." I bit my lip. "I just remembered I saw someone running along the dock yesterday too, long after I'd sent everyone home. It was just before I went out to move Oliver's boat and the storm got so bad."

Benjamin swore softly. "I shouldn't have left you alone. I knew you wouldn't go home."

"It was my choice to stay," I said. I stared at him until he looked away.

"Right. It's just I worry about you." He bit his lip.

Roland cleared his throat. "Who was it you saw, Fin? Did you get a look at him?"

"No idea." I shook my head. "Honestly, the rain was bad enough by then I couldn't even tell if it was a man or a woman. And the person was hunched over. I couldn't hazard a guess as to how tall they were. If they hadn't been wearing the bright yellow rain gear, I might not have seen them at all."

Roland nodded. "Okay. Morey, let's go see DS Scott. He's probably wondering where we've been."

The door opened and DS Scott walked in before Roland finished speaking. "No need. I got tired of waiting. I had Stewie come get me with the kayak. Where are we with the investigation?"

Roland gave Dane a recap of what we'd learned thus far, which wasn't much. We had a lot of "could have been…" and I thought I saw…" but nothing really concrete to report.

When Roland had finished his recap, Dane walked over and looked at Benjamin's head wound. He nodded. "I agree with your assessment of the cause. Probably not from the storm." He turned to me. "Fin, where are the other members of your team? I thought you were going to assemble them here." He looked around. "I don't see very many people."

I nodded. "This is everyone on site today. We're closed, so most of the crew is off, cleaning up their own homes after the storm. Besides Benjamin, Stewie, and me, the only employees here are a couple of people from the maintenance department. Your team and I got distracted by Benjamin's injury, and then by talking about the prowler I saw in here last night."

He shrugged. "Okay. Letting Stewie leave the infirmary to answer his phone was the right call. Otherwise, I'd still be sitting on that boat. But where is he now? He should have come right back." He glared at Roland as though Stewie being out of the infirmary was his fault. Dane was usually more guarded. Being stranded out on the boat with Cara's body must have put him in a foul mood. "May I see the rain gear you found, please?"

I handed him the plastic bag and then went to the supply cabinet to grab a clean sheet from the neatly folded stack. I handed the sheet to Dane.

"Roland, you have your kit?" he asked.

Roland lifted the handle of the case containing his forensic tools and nodded. "Right here, Boss."

Dane shut the blinds and closed all the doors while Morey vacuumed an open space in front of the nurse's station. When he finished, Dane spread the sheet.

Roland flipped off the lights and shone a black light over the sheet. "Looks clean."

Dane opened the plastic bag and carefully removed the oilskins. Morey took the now empty bag from him and put it inside an evidence bag. Dane unrolled the oilskins, and Roland shone his blacklight on each piece. The pants came up clean, but a few small dots on the left wrist of the jacket glowed in the light. I knew that meant blood.

Dane used a pen and carefully poked at the jacket's zipper placket. The front of the coat fell open and I saw the nametag sewn inside the neck.

Even from several feet away I could read it.

Oliver Russo.

Before I could decide what this might mean, the infirmary door burst open. My brother rushed into the room. Everyone fell silent.

He looked at each of us in turn. "Why is there a guard on my boat? Why am I not allowed to board it? It's my property." He glanced at the rain gear spread on the floor. "And what are you doing with my oilskins? What the heck is going on here?"

He walked over and put his face close to mine, eyes blazing with fury. "What are you up to now? Isn't it enough you conveniently forgot to send my boat to drydock? Now you're trying to claim ownership or something?" He was shouting, and his fists were clenched at his side.

Out of the corner of my eye, I saw Morey put a hand on Benjamin's arm to keep him from getting out of bed. Which was a good thing. We didn't need anyone else to join in this fight.

I had never seen Oliver in such a rage, never seen him act as irrationally as he'd been acting the last few days. One minute he was his usual self and the next he was screaming in rage. What could be going on with him?

Stewie's words about the mental health issues that seemed prevalent in Oliver's biological family ran through my head. I held his gaze with my own. "Calm down, Oliver. Nobody's trying to take anything away from you."

Dane casually inserted himself between Oliver and me. "When was the last time you saw your mother?"

"Which one?" Oliver shouted in reply. "I have two, you know."

Dane's voice was soft and soothing. "Yes, I know. I'm talking about your birth mother. Cara Flores. When did you see her last?" Dane gently put his hand on Oliver's shoulder.

Oliver inhaled deeply and lowered his voice when he replied. "I saw her in New York, while I was at school. She said she might want to come back to the Caymans, stay a while. She didn't want to stay at a hotel because it would be too visible, and she knows you have it out for her. I told her she could stay on my boat if she came back, but I haven't heard from her since before the storm."

His unjustified rage returned, and he shook off Dane's hand. "Is that what this is about? You're harassing me to get back at my mother? Cara's not dealing drugs anymore. Leave her alone, will you? And leave me alone too." Oliver strode away toward the infirmary's door.

Dane spoke softly. "Oliver, I'm sorry to tell you Cara Flores is dead. We found her body on your boat this morning. I'd like you to come down to the station to answer a few questions."

Oliver stopped still. When he turned around, I could see him struggling to take in the meaning of Dane's words. "She drowned when the boat capsized?" he said.

"No. She was murdered. We found her body tied up in the engine compartment."

"No. No, she wasn't murdered. She was fine when I saw her last,' Oliver said.

"You were with her last night?" Dane said.

"No, not last night. A few days ago. She was alone. And now she's dead?" Oliver seemed to be having trouble believing what Dane had told him.

Without warning, Oliver lunged for Dane and clasped his hands around the policeman's throat. "You're lying," he shouted. "Stop it right now. My mother is still alive. She has to be." His hands tightened, and the veins on the backs of his hands popped out from the pressure of his grasp.

Dane quickly broke Oliver's grip, and Morey and Roland each grabbed one of Oliver's arms and pulled him back. Tears streamed down Oliver's face.

Dane cleared his throat. "Oliver Russo, you are under arrest for assaulting a police officer and for resisting arrest. And the murder of Cara Flores." I knew he was fond of Oliver, and sorrow glinted in his dark brown eyes when he spoke.

Morey and Roland cuffed Oliver, who stared vacantly at the ceiling, seeming unaware of the gravity of his situation. Dane bent down and carefully folded the sheet with the rain gear inside it. He stuffed the whole bundle in an evidence bag and followed his team out the door as they led Oliver away.

Chapter 8
Doc Returns

E ugene, Benjamin, and I were shocked at the turn of events, and it took a few seconds for us to come to grips with what we'd just witnessed. When I'd recovered sufficiently, I pulled out my phone to call my father. He's a lawyer, although he doesn't practice law. Even so, he'd know what to do.

Fortunately, the cellphone infrastructure was working again. At least for the moment.

"Newton, I need you here now. Cara was murdered on Oliver's boat, and he's been arrested. He's been acting strange, flying into a rage for no reason and then a few minutes later he's like his usual self. Something weird is going on with him, but I can't imagine what's causing it. Anyway, whatever it is, he needs a good lawyer."

Newton was quiet for a moment, and I knew he was remembering the time when he and Cara had been lovers as well as co-workers. Those days were far in the past, but they'd been an important part of his life. When he'd gotten a grip on his emotions, he spoke. "Take it easy, Sweetheart, and don't worry. I'll be there as soon as I can, and meanwhile, remind Oliver not to say anything to anyone until I get there."

Newton disconnected without saying goodbye, but I knew that was because he was already mentally working on the issue. He was single-minded when he focused on something important, and I'd come to realize nothing was more important to Newton than his family.

Benjamin slipped out of his bed and stood beside me. He reached out to touch my hand. "It'll be okay. We both know Oliver had nothing to do with his mother's death."

Eugene and Stanley were huddled at the nurses' station when the infirmary door opened, and Doc walked in.

"I got here as fast as I could." She looked at Benjamin standing beside me. He was so weak he was swaying on his feet. "You should be in bed," she said to him, her voice stern.

He nodded and climbed back under the covers while Doc snapped on a pair of gloves to run a quick exam. She shone a light in his eyes to check his pupils, then she asked him to follow her moving finger. She tested his reflexes and listened to his heart and lungs. "I think the concussion has resolved, but I'd like you to spend another night here. Now let me take a look at the wound." She gently removed the bandage.

"This doesn't look like it happened when the roof collapsed. Looks more like a horizontal blow from the left side," she said to me. "This happened in the lobby?"

Benjamin and I both nodded.

"There's no way the storm caused this," she said. "No wind would have been blowing through the lobby in that direction."

"That's what Dane said, too," I told her.

Stewie walked in just then. "Ready to go, Doc?" he said.

"No, sorry. I'm going to stay here. Benjamin needs someone to watch him."

"I'll stay too." Stewie and I both said the same thing at the same time.

She smiled. "Stewie, you can stay to keep me company. Fin, you go home and get some rest. From what I hear, you've had a tough couple of days. You must be dead on your feet."

I bit back a yawn. "I'm fine," I said. "And I have a lot of work to do here to clean up."

"We've got it covered. Where will RIO be if you collapse from exhaustion? There's no one else who can run this place. Go home and rest," Eugene said. "C'mon. I'll walk you to your car."

I'd left my Prius inside RIO's loading dock to keep it sheltered from the wind. It was undamaged and ready to go when Eugene and I got there. But when I left RIO's grounds, the roads were increasingly bad—awash with sea water and rain, covered with fallen limbs and debris, abandoned cars blocking the travel lanes. I decided to spend the night in Newton's condo because it was a lot closer to RIO than my house in Rum Point. And that way, I could talk to Newton as soon as he arrived.

Chapter 9
Newton Comes Home

I parked the car in a visitors' spot in the covered garage at the complex where my father lives when he's on the island and took the elevator to the penthouse. When I walked into his home, the place was dimly lit by the slanting rays of light peeking through the shutters. His staff had obviously taken pains to stormproof the wall of windows that looked out at the ocean, and he was high above the level most of the flying debris had reached. There'd been no damage.

I dropped the canvas tote bag I used instead of a purse on the table beside the entry and headed to the kitchen. Newton was out of town, so there probably wasn't much, if any, fresh food in the refrigerator, but the freezer was always stocked with frozen gourmet meals. I rummaged around until I found something that looked appetizing and popped it in the microwave.

Even reheated, the food tasted wonderful, and I realized I'd barely eaten anything since before the storm. Eugene and Doc had been right. I needed to take better care of myself.

I found a plastic bin of homemade cookies in the freezer, and I nuked a couple of those for dessert. I was contemplating the crumbs while considering reheating a few more of the frozen cookies when I heard the front door open.

I rushed down the hall and into my father's arms. "You made good time."

"The benefits of having a private jet. Maddy's at her place freshening up, but she'll be here in a few minutes. You can fill us both in, and then we'll go talk to Dane and see if we can get Oliver out on bail."

"Hungry?" I asked.

"No, we ate dinner on the plane. But it smells like cookies in here. Have you been baking?" He looked at me in surprise.

It's well known I'm no cook. Unless I eat out with friends, my dinner usually consists of a pre-made sandwich from a convenience store, and my idea of baking is to pick up some hot-from-the-oven cookies at the café at RIO.

"Nope. Found some frozen dough and nuked a few cookies for dessert. Want some?" I grinned at Newton. Even at his age he could eat anything he wanted, and he still looked like a male supermodel.

"No thanks. I'm too stressed to enjoy them right now. Maybe when we get Oliver back where he belongs."

The front door opened, and Maddy walked in. Her white-blonde hair was pulled up in a messy bun, and there were shadows under her turquoise eyes. She looked exhausted, but her back was straight. She's a beautiful woman, and although she's petite and delicate-looking, she's actually as strong as a bull. Otherwise, she never would have been able to manage RIO by herself all those years.

I rushed over to give her a hug, and as soon as we touched, I knew everything would be okay. Maddy has always been my rock. I love Newton dearly, but he wasn't there for twenty-plus years while I was growing up. Maddy and her late second husband, Ray Russo, had raised me, and I considered myself lucky to have had Ray in my life while Newton was away.

Killer Storm

Maddy knew instinctively I'd be blaming myself for Cara's death, Oliver's troubles, the destruction at RIO, even the storm itself. She brushed the hair back from my forehead. "First, you need to know you did nothing wrong, and nothing happening is your fault. We'll get to the bottom of this, and everything will be fine. You'll see."

Newton broke in. "That's true, but the best way to prove that is to find out who really murdered Cara Flores. Fin, can you tell us exactly what went on? I'd like to know all the facts before we go see Dane."

Newton and DS Scott had an uneasy relationship. They were not quite enemies, and in fact, they'd been well on their way to becoming friends until Newton and Maddy suddenly remarried, putting an end to Dane's budding relationship with her. Now there was always a competitive undercurrent to every conversation between Newton and Dane, and I worried about the effect that might have on our bid to free Oliver.

We all took seats, Newton and Maddy on opposite corners of the long leather sectional and me sitting in the Eames chair across from them. By now, I was getting good at telling the story of the storm, Benjamin's accident, and finding Cara's body. I was able to fill them in quickly without missing any of the details.

When I finished, I bit my lip. "But I'm worried about Oliver. He's been acting erratically. One minute he's the Oliver we all love, and the next minute he's in a rage, screaming at people for no reason. Then he's back to normal again. There doesn't seem to be a reason for the behavioral changes—at least, nothing that could account for the extremes."

Maddy and Newton exchanged glances. "Could Oliver be taking drugs?" Maddy asked after a moment's hesitation.

"I doubt it," I said. "He saw how drugs killed his friend Dylan, and even though Oliver didn't take any drugs voluntarily, the drugs he was given back then nearly killed him too. He's doing well at school, and his relationship with Genevra seems fine. There's no reason for him to turn to drugs."

Newton stood and walked to the glass wall to stare out at the ocean from between the slats in the storm shutters. "From her actions over the last few years, I've started to think his mother may have been insane. His sister Lily is crafty enough to hide it most of the time, but she is definitely insane, and she and Oliver are twins. Could it be something genetic causing his personality shifts?"

Maddy bit back a sob. "No. Please, no. He's such a sweet young man."

Newton came back and put his hand on her shoulder. "He's our son now. Whatever it is, we'll help him through it." She reached up and touched his hand.

Newton jumped at the touch. "Let me go put on my lawyering clothes and then we'll head to the station. See what we can do to get him out," he said. He walked down the hall to the master suite.

Maddy took a deep breath. "I wanted to tell you what a great job you've been doing running RIO in my absence. I'm impressed, especially with all your other responsibilities. Thank you."

I smiled at her. "Thanks, Maddy. But I've been meaning to talk to you about that. I need an assistant. Since you took June to Woods Hole with you, I feel like I'm drowning. I need help."

She shrugged. "Then hire someone. Do whatever you need to do. I left you in charge."

"Budgets?" I said. Despite the periodic infusions of cash from Newton's personal fortune and the revenue we generated from our annual documentaries, our dive operations, and the aquarium attendees, RIO was always operating without a financial cushion because we used every penny to fund research.

She smiled at me. "Tell Benjamin to find the money somewhere and transfer it to your department. If he can't free up the funds, then we'll find another way. RIO can't afford to have you drowning in administrative work when you should be creating. Creativity is your gift."

I felt like a giant weight had fallen off my back. "I love you," I said to her.

"And I love you."

Newton came back into the room, dressed in a bespoke suit that whispered of wealth. His silver hair, perfectly cut, gleamed in the slanting sunlight streaming through the slats of the stainless steel hurricane shutters that had protected the window wall. He wore a Patek Phillippe watch on his wrist, and his gleaming leather shoes were handmade. He looked like the world's most successful lawyer —or maybe the world's most successful male supermodel. "Ready?" he asked.

Maddy and I both rose, but I hung back. "I don't know if I should go with you. My presence seems to set Oliver off. I think he's upset with me."

Newton reached out and took my hand. "Then he'll have to get over it. We're a family, and family sticks together."

Chapter 10
Police Station

W e walked into the Cayman Police station on Elgin Avenue a few minutes later. Newton asked the sergeant at the main desk for DS Scott. The sergeant rolled his eyes. He was familiar with Newton from a few years back when I'd had my own legal troubles, and he knew Newton wouldn't put up with any delays. He picked up his phone.

Within a few minutes, DS Scott came out to the lobby. He clapped Newton on the shoulder and shook his hand. He looked at Maddy and said "Hello," as though they were strangers, not past lovers. He turned to me. "Fin, you look beat. I thought you were going home to rest." His voice was kind.

"I went to Newton's instead. My brother's in trouble," I said. "No way could I rest."

Newton spoke up. "I'm Oliver's lawyer. When can I get him out of here?" He reached into an inside pocket of his suit jacket for his checkbook.

"Leave your checkbook right where it is," said Dane. "No bail on murder cases. Nothing I can do about that."

"You could have held off on making the arrest," Maddy said, anger in her voice. "Did you rush it just to get back at me?"

Dane looked at Maddy for a long minute before he spoke. "Maddy, last I heard, you're married to Newton, making our former relationship water under the bridge. But I still care about Fin and Oliver. His biological mother was murdered on his boat. I saw him threatening Fin, and I was afraid for her. He even attacked me in front of witnesses." He shrugged. "This was the only way I could be sure of keeping Fin and Oliver apart until I could figure out what's going on with him. And it will keep him safe too if there's more to this crime than seems apparent at first, and I think there is a lot more here than meets the eye. You know Oliver's twin sister is back in town?"

Maddy went pale. "Lily's here on the island? Why? Where is she?"

"That I don't know, but we're on the lookout for her." He turned to stare at me. "And we're looking for Alec Stone too. His boat's in the marina, but nobody has seen him around town. Watch your back, Fin, and call my cell if you see or hear anything that makes you uneasy."

I shivered at the idea that Alec Stone, my vile ex-husband, and his homicidal girlfriend were back on Grand Cayman. "Will do," I said.

Newton put his arm across my shoulders. "Why don't you stay at my place until this is resolved? That way, we can keep you safe." Then he turned to Dane. "Are you sure there's really nothing you can do about Oliver? For real? Ankle monitor? Security guards?"

Dane shook his head, and I could see the pain in his eyes. It was obvious he was taking no joy from Oliver's arrest. "He's safer in here than he is out there," said Dane. "It's for his protection as much as anything else."

Newton turned toward the door, and the three of us left the police station without seeing Oliver. When we arrived at the building where Newton and Maddy had their respective condos, we walked to the elevator, but I didn't get in with them. "I'm going to check on my house. Then I'm going to stop by RIO, but don't worry. I'll be back soon," I said.

"Do you think it's a good idea to go alone, knowing Lily is on the island?" Maddy asked.

"I'll be fine. Nothing bad will happen to me. You know I'm the luckiest person in the world," I said.

"You can't always rely on good luck to just happen," she said. "Sometimes, you need to be smart about it. Give your luck a little helping hand. Like staying here where it's safe when there's a killer on the loose."

"I'm just going to check. And Chaun is right down the street if I need help." I said, giving her a hug. My friend Chaun is a tech genius, but even I know he isn't likely to strike fear into anyone's heart—especially if the person he's trying to scare knows what a sweet guy he is.

Maddy laughed. "Chaun—all four foot eight and ninety pounds of him? Doesn't sound like much protection to me. What's he going to do, pester the bad guys to death with his questions?"

Newton took her hand. "Let her go. She's a grown woman and she can make her own choices. And she's just going to check things out and come right back. Call us if you need anything, Fin." He winked at me and then pushed the elevator button that would whisk them to the penthouse level.

Sometimes I think it's easier for Newton to see me as an adult because he wasn't around during my childhood. And although Maddy spent years teaching me to be self-reliant, I think it's harder for her to let go, especially since Ray died.

I walked across the cement floor of the garage to my Prius and unlocked the door. I was deep in thought about what was going on with Oliver and the return of his sister Lily but paying attention as I drove to Rum Point. The roads were still a mess, with stalled out cars, downed tree limbs, and trash blocking the way, but I made good time anyway.

From the driveway, the house looked untouched, and I breathed a sigh of relief that I hadn't suffered heavy storm damage. I went inside, and everything there seemed fine. Even though my house hadn't sustained any destruction during the killer storm, the last few days had been extremely stressful.

When I'm stressed out, nothing calms me down like being in the water. The ocean is my happy place, so I decided to take a quick dive at my favorite dive site before I went back to work at RIO. It would give me a chance to take some photos of the storm damage that occurred below the surface.

I packed my camera and a shorty wetsuit in my gear bag and grabbed a couple of scuba tanks from the stack in my breezeway. I loaded up the trunk of my car and drove the short distance to the deserted parking lot at Rum Point. After parking, I pulled out a tank and set up my regulator—the equipment that lets a diver breathe air from the tank. Then I wiggled into the wetsuit.

I was just about to shut the trunk lid when I felt a hand on my shoulder. After everything that had happened recently and my concerns about Alec and Lily being back on the island, the touch startled me, and I jumped away with a loud scream. I swung my arm around and whacked the person who'd been standing behind me with the stiff fins I carried in my hand.

"Ow," yelped a familiar voice with an Australian accent. "What did I do?"

"Liam?" I said when I recognized the man I'd thought was an attacker. "You scared the heck out of me. Don't you know better than to sneak up behind a woman alone in a parking lot?"

"Well, I do now," he said, rubbing his bruised cheekbone. "But I wasn't trying to sneak up on you. I knew you'd be here sometime today. I decided to spend the day working on the restaurant's patio hoping to see you. The restaurant's closed. It was quiet and serene."

Killer Storm

He smiled. "If you hadn't come here today, I'd have been happy just to have spent a great day working by the sea. But I got lucky. I saw you pull in. I didn't realize you hadn't seen me, and the sand must have muffled my footsteps when I walked over. I'm really sorry. I didn't mean to startle you."

It was only after Liam finished apologizing that I noticed his bicycle in the bike rack near the far edge of the parking lot. Two scuba tanks were strapped into a milk crate on the rear platform, and a gear bag hung off the handlebars. "Sorry about your face," I said. "I think you'll probably have a black eye soon."

He shrugged. "My own fault. May I dive with you?"

I was thrilled to see him, but I didn't want him to know it. "It's an open ocean."

He smiled again, and I knew he realized I was happy to have him here. "Okay if I leave my work stuff in your car? There's no way to lock it up on a bicycle."

I nodded, and he trotted back to the restaurant's patio and returned with the leather satchel he used to carry his computer when he was working away from the office. He dropped it in the back of my car. Then he quickly set up his dive gear, and together, we walked toward the water.

The waves were a little higher than usual, and the water was silty with bits of seaweed and broken coral swirling through it. It didn't look as though we'd have much visibility on this dive, but I didn't care. I loved diving with Liam, especially here at this site.

We used our snorkels to swim to the guide ropes marking the boundaries of the designated swim area, then we switched to our regulators and ducked underneath the ropes. Once we got down to about twenty feet, the surge we'd noticed on the surface became negligible, but the visibility was only marginally better than it had been in the shallows.

We followed the sandy underwater path that led to the wall, enjoying the sight of hundreds of garden eels swaying in the current and ducking into their burrows at our approach. The sand chute meandered through clusters of bright orange brain corals and brilliant red sea fans.

Most dive sites consist of a flat or nearly flat reef with beautiful corals and abundant small sea life. The flat part of the reef usually drops off almost vertically at somewhere between forty and one hundred feet, depending on the site. Here at this site, the drop off happened at about fifty feet, and the vertical wall continued straight down for thousands of feet.

Liam and I dove this site together often, and we always followed the same profile. We kicked along the sand chute, looking for signs of Suzie Q, the resident Southern Stingray. We'd been watching Suzie Q for a couple of years now, and she'd been watching us right back. By now she probably knew we weren't predators, but she still kept a wary eye on us.

I didn't blame her. Life in the ocean could be perilous.

Liam was swimming on my left, and he reached over and touched my arm. He pointed to his left and down, and when I looked in that direction, I saw her.

She'd gotten larger over the years since she'd first made this location her home. Her wingspan had grown to about five feet across. She was settled into the white sand, the faint outline of her body and her hooded eyes following our every move the only signs of her existence.

Liam and I always pretended not to see her because we knew from experience she'd swim off in a nano-second if she thought we were looking at her. We watched her using only our peripheral vision and continued on our original path to the wall. Even so, as we drew abreast of her hiding place, Suzie Q rose, shook off a few grains of sand that were still clinging to her wings, and glided away with such gracefulness a prima ballerina might envy her movements.

Killer Storm

By the time she'd faded from view, we'd reached the drop off where the reef top transitioned to the wall. After testing the direction of the current, we headed to the right, staying close to the wall to avoid the current. The visibility was better as we went deeper, but we stayed above seventy feet, peering into nooks and crannies in the coral to see what we could see.

We knew there was a cleaning station along the reef at about sixty feet. A cleaning station is a spot where fish stay perfectly still while the specialized shrimp manning the station clean their teeth and gills, removing and eating parasites, debris, and dead scales. The cleaner shrimp provide an important service, helping to keep the fish healthy and clean, while the shrimp benefit from the ready supply of food. It's not unusual to see fish lined up waiting their turn near the most popular stations.

If there's no fish in line, a diver can sometimes get a manicure at a cleaning station by extending a hand and holding it steady while the shrimp do their work. The shrimp will scurry over the hand and remove hangnails and dead skin. The cleaner shrimp are very good at their jobs—it doesn't hurt a bit.

But today there was a line at the cleaning station, including a mid-sized grouper, a barracuda, and a moray eel. Liam and I passed by without stopping.

A short time later, we reached our turnaround point when the air pressure in our tanks reached fifteen hundred PSI. We ascended about ten feet and then began a leisurely swim along the reef wall, ascending slowly until we arrived back at the sand chute.

We headed to shore, following the gradual slope of the reef toward the shallows. We stopped at between fifteen and twenty feet of depth for a few minutes to let our bodies release some of the excess nitrogen we'd absorbed while breathing compressed air from our tanks, then we swam slowly the rest of the way to shore.

We stood up in waist deep water. Liam held out an arm for me to balance on while I removed my fins, then I did the same for him.

We waded to shore and crossed the sand to my car where we removed the rest of our gear.

"Great dive," Liam said. "Thanks for letting me join you." He smiled, and the corners of his blue eyes crinkled in that way I loved. "Are you up for a second dive?"

I regretted telling my family I'd come right back, because I wanted to stay here with Liam, but I knew if I stayed away much longer, Newton and Maddy would get anxious knowing Lily was on the island. "Sorry," I said. "I've gotta get back. But would you like a ride? It can't be easy riding a bike with all that stuff on the back."

He threw back his head and laughed. "Too right. I thought I'd break my neck going around the curves and through the standing water. And lucky there aren't many hills on this end of the island, or I'd still be pedaling. I'd love a ride. Thank you."

We stowed Liam's gear in my trunk, and he used a bungee cord to secure his bicycle to the rack on the back of my car. The rack was a relic from the early days of our relationship when a bicycle had been his only form of transportation—before I knew he was a tech millionaire many times over.

Chapter 11
The Drive

Sometimes, when I remembered how our relationship had ended, being with Liam felt awkward and uncomfortable. Other times, like today, it was pure joy, as it had been when we'd been a couple. I missed those days—missed his easy wit, and his keen intelligence. I didn't know if I'd ever get over the way he'd left me, but I also knew I'd probably never get over loving him.

"Should I drop you at Quokka HQ?" I asked. "You must be busy."

"Actually, if you wouldn't mind, I need to talk to Newton. Would you drop me at his place?"

"No problem. I was going there anyway because I'm staying there for a few days." I concentrated on my driving for a bit before I spoke again. "What did you need to talk to Newton about?"

"Oliver's arrest. Lily's return. Your safety," he said. He'd turned his head to look out his window. I couldn't see the expression on his face.

"How'd you know?" I was always amazed at how much Liam knew about what went on around the island. Of course, he ran a media company, and one of his most popular titles was a weekly news sheet that covered Cayman events, so he had lots of feet on the street to keep him up to date.

He looked uncomfortable for a moment. "Don't get mad. I have an agent assigned to Lily and Alec. I like to know where they are. That way I can always be sure you're safe."

"But you didn't have someone on Cara?" I asked.

"Nope," he said. "I couldn't imagine she'd be brazen enough to return to the island. I didn't think it was necessary. I wish I had, though, then Oliver wouldn't be where he is right now. I regret the oversight."

I took a deep breath, thinking of the two unexplainable people I'd seen at RIO during the storm. Or maybe I'd seen one person twice. There was no way to know at this point, but I wondered if Liam might have some insight. "Do you have an agent watching me too?"

"No. I'd like to, because I want you to be safe, but I know you'd never allow it. And if I did it without telling you, that would be an invasion of your privacy, and I love you too much to betray you like that. I learned my lesson." He looked at me and smiled. "Besides, I know you can take care of yourself."

My heart hammered when Liam said he loved me, but I had to admit I didn't know what the word meant to him. He'd gone back to Australia to finalize his divorce from his first wife, and I hadn't heard from him for the whole year he'd been gone. Because of my insecurity about Newton leaving me when I was a toddler and not coming back into my life until I was an adult, Liam's unexpected disappearance had really thrown me. Then with no warning, Liam came back, expecting things to simply be the way they'd been when he left.

His staying away with no communication nearly killed me, it hurt so bad. And I'd been angry at his assumption I'd drop everything to be with him when he came back. But now, I wondered if refusing his marriage proposal had hurt me as much as it had hurt him.

Killer Storm

I'd been working on a relationship with Benjamin Brooks for more than a year, but Liam's shadow was always there between us. Same for the short-lived attempt Justin Nash had made to kindle a romance with me. I'd been living my life in a sort of limbo, loving Liam but afraid to commit to him for fear of being hurt, and just as afraid to totally cut him out of my life. This indecision wasn't like me.

After Liam's use of the charged word 'love,' we rode in silence until I pulled into the garage at Newton's condo development. Liam and I walked toward the elevator, and while we waited for it to arrive, he turned to me.

"Is there any hope for us at all?" His voice cracked when he spoke.

I inhaled, a long, deep breath. "Honestly, I don't know."

"Is it because of Benjamin?" he asked. "Are you in love with him now?"

The elevator doors opened, and we stepped inside. Neither of us spoke during the ride to the penthouse, which seemed to take forever. My mind was racing during the trip, trying to decide how to answer Liam's question. When we finally reached the top floor and stepped out into the hall, I turned to him. "No, I'm not in love with Benjamin. Not the way I was with you. But I do love him. It's complicated." I didn't want to admit to Liam that his ghost haunted all my romantic relationships.

I quickly covered the few steps to the door of Newton's penthouse and went inside. Liam paused a moment and then followed.

Newton and Maddy were sitting on the big leather sectional. An untouched bowl of popcorn sat on the glass coffee table in front of them, surrounded by Newton's law books. More books were scattered all around them. Balled up pieces of paper littered the floor.

Both Newton and Maddy were meticulously neat, so seeing them in the midst of this chaos made it clear how worried they were about Oliver. I felt a moment of guilt for taking the time to dive and

87

leaving them to deal with this problem on their own. Then I realized my head was clearer than it had been in days. For the last few weeks, I'd been too busy to dive, and the stress had built up until I'd been as taut and tense as a snare drum.

The ocean is my happy place. It's the only place where life makes sense, and I could always think clearly. I'd needed that dive, the same way a desert needs rain. I refused to feel guilty for taking care of myself. And besides, neither of my parents seemed to notice how long I'd been gone. They were focused solely on freeing Oliver and clearing his name.

"Do you know where Lily is?" Maddy said when she looked up and saw Liam standing in the entry.

He shook his head. "No, but I know where Alec is, and they're usually not very far apart. He's living on his boat at the yacht club. Supposedly he's in town to search for a property. He claims he's moving *Your World*'s headquarters here from New York. Which makes no sense."

At one time, *Your World* had been the premier magazine for ecotourism and nature photography. I'd once had a monthly column in it, but I quit when my ex-husband took over as editor-in-chief. He'd wanted to share credit for all my work that he published in the magazine, but I wasn't dumb enough to fall for that line again. And predictably, under Alec's leadership, the magazine's circulation had dropped. The rumor I'd heard around the Quokka Media office was that *Your World* was in deep financial trouble. I felt sorry for the company's staffers who were in danger of losing their jobs, but I couldn't muster a single iota of concern for Alec.

"You set up Quokka Media here, and all your titles are doing great. Why doesn't it make sense for Alec's company to move here too?" I asked, genuinely puzzled.

"This is a small market. He'll be struggling to find experienced talent, and if the rumors about his finances are true, he won't be able to match my pay scale." Liam shrugged. "He's smart enough to know that which is why I think that story about relocating his head-quarters is just a smokescreen. He's working on something else. And I'd bet it has something to do with the trouble Oliver's in."

Maddy had great faith in Liam's business acumen and his ability to reason even with limited information. That's why she'd hired him as RIO's CFO while I still thought he was a penniless valet. Her eyes shown with hope. "Walk me through your thoughts, please," she said.

"First, Alec and Lily have been together for a couple of years now. We suspect, but have no proof, Lily was working with Cara when she was selling drugs to the RIO team. If Lily was involved, Alec probably was too," he said.

He held up two fingers. "Second, Lily has been smart enough to stay off the island since then. If she's back, something big brought her here, and it isn't just the opportunity to hang out with Alec."

"Third," he paused here and looked at me with concern in his eyes, "they both have it in for Fin. And since Oliver's been adopted, they probably have it in for him now too. We know Lily is ruthless. She would have let Lauren kill Oliver when we were on the treasure expedition. Her own twin brother." He shook his head.

Maddy was following along with Liam's logic, but Newton didn't seem convinced. "Why now? And why kill Cara? And why try to blame Oliver for it?"

"That's the key question, isn't it?" Liam said. "My guess is Alec is short on cash. Selling drugs generates lots of cash, and he wanted to cut out the middleman—Cara. And Lily may be punishing Oliver for letting himself be adopted. She may think he abandoned her. And she knows he and Fin are close, so it would hurt Fin too if Oliver went down for the killing."

Maddy groaned. "We adopted Oliver because we love him, and to give him people to rely on in an emergency. It never occurred to me the adoption would set Lily off." She turned to Newton. "We have to find Lily and get her to tell the truth."

Newton patted her hand. "Don't panic, Maddy. This is just a theory. And Dane is looking for Lily. He and I may have our differences, but Dane is a good man. He'll find her." He looked at me. "I'll have Justin start tracking suitable real estate available for sale or lease. Even if it's just a smokescreen for Alec, he'll need to at least pretend to look at property or his board of directors will get suspicious. We can keep an eye on the properties. That way we can pick up his trail when he goes to see one. We can set a watch in case Lily comes along with him."

Maddy and Liam both nodded.

"Good idea having Justin focus on the real estate angle. It would be too obvious if you or I started nosing around," said Liam.

"Exactly." Newton turned to me. "Fin, I know I said Justin was too busy to take this on, but with this added work and Oliver's arrest, you'll need to work with him on the funding for repairs to RIO. Let me know if he seems overworked to you and I'll figure something else out."

"Will do," I said. "But although I hate to say it, I think Liam's theory is all wrong. Alec's parents were addicts, and he always said drugs ruined his life. None of you know Alec as well as I do, and I don't believe he had anything to do with Cara's drug operation. Lily might have had a hand in it, but it's the one skeevy thing Alec would never get involved in."

"You could be right," Liam said. "Maybe he really didn't know what Cara was up to. But he still bears watching."

"No question about that. He's a trouble magnet. But now, if you guys don't need anything else, I'm exhausted and I'm going to bed. Liam, you can take my car to get home. I'll pick it up tomorrow." I tossed him my keys.

Chapter 12
Taking Care of Business

I slept well that night, and as usual, I was up before dawn. I dressed quietly and headed off to RIO without seeing Newton or Maddy. RIO's atrium was dimmer than usual, because Eugene and his team had covered the shattered glass roof with blue tarps in case it rained again before they could permanently fix it. I nodded when I saw it, impressed by his efficiency.

I stopped in at RIO's café to pick up a cup of coffee and a fresh blueberry muffin to start my day, and to say hello to the hard-working staff. Marianna, the kitchen staff manager, was just putting out a fresh urn of iced tea.

I walked over and smiled at her. "I'm glad I caught you, Marianna. I wanted to thank you and your team for all the good work you put in. The food is always terrific, and your staff are all pleasant. Keep up the good work."

"Thanks, Doctor Fleming. It's nice of you to say that. I'll let the staff know."

"Please, call me Fin," I said. "I also want the café to give free food to anyone who comes in today—give them whatever they want. The entire staff has worked hard on storm prep and cleanup, and they deserve a token of our appreciation. And by the way, even if the people who come in are tourists or locals, we don't know how the storm may have affected them, so everybody gets free food today. Just keep a list of what we give out and put it on my tab." I grinned at her. "I took quite a bit of food while we were shut down because I was staying here keeping an eye on things. I'll bring the list over later and you can add it to the list. I'll pay for it all at once."

She nodded approvingly. "That's really nice of you. Your mother and Ray would be proud of what a fine young woman you've grown up to be."

I swallowed the lump in my throat, took my coffee and muffin, and left the café. I realized Roland must have finished his forensic work, because Eugene and his team had done a terrific job of cleaning up the storm damage in the halls. All the debris had been swept away, and the floors were washed. The removable hurricane shutters had been taken down on the windows that were still intact, and the ceiling had been covered with blue tarps in case of rain. It was much darker than usual, but at least the building was weather-tight.

I flipped the lights on in my office and smiled. I loved my office here at RIO. The salt-crusted clear storm shutters were still up, making everything outside, even the ocean, seem blurry and indistinct. But the office itself was neat and tidy. All my books were in place in the bookcases, and the giant picture of Maddy facing down the great white shark was hanging in its place of honor behind my desk.

The version of the photo hanging here now was even larger than the original had been. A small spotlight highlighted the nearly life-sized photo, and the subtle colors glowed in the soft light. The print now stretched almost wall to wall behind my desk. It looked spec-tacular.

The photo was definitely one of my finest pieces of work. No wonder it had won all those prizes, I thought with pride. I had been surprised and pleased when Newton had commissioned the huge print last year after Alec had destroyed my original version in a fit of rage. I was even more delighted when Newton had hung the print in my office.

I dropped my canvas tote bag into a desk drawer and looked at the neat stack of papers on my desk. I saw Eugene and Stanley had compiled a preliminary list of repairs and some rough estimates of the costs. I put it aside until I finished my most important task of the day.

I booted up my computer and wrote a quick job description for an assistant. I sent it off in a quick email to the head of HR asking her to find some candidates. I wanted to get started interviewing right away. In an effort to get the process moving quickly, I wrote a help wanted ad and sent it in another email to the Cayman Compass, and then I posted the same ad to the "we're hiring" page of RIO's website. That was as much as I could do at the moment to resolve my urgent need for a helper, so I turned to my other priorities.

I picked up the list of repairs Eugene and Stanley had compiled. I knew it was too soon to have found everything that needed repair or replacement, or to have any binding estimates on costs, but it was a great start on identifying the most critical repairs. I was lucky to have them on the team. Once I'd reviewed the list of projects, I sent an email to Justin Nash, Newton's assistant, asking for a meeting later in the day to discuss the funding requirements.

The meeting was a formality. Since I was nominally Justin's boss in Newton's absence, I could have just told him the amount I wanted and had him transfer it. But I wanted to be sure he was on board, so he'd do all the paperwork correctly and get the money to RIO as quickly as possible. It seemed like a good idea to discuss RIO's needs with him and ask for his advice on the tax ramifications and the best timing of the new donation as well.

Chapter 13
Early Morning Dive

I took a last sip of my cooling coffee and thought about heading to the café for another cup—and maybe another one of those terrific blueberry muffins. Before I could lock my computer, Benjamin and Chaun walked into the office bearing coffee and muffins.

I laughed. "You read my mind."

"Hurry up and drink your coffee. We want to get in a quick dive before the day gets busy." It was barely six AM. Chaun could be pushy, but he always meant well.

And to be honest, I'd just been thinking about trying to get in a dive before things got hectic around the office. I had been mulling over the idea of showing the underwater destruction the storm had left in its wake as the topic of my monthly *Ecosphere* column, and I wanted to get some shots before the sea began its own repair cycle.

"Good idea." I took a gulp of the coffee and broke off a small hunk of the muffin. "But have you been cleared to dive yet, Benjamin?"

He colored. "No. I was hoping you wouldn't ask. Doc told me to wait a few days and not to overdo it. I guess I'll wait here and try to get some work done."

"Good. *Tranquility* isn't back from drydock yet, so we'll have to make it a shore dive. Let's go." *Tranquility* is my boat, bequeathed to me by my late stepfather, Ray Russo. I loved the boat not only because it was a terrific boat, but because it was a lasting connection to Ray.

We walked out RIO's back door onto the back lawn, which was now as barren as a vacant lot. Stanley was out working already. He was raking up debris and the scattered shells that had once defined the walks.

I stopped to say good morning. "You're out early today," I said.

"Best to get the outdoor tasks done before it gets too hot," he replied. "And I think it's going to be a scorcher." He dropped a few bits of broken shell into a nearby bucket. "I'll hose these down later to see how well they clean up. We may be able to reuse some of them, but we'll have to supplement with new material too. We lost a lot." He looked around, shaking his head. "We'll need all new plantings too."

"It's okay, Stanley," I said. "We'll be fine. And thank you for all your hard work, both here and in putting together the repairs list. I appreciate it."

He smiled. "Thanks. Now I've got to get this area raked before the sun gets too hot. See you later." He started raking again.

Chaun and Benjamin had kept walking toward the dive shop while I'd been chatting with Stanley. They'd already signed out the tanks for the dive.

Stewie was inside the shop, washing down the rental equipment. He'd used a nail gun to tack tarps over the holes in the roof and the walls, and he had disassembled the compressor to give it a thorough cleaning before using it again for filling tanks. I was always impressed at the change in Stewie over the last year or so. He turned and smiled at me.

"You sure we're not going to need these tanks for something more important?" I said. "It'll be a while before the compressor's fixed, won't it?"

"No, you're good to go. I filled as many tanks as I could before the storm and put most of them in the storage shed, and there are some additional tanks in Eugene's maintenance room because I ran out of space. And between the two of us, Eugene and I should have the compressor going again in a day or two. I know you're on deadline for your *Ecosphere* column, so go for it. We'll be fine here for a few days, and if we do end up needing more tanks, I'll run some empties out to the *Omega* and use their compressor."

"Thanks, Stewie. It's good you're on top of things. I'm proud of you."

"Any news on Oliver?" he asked.

"Not yet. Newton's working on it with Dane and Liam. It'll be fine." I hoped I was telling the truth about the outcome.

Benjamin and Chaun were at the water's edge, and Chaun had finished setting up his equipment. I quickly slid the tank into the straps on my buoyancy control device—BCD—and attached my breathing regulator to the tank.

I had brought my favorite camera because I wanted to photograph the damage to the dock as well as to the ocean floor and the sea life. Chaun and I donned our masks and fins and shuffled into the water backwards. Walking backwards made it easier to walk if we didn't have to worry about the long blades of the fins burying themselves in the sand. When the water reached our waists, we turned and began to swim.

We swam past the ruined dock's concrete footings, and I photographed the eerie sight of the footings sitting on the ocean floor with no dock attached. A few forlorn pieces of wood lay scattered on the bottom, some with nails protruding or bits of rope or steel cleats still attached, but most of the former dock had been flung up onto the beach. After I took the photos, Chaun gathered up some of the debris so we could remove it when we emerged rather than leave it there where it might injure someone, and then we continued swimming out to deeper water. I knew the storm had been bad, but I was still shocked at the damage to the sea floor and the fragile coral.

Deep gouges wracked the sandy bottom. Bits of coral and gravel were everywhere, rolling across the bottom with the rhythm of the waves. Large pieces of delicate fan coral lay on the sand, and my heart broke when I saw a once magnificent elkhorn coral smashed to bits. I photographed it, even though the sight made me want to weep.

But the fish and all the other sea creatures were out in full force. There was no shortage of subjects for my pictures. Because there was still so much silt suspended in the water, the visibility was nowhere near its usual level of clarity, but the reduced visibility had emboldened some of the night feeders, who were out hunting, along with the usual day creatures like parrot fish and wrasse. Some reef creatures that normally never met because of their different schedules ended up in the same shot, which would make interesting and novel images for my column.

I saw a small brown octopus leave his usual hideout in a coral crevice and scurry across the sand. I videoed his loping, gliding, backward travel. A green moray eel poked out of his own lair, extending nearly six feet into the open, an unusual action for these normally shy creatures. Obligingly, he opened and closed his jaw repeatedly, making him look extremely menacing, even though I knew morays actually did that to increase the flow of water around them to compensate for their small gills. Two small crabs in lockstep scurried away at our approach, and I caught that shot as well.

We dropped down over the edge of the wall. Much of the protruding corals—the elk horns and sea fans—that lived near the top of the reef had been detached by the storm's fury, but as we descended, we saw less destruction. Life below sixty feet was continuing as though there had never been a storm.

I drifted slowly along the wall while I concentrated on taking pictures. After a few minutes I heard a clang of metal on metal, and I knew Chaun was banging his tank to let me know he was running low on air. I turned and the two of us swam slowly up the wall and back across the reef to the shallows.

We were swimming slowly along the sand at around twenty feet of depth when I saw something bright green lying on the ocean floor. I swam over and picked it up. After examining it for a moment, I realized it was a Fleming Environmental employee badge on a lanyard.

Fleming Environmental used these electronic badges to control employee and visitor access to the building's entrance and to various places inside. The cards also functioned as a security device for logging in to company computers, and they controlled access to various files and applications. There was no picture or any identifying information on any of them.

At first, I thought it must belong to either Oliver or Justin, because they both spent a great deal of time at RIO. Then I realized many of the other employees of Fleming Environmental swam or moored their boats in our marina or dove from our shore dive entry point along the ironshore. The device could have belonged to any number of people. I put it in the pocket of my BCD to keep it safe until I could return it to Newton. Then I resumed swimming toward shore.

We stopped to gather the debris we'd placed near the dock's fittings and carried it out with us. When we emerged from the water, I still had more than half a tank of air left, while Chaun's was nearly empty. I was sorry I'd had to cut my dive short, but it didn't really matter. I'd taken the pictures I needed for my *Ecosphere* column. I had a busy day ahead, and as much as I wanted to, I shouldn't spend more time diving just now if I wanted to get everything done.

Stewie was waiting for us on shore with a barrel for us to drop in the debris we'd gathered. "I'll take care of this later today," he said. "I know Eugene has a lot of junk he picked up that we need to dispose of too."

I thanked him, and then Chaun and I dropped our gear in the rinse tank outside the dive shop and swirled it around to clean the salt water off. We brought the empty tanks to the rack near the compressor, careful to ensure we left the dust caps hanging loose so Stewie would know they needed to be refilled. Then we stored our equipment in our wooden lockers and headed to the showers in the pool house. It was barely eight in the morning.

Chapter 14
New Hire

After a quick shower, I was sitting at my desk ostensibly working on selecting the shots for my *Ecosphere* column but mostly worrying about Oliver and trying to figure out who murdered Cara. I could think of a lot of reasons people might want her dead, but none of the people with reasons were the type to act on their issues violently.

I was concentrating so hard I didn't even notice when Genevra Blackthorne walked into my office. It wasn't until she cleared her throat softly and said my name that I looked up.

"I'm sorry, Genevra. I didn't realize you were here. Is my column late? I was just working on it. I should be done with it later today."

Genevra smiled. "No rush. It's not due until next week."

"Whew. That's a relief. I've been so frazzled lately I've decided to hire an assistant to help keep me on track. Did I forget we had a meeting? Or is it something to do with Oliver? Is he okay?"

Genevra bit her lip. "Oliver's fine, as far as I know. And you and I didn't have a meeting scheduled, but I'm hoping you can spare a few minutes to talk to me about that assistant role you're looking to fill."

"Sure. Do you have someone you think I should talk to?" I pushed my computer aside and picked up a pen to take down the contact details I assumed she was about to give me.

"Well, yes, I do." She blew out a breath, making her auburn bangs float above her forehead. "Me. I want you to interview me for the job."

My jaw dropped open. "Wow. That's a surprise. I didn't realize you were thinking of leaving Quokka Media. Liam will be devastated."

"Maybe. Maybe not. I think he'd be fine with it as long as I'd be working with you. He'd do anything to make your life easier, you know."

"That's nice to hear," I said. "But speaking of hearing, how did you find out about this so quickly? I only posted the job an hour ago."

She looked at her shoes, a stylish designer brand I recognized as crazy expensive. "I had an alert set up for new listings on RIO's job board. I couldn't believe it when I saw the posting this morning. It sounds like my dream job."

"Have you been unhappy at Quokka? Why do you want to leave?" I was puzzled. We'd worked well together, and she'd never given the slightest hint she was unhappy with her role there.

"No, not unhappy at all. I've loved working with you and Liam, and you've both taught me so much about the environment and the oceans." She bit her lip again. "You're good at everything. I want to learn from you."

That made me laugh. "Genevra, I just told you how I'm drowning here. You know I rely on you to do most of the work on *Ecosphere*. Even though I'm supposed to be the managing editor, you're the one who does all the managing. What will you gain by coming here?"

"This is a perfect role for me. I can help you with all the RIO stuff you always complain about—the budgets and the approvals and the research grants. I love that stuff, and I'll still manage *Ecosphere* for you if you want me to. And maybe you can teach me to dive if you have some time…" Her blue eyes were huge and pleading.

"I'll teach you to dive no matter what. You don't have to change jobs to take a dive class with me. They're open to the public, you know. Although I'd be happy to give you private lessons, if you prefer." I fidgeted with my pencil. Genevra was the ideal candidate. An Ivy League graduate with an MBA. A few years of experience managing projects, but not enough that RIO would be stifling. I liked her, and I never in my wildest dreams would have expected someone of her caliber to apply for the job. There were just two things standing in my way. Liam. Oliver. And, oh yeah, her salary. So, three things.

I decided to approach the easy problems first. "You know Oliver works here as well as at Fleming Environmental. How do you think you working here would affect your relationship with him?"

She paused a moment to think through her answer. "Honestly, I don't believe it would bother either one of us if we worked together. We wouldn't have too much interaction given the difference in our roles. He mostly does dive operations, right? And he's spending more of his time at Fleming Environmental, anyway. He loves learning about investment strategy."

I nodded. "And Liam? He's very important to RIO. Very important to me personally. And you're very important to Quokka Media. What will he think if you leave his company to work here?"

"He'd think it was brilliant." Liam stood in my office door, his blonde hair shining in a stray sunbeam peeking through the shutters that covered my shattered windows. "I'm all for it."

"Eavesdropping again, Mate?" I said in a poor imitation of his Aussie accent.

He grinned. "Didn't mean to, but I just happened in at the critical moment. I'm all for whatever makes your life easier, Fin. And if it makes you happy too, Genevra, that's just icing on the cake for me."

"The last issue is your salary. Did you see the range on the job posting? The pay scales here at RIO are different than at Quokka Media. I probably won't be able to match what you're earning."

Liam broke in. "Don't mind me butting in again, but if Genevra is going to continue managing *Ecosphere* for you while she works at RIO, Quokka will make up the difference in salary. With your permission, of course."

I drew in a deep breath. "You're sure this is what you want?"

She nodded, eyes shining. "It is."

"Okay then, you're hired. When can you start?"

Chapter 15
Liam Leaves

Genevra and Liam huddled in the hall for a moment and agreed her last day working for him would be a week away. She was bouncing with excitement when I asked her to drop by HR on her way out to get started on her paperwork to join RIO. She thanked me and left, leaving Liam and me alone in my office. He sat in one of the visitors' chairs.

"What brought you by so early this morning?" I said. "Things slow in the media biz?"

"No, everything is fine, but I have to go out of town for a few weeks. I didn't want you to think I'd abandoned you again, especially with Cara's murder and Oliver's troubles hanging over you."

Liam had left me a while back, ostensibly to finalize a divorce from his first wife. The problem for me was he'd stayed away for over a year with no communication. His departure had been in the middle of uncovering the drug problems at RIO, right as we were closing in on Cara and Lauren. Was the timing of his departure this close to their recent return merely a coincidence, or was it tied in with the drug dealing women?

Of course not. How could it be. I tamped down my suspicions.

Before he'd left last time, we'd been talking about building a life together. He'd returned, expecting us to pick up exactly where we'd left off, but I was uncomfortable. It wasn't like he'd been on the moon. He could have used his cell phone or email if the thought of me had ever crossed his mind, but he hadn't. It rankled all the more because he'd never explained his lack of communication or what had kept him away that long.

I mulled over his announcement. I was happy he'd let me know he was leaving town for a while. I knew his ex-wife had been living in the remote outback with no phone or email. He'd had to track her down across some rugged, desolate terrain. He'd had to find her before they could agree on the terms of their divorce. Maybe he really had been caught up in finding and divorcing his wife and couldn't call me. Although he was also starting up Quokka Media and its flagship periodical *Ecosphere* during the same time. He must have been able to communicate with the outside world when he'd needed or wanted to.

I knew he'd done the whole media thing—and *Ecosphere* in particular — for me, to give me an outlet for my underwater photography that hadn't been tainted by my nefarious ex. But even so, it wouldn't have killed him to call occasionally while he'd been gone. Now I was scared about him leaving again, but I knew if I wouldn't commit to him, I had no right to be upset.

"Is this the right time for you to be going out of town? With Genevra leaving Quokka, and Oliver in trouble over Cara's murder, friends and family might need you," I said. "*I need you*," I thought, but didn't say out loud.

Liam smiled as though he'd heard my unspoken words. "Nobody actually believes Oliver killed his mother—not even Dane Scott. But Oliver's been acting erratically, and letting his temper run free when he shouldn't. He's in jail partly to give him a chance to cool down, but mostly to protect him from his psycho twin sister Lily. Or whoever it is who tried to frame him for the murder."

I nodded. Dane had said the same thing, so I knew that was the reason Oliver was in jail. And since I'd told Liam there was nothing but friendship between us now, I also knew there was no real reason why he shouldn't leave Grand Cayman any time he wanted to go. Trying to feign indifference, I turned the conversation back to his impending departure.

"Where are you off to? Planning to start another groundbreaking company?" Liam was a brilliant thinker and a serial entrepreneur. If he'd said he was starting a new company, it wouldn't have surprised me.

But what he said did surprise me. "I'm heading to Switzerland. There are some financial things I need to take care of. And I might spend a few days skiing. Drink some hot chocolate. Climb a mountain. Relax a little. I need a vacation."

My mouth dropped open with surprise that anyone would need a vacation from our idyllic life here on Grand Cayman, but Liam was always full of surprises. "I didn't know you skied. Or climbed mountains."

"It's mostly the financial thing," he said, "but while I'm there I should take in some of the local attractions, don't you think?

I nodded. "Of course. Have fun." I bit my lip to keep it from trembling.

"I'm leaving tonight. But I'll call you," he said. "Every day." He leaned across my desk to touch my hand. "I promise."

Chapter 16
Justin

I'd already done a preliminary cut of the video of the brown octopus I'd seen on the dive with Chaun. The octopus had obligingly changed color several times, and then miraculously oozed into a tiny crevice in the coral. These beautiful creatures fascinated almost everyone, and I was considering using the video in RIO's foyer to entertain people while they waited in line to tour the aquarium. I'd put it aside for a while, so I'd have fresh eyes for the final edit, and now I was choosing the photos I wanted to include in my *Ecosphere* column when my phone rang.

"Fin, it's Ralph, the lobby security guard…"

"I know who you are, Ralph. What's up?" I asked.

"There's a mister Justin Nash here to see you. He said he usually just goes straight to your office, but during orientation you told me not to let anybody go into the office wing if they don't work here, so…"

"Quite right, Ralph. Thanks for being diligent. I'll come get him." I hung up the phone and stuck my feet into the flip flops I'd kicked under my desk. I knew being stopped would annoy Justin, but he'd taken liberties with RIO's equipment before, and in the past, he'd roamed the premises at will, even going into restricted areas.

He was Newton's assistant, so it wasn't that I thought he was up to no good, but it set a bad example for other visitors. We'd had enough incidents with unauthorized people causing damage that it made sense to put a hard and fast rule in place. Stopping visitors was the whole reason we'd hired Ralph to work the lobby. I was glad to see him taking the policy seriously, even though Justin was well known to us.

Justin was standing very close to Ralph, arms crossed and looking completely disgruntled. When he saw me, he said. "Tell this guy who I am. He doesn't need to stop me and make me wait for someone to pick me up like I'm a complete stranger. I've always been able to come and go without an escort."

"Sorry, Justin. New rules. If you don't have an employee badge, Ralph's job is to ask you to wait for an escort." I raised my shoulders in a "there's nothing I can do" gesture.

"But you're the boss. And I'm not just anyone. Tell him to let me through." Justin was clearly annoyed, and not above making a scene. Ralph was biting his lip and eyeing me fearfully.

I shook my head. "No can do. It's Ralph's job to stop people. It would be too much of a burden to expect him to decide who can enter without an escort and who needs to wait while he tracks one down. His instructions are, unless someone has an employee badge, they are restricted to the public areas of the building. I'm pleased to see he's following those instructions to the letter. Exactly as he should."

Both Ralph and Justin stared at me incredulously. Ralph because he'd obviously been expecting to be reprimanded, even though he'd been following my orders, and Justin because I'd actually dared to restrict his access.

Justin sputtered. "This is ridiculous. I'm going to speak to Newton about your new policy."

"Go right ahead, but as you know, Newton doesn't have any management authority at RIO. He's one of our major donors, but that doesn't give him the option to change our rules." I paused a moment. "And let me remind you I do have the authority, both here at RIO as well as at Fleming Environmental." I looked at him meaningfully, hoping to remind him without having to say it, that I was, in fact, his boss at Fleming Environmental.

I turned to Ralph and winked. "Please give Mr. Nash a visitor's badge."

Justin gaped. "You could issue an employee badge with a snap of your fingers if you wanted to."

I nodded. "I could. But you're not an employee. And really, Justin, is this the hill you want to die on?"

He flushed and looked away. Ralph held out a visitor's badge and Justin snatched it rudely from his hand. "Shall we meet in your office?" he asked haughtily.

"Sure. Do you want coffee or anything from the café before we head there?"

His nostrils flared. "I'm good, thanks."

We walked down the hall toward my office. Justin gawked at the damage to the windows and floors. "RIO really got hit hard in the storm, huh?"

"We did. And Eugene, Stewie, and Stanley are doing a great job of getting us back up and running. But that's what I wanted to talk to you about. We'll need a cash infusion from Fleming Environmental to cover the costs of repairs. I have some estimates to review with you."

We entered my office and sat at the small round table in the corner. I handed Justin a copy of the list of repairs and estimates Eugene and Stanley had prepared. "Remember, this is just preliminary, but I think it will cover most of the repairs." I paused a moment. "Unless something unexpected crops up."

He frowned. "Shouldn't you wait until you're sure how much you'll need? You don't want to go back to the well too often."

I shrugged. "It's Newton's well I'm drawing on, and this is what he asked me to do. He's my father as well as the founder of Fleming Environmental. I'm sure he'll be fine with it if I end up needing more money later. We need at least some of the funds to get started anyway. We might as well go for it all at once. That way I don't have to keep bugging you."

He tapped his pen on the number at the bottom of the page. "This is a big number. I don't think there's enough free cash in Fleming Environmental Investments' accounts. We might have to draw from Newton's personal funds, and remember I've told you before I was worried that he was outspending his assets. I'll want to check carefully to make sure he doesn't leave himself strapped. Do you have his account access information handy? It will really help accelerate the transfer of funds if you do."

I'd forgotten about Justin's prior questions about Newton's personal finances until he mentioned it just now. A while ago, Justin had hinted to me on several occasions Newton was running short of funds. It had been when my friends Gus and Theresa had been kidnapped, and Newton had offered to pay the ransom, but luckily, it hadn't been necessary for Newton to step in.

I looked at Justin, puzzled. "No, I've told you this before. You know I don't have access to his personal accounts, just the Fleming Environmental funds. And I'm surprised you think an amount this small would wipe out the business accounts of a multi-billion dollar company. And as far as Newton's personal accounts—not that it should be your concern—Newton's a multi-billionaire. It's pretty hard to outspend your assets when you have that much money. He's not worried, but I'll talk to him about it. Or you can talk to him since it seems to be a problem for you."

Justin gathered up his papers and tapped them on the table. "No, don't bother him with this. I'll shuffle some allocations around and it should be fine. I'll call you if I have any questions. Otherwise, I'll get the funds transferred to RIO by the end of the week." He smiled. "Gotta run. Lunch later this week? We could go to Nelsons in my electric car. I know you love the car, and you love to eat at Nelson's."

There was so much wrong with Justin's last few sentences. He'd been trying to start a relationship with me for a couple of years now, but I had all the love interests I could handle between Liam and Benjamin. I'd tried everything I could think of to discourage him, but he never seemed to get the message.

I found his expensive car ostentatious, and I was always embarrassed to ride in it. The thing cost well into six figures, and it was just too pretentious for me to be comfortable with. And Justin was always bemoaning the size of the payments, making me wonder why he'd bought such an expensive vehicle if he couldn't afford it.

And he never seemed to catch on to the fact I actually dislike going to Nelson's. It's owned by Stefan Gibb, the man I'd once thought was at least partially responsible for my stepfather's death.

Stefan and I had a cordial relationship now, but I didn't like spending time with him, and I didn't like to patronize his restaurant very often, especially because he comped everything I ordered, every time I went there. I couldn't help thinking that because it was free, Justin enjoyed taking me to Nelson's even more than he would have otherwise. At least this time I had a good excuse for saying no. In fact, I had several good excuses.

"Sorry, Justin. I don't have time. Everybody at RIO is working double shifts to help get us back up and running after the storm. My *Ecosphere* column is due this week, and I'm running behind. Between the aftermath of the storm, Maddy being away so long, and Oliver sitting in jail, I haven't got a free moment. Any time I do have, I need to spend working on clearing my brother's name. I can't justify going out for a long lunch. Maybe another time."

Justin opened his mouth, and I sensed he was going to try to cajole me into joining him. This time, I was saved from having to come up with even more excuses by the arrival of DS Scott.

"Hello, Justin. Fin, I hope you can spare me a few minutes. I have some questions and a few ideas I'd like to discuss with you. Is this a good time?"

I swallowed my sigh of relief. "Sure thing, Dane. Justin was just leaving. And Justin, unless I hear from you before then, I'll expect the funds to be in RIO's account by Friday. We good?"

He nodded and stood up. "If you're sure you're not going to be free for lunch...?"

I shook my head. "Sorry."

"Okay then. I'll get right on the transfer and let you know if I run into any problems."

Dane watched him saunter down the hall toward the lobby, then he looked at me. "You two dating? I thought you were seeing Benjamin Brooks."

Last year when Dane and I worked together to solve the kidnapping and he and Maddy had been dating, we'd become very close. I wasn't surprised he felt comfortable questioning my love life. "Nope. Not dating Justin. We work together at Fleming Environmental, that's all. And it's just a casual thing with me and Benjamin."

Dane nodded. "Good to know. Mind if I sit?" He crossed the few steps to the corner table and sat in the chair Justin had just vacated.

"We got the DNA swabs results from the oilskins you found in the basement. As you'd expect, since they're his, some of the DNA belonged to Oliver." He looked at me. "But we identified a couple of other people too. Is there anyone who might have borrowed Oliver's raingear? I checked with him, but he doesn't remember ever lending it out."

"Everybody keeps their foul weather gear in their lockers in the pool house unless they're assigned to the *Omega*. Then they usually keep it aboard ship."

The *Omega*, RIO's research vessel, was a more-or-less permanent home to about fifty RIO employees, but the ship housed more than 200 of us when we were working on our annual documentaries. "It could have been anyone. It doesn't rain hard often here, and Oliver's been away at school off-and-on for the last few years. There's no way to even guess when or if someone might have borrowed Oliver's gear. Don't the police have a way of finding out who the mystery DNA belongs to?"

"Our DNA lab doesn't have a match, but that just means whoever it belongs to doesn't have a criminal record. At least, not here. We can coordinate with other labs if we have to, but it might make more sense if we run a series of elimination tests on the RIO staff and frequent visitors to see if a match pops up. What do you think?"

I nodded. "You know we'll do whatever it takes to prove Oliver is innocent, so no problem. Can we do the swabbing here on site, or do I need to send everybody to your lab?"

"No, not everybody," he said. "We know whoever wore the slicker is a male. We only need to test male employees. And only those who worked here after Oliver bought the oilskins. He said he thinks he bought them through RIO. Will your records tell us how long he's had them?"

"Yeah, I'll get someone to go through the purchase records and see what we can find out." I knew there was no one else with the bandwidth to do this. It was one more thing that would end up on my to do list. But if tracking down the date Oliver received his raingear would help clear my brother, I'd put my heart and soul into it. I made a note on my to do list before I spoke again. "Any news on Lily? Or Alec?"

He sighed. "No. We've been on the lookout for Lily, but nobody's seen her. We know Alec is living on his boat at the yacht club. We've seen him go in and out of commercial buildings with a realtor almost daily. His story that he's here looking for a new headquarters building may be true. I wish we had a sample of his DNA though. It would set my mind at rest if I knew he wasn't involved."

I shook my head. "Even if it isn't his DNA in the slicker doesn't mean he's not involved in this somehow. Just means he's too smart to do any of the dirty work himself."

"Probably true, but even so, I wish I had a sample of his DNA. We might get lucky."

"Maybe. By the way, how is Oliver doing? Does he need anything? Can I see him?" He hadn't been my brother long, but I'd loved him as though he were part of my family for years before Maddy and Newton adopted him. He and I shared a love of the ocean and the outdoors—and Ray. It hurt me to think of him stuck in a jail cell.

"Maddy brought him some clothes and toiletries this morning, plus a few books. I don't think he needs anything else, but a visit from his older sister might cheer him up. You can see him whenever you want."

"You're being pretty lenient with a murder suspect," I said.

He flushed. "Yes, I am, but even though the evidence to date points to him, I don't think Oliver is a murderer. And I certainly don't think he'd ever kill his biological mother. In truth, he doesn't deserve to be in jail any more than you or I do. I'm mainly concerned because his evil twin sister Lily is in town. Now her, I can see killing Cara—or anyone else who gets in her way."

He stared through the storm shutters still obscuring the view through my window. "No, Oliver's in that cell as much to keep him safe as to keep him from leaving the island. That's one reason I want to solve this case as fast as I can." He rose. "Be careful, Fin. You never know who's out there."

Chapter 17
Cookies

By now it was late afternoon. I'd been at work since before five in the morning, and I felt as though I hadn't accomplished any of my goals for the day. I needed to go through all our purchase records to see if I could find out when Oliver bought his raingear, and I'd promised Genevra I'd have my column ready by the end of the day. I groaned.

I hadn't had anything to eat or drink since the coffee and blueberry muffins before the dive this morning. I was starving and so thirsty my mouth felt like the Sahara. I slumped over my desk with my head resting on my arms. I needed water, and I needed to eat, but I was too beat to go in search of food.

Something cold rolled across the back of my neck and I stretched into it without lifting my head or opening my eyes. "I hope that's a bottle of water and I hope it's for me," I said.

"Right on both counts. This turkey club sandwich is for you too. The chocolate chip cookies are mine, although if you eat all your lunch, I might share some with you." Benjamin placed a covered plate on the desk in front of me, along with a bag of chips, and the bottle of icy cold water.

"My hero," I said as I lifted the cover off the sandwich he'd brought. It was my favorite kind, and this one was a feast for my senses before I'd even taken a bite. The toasted bread was a soft golden brown; the tomato slices were a bright and cheery red; the lettuce was a crisp and vibrant green. The sandwich was sliced diagonally across the bread, and the smell of the bacon and turkey was heavenly. It was one of the most beautiful—and welcome—sights I'd ever seen. Wasting no time, I picked up one half and took a bite. I may have moaned, but I'll never admit it.

Benjamin sat in the visitors chair across from me and nibbled on a cookie. He watched me eat with a small smile on his face.

When I'd placed the last potato chip crumb on my tongue with the tip of my finger, he handed me the bag of cookies.

"You earned them," he said.

I took out one cookie and left the bag on the table between us. "Why don't you have another one or two? I can't possibly eat them all," I said.

But then I did manage to eat them all, and Benjamin laughed until tears rolled down his face when I balled up the empty bag. After a few seconds of watching him laugh, I joined in, realizing I was suddenly happier than I'd been in months.

Chapter 18
Visiting Oliver

B enjamin and I were still laughing when Eugene walked into my office. "What's so funny?" he asked. "Things have been pretty serious around here lately, and I could use a good laugh too."

Benjamin swallowed hard. "Fin ate all the cookies." He dissolved into laughter again.

"That's no big deal. I've been watching her eat all the cookies since she was a little girl. You'd never know it to look at her though."

He smiled at me, and I realized I'd known Eugene nearly my entire life. He was a nice man, and he's been a good friend to Maddy—as he was to Ray while Ray was still alive.

I bit my tongue to stop the giggles. "What can I do for you, Eugene?"

"The lumberyard is here with the materials to rebuild the dock, and they want a check. Normally they'd send us an invoice, but after the storm there's a lot of demand for lumber and cement. They could charge us double or triple what they usually do. As it is, I had to agree to a ten percent surcharge and payment on delivery. I hope that's okay."

I nodded. "We've got to rebuild, so whatever it takes. Just try to keep the surcharges to a minimum," I said.

Benjamin stood. "C'mon, Eugene. I'll cut you a check." He turned to me. "Will I see you later?"

"No, sorry. Right now, I'm going to visit Oliver and then I'm headed home. I need to get some sleep, and my *Ecosphere* column is due today." I smiled. "But thanks for the sandwich. And the cookies." We both burst out laughing again. Eugene smiled and shook his head. He left my office and walked down the hall. Benjamin stepped through the door, then turned back and waved goodbye before he followed Eugene toward his corner office.

I shook my head fondly and pulled the canvas tote bag I used as a purse out of my bottom desk drawer. I emailed myself the notes I'd been making about my *Ecosphere* column, so I'd have them to work from when I reached my home office. Then I hurried toward the main door.

The smell of chocolate chip cookies baking wafted from the café out into the lobby, and I rushed inside to pick up a half dozen cookies for my brother. He could probably use something to cheer him up. I thanked the lady behind the register, put the bag of cookies carefully in my tote, and raced to my car.

It was a short drive from RIO to the detention center on Fairbanks Road. The cookies were still warm when I arrived. Apparently, DS Scott had told the staff that Oliver was allowed unlimited visitors. The sergeant on duty at the desk asked me for my ID, even though he knew me. I didn't complain, just handed him my ID card and my tote for his inspection.

While he was logging my information into his records, Noah and Austin Gibb entered the lobby from the door that led back to the cells. Noah and Austin were Stefan Gibb's younger brothers, and they'd become good friends with Oliver while we were on the treasure expedition. I was glad to see they'd remained friends in the intervening time.

Killer Storm

I waved to them, and they came over to say hello.

"Thanks for coming to visit Oliver. You've been good friends to him, and I appreciate it."

Both boys blushed, but they smiled.

Noah, the elder of the two, spoke. "He's a good guy. And you and the others at RIO saved our brother's life that time. We'll always be grateful to you. And Oliver's part of RIO, as well as our friend. We know he's innocent, so of course we'd visit him." His voice cracked. "Dylan didn't live much longer after the drug overdose, thanks to that witch, but at least we had a little more time with him. And we're always grateful she didn't get Oliver too."

I wasn't sure whether Noah was referring to the woman we'd found in the sunken ship, who legend had it was a witch, or to Lauren Foster, the notorious drug dealer who'd dosed his brother Dylan with lethal drugs, or to Cara Flores, Oliver's biological mother. In my book, each of those women had earned the epithet of witch— and probably a much stronger word.

Austin's eyes looked haunted by the memory of his dead brother. "I miss Dylan every day, but Oliver's become almost like another brother to us. Almost like he was sent to fill Dylan's place in the family. We'll do anything we can to help him prove he's innocent. We know he'd never kill anyone. And right now, he's pretty broken up about losing his biological mother."

I pulled Austin into a hug and patted his back. The youngest of the brothers, he was barely twenty-one, and he, Dylan, and Stefan had been on their own for many years. Stefan, the eldest, had tried to fill the role of both mother and father to his brothers, but money had always been tight, and he'd been away at sea for long periods. The Gibb brothers were always hungry for affection.

After a few seconds Austin gulped and pulled away. "Thank you. I needed a hug."

He shuffled his feet. "I was going to call you today to see if you need any extra help with the storm cleanup around RIO. Or at your place. Or with any of the boats. I'm willing to pitch in wherever you need me."

I thought about it for a second before I answered. "Thanks, Austin. That would be great. I can pay you an hourly rate for any time you put in."

Because Dylan Gibb had died aboard the *Omega* and because the boys had once helped save Oliver's life, RIO had given the Gibb family the salvage reward we'd earned from recovering the Queen's Tiara treasure. I knew Austin didn't really need the money I could pay him. On the other hand, I wouldn't take advantage of him by letting him work for free. "Can you come by tomorrow morning? I'll ask Stewie and Eugene to figure out where you're most needed."

"Me too?" asked Noah.

"Sure. We'll take all the help we can get." I said. Behind them, I noticed the sergeant motioning to me that I was approved to go in to see Oliver, so I added, "I have to visit Oliver now, but I'll probably see you tomorrow at RIO."

The boys high fived each other, said goodbye, and left through the main entrance, while I picked up my bag from the sergeant and went through the door leading to the cells.

I walked through the dimly lit corridors and felt sorrow that Oliver was stuck in this dismal place. I knew I had to redouble my efforts to prove his innocence.

All the cells I passed were empty until I reached the end of the hall, where Oliver was being held. He was alone in his cell, lying on his back in the uncomfortable looking metal bunk suspended from the cinderblock wall. He was so tall his feet hung over the end of the bed. The pad on the cot looked thin and lumpy, and there was no pillow. He had the threadbare blanket draped over his shoulders.

His hands were behind his head and his eyes were closed. I thought he was asleep, but then he gave a small sob, like he was trying not to cry. Tears slid down his face and ran into the white ear buds he wore. I said his name, raising my voice a little, hoping he'd hear me over the noise of whatever he was listening to.

The second time I said "Oliver" he sat up, dashed the tears off his face and pulled the tiny speakers out of his ears. "Fin! You didn't have to come." He looked sheepish for a moment. "But I'm really glad you did. I owe you a huge apology. I've been acting like a jerk, and I don't know why." His voice broke, and I thought I saw more tears in his eyes, but it could have been a trick of the light.

The cynical side of me remembered his twin sister was a sociopath who could generate tears on a moment's notice, without any provocation whatsoever. Then I shoved that thought aside. This was my friend Oliver, my adopted brother, and I loved him.

I pulled the bag of cookies out of my tote. "I brought your favorites. They're still warm."

He reached through the bars and accepted the bag eagerly. Then he remembered his manners. "I'm happy to share. Would you like one?"

That set me to laughing, and Oliver joined in, even though he probably had no idea what I found so funny. By the time I stopped giggling and told him I had just eaten a whole bag of cookies by myself, he and I were back on our usual good terms. Oliver was no longer overwhelmed by grief. At least for a while.

There was an uncomfortable looking folding chair across from Oliver's cell, and I dragged it nearer so we could talk without shouting. "I want to help. I can investigate or do errands. What do you need?"

He looked up at the dingy ceiling and I thought for a moment he would cry again. Then he said, "I'm just grieving. My biological mother is dead. She wasn't a great mother, but in her own way, I know she loved me. And I loved her. I can't believe anyone would think I could kill my own mother." His voice cracked and he swallowed hard.

"I don't think that." I thought for a split second about whether I should tell him this next bit or not. Had Dane said it in confidence? I didn't think so. "DS Scott doesn't think you did it either. He brought you here partly because the early evidence points to you, but mostly to keep you safe. He's concerned about Lily or some of your mother's unsavory friends coming after you. Keep your chin up. Things are not as bad as they might look. We'll get you out of this."

Oliver let out a huge sigh—so big I thought he might have been holding his breath since they arrested him yesterday.

"Hey, we do have one lead," I said. "Did you ever lend your rain gear to anyone else? And do you remember when you bought it?"

"Sure" he said. "While we were on the treasure expedition, Austin, Dylan, and Noah borrowed it. Maybe Stefan. Todd borrowed it too." He paused for a quiet moment, remembering his late friend Todd who had turned out not to be much of a friend.

Then he continued. "I don't remember ever lending it to anyone while at RIO, but you know everybody's rain gear is all just hanging there in the locker room. There's nothing to stop anyone from using somebody else's stuff if they wanted to. Although, most people who work at RIO would probably ask permission if they wanted to borrow it."

"I agree," I said. "Dane is going to do some DNA tests on current and past RIO employees. It would help if you could narrow down when you bought it. That way we could eliminate former employees who left before you acquired it."

"Hmm, I think I got it just before we left on the treasure expedition. Maddy wanted to make sure I had everything I might need for the trip, but I never used it while we were away. Remember, I rode out the storm with you and Newton on the *Tranquility*. I remember though I put the slicker in my footlocker and loaded it on the *Omega* the same day it arrived." His face brightened. "So it wasn't that long ago I got it. There can't be many people who've worked at RIO in that short a time."

I didn't want to disillusion him, but it had been more than two years since that expedition. And although the research staff usually stayed for several years while they worked on their projects, the rest of the staff was more volatile. People who worked in the café, the aquarium tour guides, the maintenance crew, the office staff—they came and went with frequency. Like most businesses, we had a lot of personnel turnover. There could be hundreds of people we'd need to track down and test—and the killer might not even have been the stealthy figure in the slicker I'd seen during the storm. I was pretty sure Dane would consider this avenue of investigation a dead end unless we found more information to tie Cara's murder with the mysterious figure in the rain.

Oliver had been steadily munching on his cookies while we talked, and now he crumpled the empty bag. There was no trash receptacle in his cell, so he passed it to me through the bars. He usually didn't eat a lot of sweets. I wondered whether his binge was driven by hunger or stress.

"Are they feeding you okay? Should I have meals delivered for you?" I asked. "I don't want you to get sick on top of everything else."

"Nah. Food's okay. Boring, and loaded with fat and salt, but okay. Don't go to any trouble. And anyway, from what you said, I probably won't be here very long. Dane will do a few DNA tests, identify the killer, and I'll be out. Free as a bird."

That wasn't exactly what I'd said, but since it made Oliver feel better, I didn't correct him. It was my job to worry about how long he'd be in here. His job was just to stay strong.

"Sorry to cut this visit short, but I have to go. Today's the deadline for my *Ecosphere* column, and I can't hold up production on the issue. What kind of an example would that set?" I smiled. "Oh, before I go, I have some good news. I hired Genevra as my assistant at RIO. She's organized I bet I'll never be behind schedule again."

He seemed surprised. "Genevra? At RIO? What about Quokka Media? I thought she loved working with Liam?"

"I did too. And she does love working with Liam, but she said she wanted some new challenges, and she wants to learn more about diving and the ocean." I noticed the frozen expression on Oliver's face, and I hoped he wasn't upset about his girlfriend joining the family business. "It's okay with you, isn't it? She said she didn't think you'd mind."

He turned away. "I don't mind. I won't keep you since you've got work to do." He lay back down on the cot, inserted his earbuds, and shut his eyes. I watched for a moment, but he didn't move or look at me.

Chapter 19
Jet Skis

B ack at home, I worked on my *Ecosphere* column until nearly midnight. I pushed send with only about three minutes to spare if I were going to keep my promise to have it to Genevra by the end of the day. Then I tumbled into my bed and slept soundly through the night.

I was awakened before sunrise by a scratching sound on my sliding patio door. For the last few weeks, Chico, my next door neighbor's free-range pet rooster had been coming over before dawn for a handout. I'd made the mistake of giving him a handful of seeds one day when he'd been pecking listlessly at the dirt in my front yard. Since then, he wouldn't even crow in the dawn until I gave him a handful of seeds. He'd seemed forlorn that day, but now it was apparent he felt like I owed him a handout, and he came over every morning to collect his reward. I had no idea what he did on the days I slept at Newton's or on the *Tranquility*.

Sighing at the loss of those last few minutes of sleep, I rose to give Chico his seeds. He gobbled them up and left without a thank you. A few minutes later, I heard him crowing loudly, heralding the dawn. At least I wouldn't be the only one getting up at sunrise.

I rushed through my morning routine so I could get to the office early. I was dragging with exhaustion, and not looking forward to a long day of desk work.

When Benjamin came in bearing coffee at six fifteen, I thanked my lucky stars Maddy had hired him a few years ago. He was a terrific co-worker and an extremely good friend. He was even a perfect boyfriend—sweet and undemanding. RIO—and I—were both lucky he was around.

"Drink up," he said. "I have a surprise for you." He was practically vibrating with excitement.

I couldn't imagine what could have made him so happy this early in the morning, but I obediently drank my coffee. "Done," I said after a few steaming swallows. "What's up?"

"It's outside," he said. "Come see."

We walked down the long hall and through the rear door next to Maddy's office. When I stepped outside, it was disheartening to see the usually pristine back lawn was still almost entirely bare dirt, even though the debris had been cleared away. What was left of the white crushed shells had been washed and placed back on the paths that led to the dive shop, the main dock, and the shore dive entry point, but we'd lost so many of the shells to wind and erosion the paths looked skimpy and unkempt.

Benjamin and I ambled down the path, but I was distraught by the sorry condition of RIO's once beautiful grounds, so I didn't notice the twin canvas-covered mounds sitting side-by-side next to a pile of landscaping supplies near the ocean's edge.

When we stopped in front of the two tarps, Benjamin was practically jumping out of his skin. I don't think I'd ever seen him this excited.

"Don't you want to know what they are?" he asked. "The one on the right is for you."

I reached over to remove the canvas covering the one on the right. As I lifted the tarp, I caught a glimpse of a bright metallic-blue finish and an aerodynamically shaped nose.

A jet ski. I dropped the canvas cover. "You know I was nearly killed by one of these a few years ago, right?"

His face fell. "I had forgotten about Lily attacking you. I wasn't around here back then. It's more like a legend than a real world occurrence to me. I'm sorry. I'll send them back."

I put my hand on his arm. "It's okay. You know me. Sooner or later, I have to face everything that scares me. Today's the day to face this fear, that's all."

"True. You're so brave you make me feel like a wimp, and you're strong, and smart, and beautiful…"

"Enough." I held up a hand. "But I can't accept this from you. It's way too expensive."

Now he blushed. "You're right about them being expensive, but these are rentals. I thought you might want to take one out for a little freediving—it would get you some time in deep water while you wait for the *Tranquility* to return." Then he slapped his forehead. "I'm so stupid. You don't freedive since Ray's death either. I'll call the rental place and have them pick them up right away. I'm sorry." He looked so contrite I felt bad for him.

"They're here now, and you probably can't get your money back. It's time I got over both my fears, and if he were still here, Ray wouldn't want to hold me back. You know I still free dive sometimes when I'm doing photography. I just don't do it competitively the way you do. And I'm willing to take a stab at riding one of these babies." I lifted the canvas again and looked at the sleek machine. "In fact, I'm sort of excited to try it out. Let's go."

Benjamin grinned. We rushed back inside to the locker rooms to change into our bathing suits. I walked outside and stuck a piece of shell in the exit doorway so it couldn't quite close all the way. That way, I'd be able to get in this way later without having to bring my keys or ID badge on the dives with me.

I thought briefly of how annoyed Eugene or DS Scott would be if either found out I was flaunting security protocols this way, but most people were still stuck at their homes cleaning up after the storm. There wouldn't be anyone around to notice the barely visible protrusion where the door's edge stuck out past the jamb.

I walked across the yard, watching Benjamin and Stewie drooling over the two personal watercraft sitting side-by-side on the shore. An emerald-green one gleamed next to the blue one. Both machines looked sleek and fast.

Stewie grinned when he saw me coming. "I'm jealous. These look like fun."

Benjamin waggled his eyebrows. "We'll let you know when we get back. You're welcome to try one out later."

"I dunno. My boss can be a real stickler, and she's determined to get this place back into shape ASAP after that hurricane."

I laughed. "Don't be ridiculous, Stewie. I bet you'd have a ball. Why don't you see if you can get Doc to go for a ride with you? I bet she'd love to try it too."

Stewie's cheeks turned pink, as they always did whenever anyone alluded to his relationship with Doc. "I bet she would at that. Thanks. I'll give her a call."

"Let me know when you're ready to go and I'll cover the dive shop for you if you think anyone will be needing tanks. And by the way, I hired Noah and Austin Gibb to work part-time on the cleanup. I'd planned to assign one of them to you. Do you have a preference?"

Stewie shrugged. "Both good kids. Either will be fine with me. Thanks. I'll see you when you get back." He helped Benjamin push the jet skis into the shallows.

Killer Storm

I had to admit freediving preparation was a lot simpler than scuba. We didn't have to lug regulators, tanks, weights, or BCDs to get going. All we needed were our lightweight fins and we were good to go.

Benjamin held out a hand to help me mount the big blue machine, but he was still holding his hand in the air while I jumped aboard, turned the throttle, and revved the engine. When I was halfway across our cove, I did a quick turn and saw Stewie and Benjamin laughing on shore. I waved my arm over my head, and Benjamin straddled his water scooter and headed out after me.

He came to a stop a few feet away. "I take it you've ridden one of these before."

I was laughing so hard I could barely talk. "Oh, I thought you knew me better than that. In all the time I've known you, did I forget to mention I grew up on the water? When it comes to watercraft, there aren't many I haven't tried before."

Benjamin slapped his forehead and laughed too. "Yup, of course I knew that. I was so excited about going freediving that for a moment I forgot who I was dealing with. But now I remember. You're Fin Fleming, world famous diver and acclaimed underwater photographer. Thank you for agreeing to let me tag along. I am humbled and honored."

"Cut it out, silly. Where shall we go?" I asked.

"I was thinking the deep wall off Cobalt Coast Resort. It's not too far away, so it won't take all day to get there. Most other dive shops don't dive there, and most shore divers either can't swim far enough to get to the wall or they don't know it's there. It's pristine. A beautiful wall dive. And a great place to freedive." Both Benjamin and I loved to dive along walls—the sheer vertical coral and rock formations that dropped straight down to hundreds or thousands of feet underwater.

"Brilliant," I said. "I'll race you." I revved the engine of my water scooter and left Benjamin behind in a spray of crystal droplets.

He tried hard to catch me, but I had too much of a head start. I was floating happily over the wall when Benjamin arrived, splashing me with spume as he swerved to a stop. "Serves you right," he said when I spluttered and wiped the salt water from my eyes.

I looked at the distant shore and the wide open expanse behind us. "How will we keep the scooters from drifting away? Are we going to dive 'one up, one down'?" I was referring to the freediving method of taking turns diving, where a diver on the surface stayed alert for problems while the other buddy dove.

"Nope," he said, opening a compartment on his scooter. "I've got an anchor. We can tether them together. I'll dive down and set the anchor in the sand. Then we can both dive at the same time." He grinned at me. "Unless you're chicken and need me to keep watch."

Benjamin was a very accomplished freediver, but he usually used scuba when we were together in deference to my preference.

"Who are you calling chicken? I don't need a babysitter. You can give me that anchor line. I'll do the honors."

Benjamin removed some lines and an anchor from the rear storage compartment. First, he fastened the two water scooters together with a short line, then he hung a small foam bumper on the line to keep the boats from crashing into each other if they were tossed by the waves. Then he handed me the anchor, which was just a bright yellow bag full of sand with a very long line attached. "You sure?" he said.

"Yup. Very sure." I took a few deep breaths to saturate my tissues with oxygen, then I turned away from Benjamin's scooter, put both legs over the side, stuck my feet into the long, rigid fins used for free-diving, and slid into the water, clutching the heavy bag.

I had to admit free diving had a marvelous feeling of freedom. No cumbersome breathing apparatus or heavy weights—other than the anchor bag. The bag's weight helped pull me down, but it was large and awkward to hold. I swam hard using one arm and both legs, looking for a good spot to position the anchor, which by design, simply sits on a sandy spot on the ocean floor.

The underwater terrain here was perfect for this. There was a large sandy swath at about fifty feet of depth, then the reef rose up into about ten feet of rocks and coral before plunging into a vertical wall that went down thousands of feet. I placed the sandbag anchor far enough away from the coral the line wouldn't bump against it.

I still felt like I had plenty of air, so I took a look around. While I was peering across the reef toward the wreck, I heard a loud thrumming. It seemed to get louder with each second that passed.

The next thing I knew, I was pushed aside, tumbled head over heels by a thick wall of water pressure. When I managed to right myself, I looked in the direction of the forcefield and saw a small submarine cresting the reef.

The submarine was the type that unbelievably wealthy yacht owners use as tenders on their yachts. It had two runners like a sled and a large clear bubble between them that gave the captain the ability to see all around. The cockpit held seats for five, although only one was occupied. The sub was painted a beautiful shade of blue, with green accents. An unfamiliar gold logo adorned one side. I watched the submarine come closer, and I could feel the cavitation of the water increasing as it approached.

It was so near me that if it had been a larger or more powerful vessel, I'd have been sucked into its path with no hope of escape. As it was, I could barely hold my position. The submarine's captain seemed totally unaware of—or unconcerned by— my presence because the sub passed within ten or fifteen feet of me. I looked at the captain, and almost gasped in a breath that might have been fatal this far underwater.

The pilot was Lauren Forster, the head of the drug ring that had targeted RIO last year. She'd worked with Oliver's mother, Cara Flores, to get drugs aboard the *Omega*, and she'd distributed drugs to many RIO employees on the island. Worse yet, she'd nearly killed

Oliver and had succeeded in killing Dylan Gibb. Sadly, she'd also been responsible for Stewie's last tumble off the wagon into the morass of drugs and alcohol from which he'd only recently recovered.

After the treasure expedition, we'd all thought Lauren had left for good when her role as a drug dealer had come to light, but she'd managed to flee the Omega before we could apprehend her. Since she was gone and all her crimes had taken place in international waters, we breathed a sigh of relief and thought to ourselves, "Good riddance."

But seeing her now, it seemed she'd merely changed her distribution method. I was still staring at her in disbelief when she turned her head and saw me hovering a few feet from her boat. Her face changed when she recognized me. Her lips tightened, and her hate-filled eyes narrowed.

She tried to steer the sub toward me, apparently hoping to hit me and render me unconscious or too injured to make it to shore, but her hands moved a split second before the boat could respond. I kicked hard at an angle away from the sub and toward its rear. When I was in the clear, I headed for the surface. I felt sure if I were on the surface, she'd leave me alone because she wouldn't want to take a chance someone would see the sub and ruin her latest drug delivery scheme.

My heart was hammering, and my lungs felt ready to burst, but I swam for all I was worth. I was moving fast enough I shot several feet out of the water when I broke the surface. I sucked in a lungful of air. "We have to go get Dane. Lauren Forster is here on Grand Cayman. I saw her piloting a Triton sub."

Benjamin didn't waste any time peering into the deep water to try to see the sub. He reached over and disconnected our scooters. "You go. I'll get the anchor and follow."

"I can't leave you out here alone. She's dangerous. She tried to ram me with a submarine." It sounded ludicrous when I said it out loud.

Lauren was ruthless. She didn't know Benjamin, but she'd know I probably knew him because it was unlikely two free divers would be diving in the same location at the same time unless they had at least a nodding acquaintance. That might be enough to make him a target for her if she was still in the area.

He spoke calmly. "You go ahead. I'll be fine. Dane needs to know as soon as possible. And I feel like Lauren being in the picture will put Oliver in the clear for Cara's murder. The sooner we get him out of that jail cell the better I'll feel. Go. I'll be right behind you."

I bit my lip, unsure what to do.

Benjamin reached over and pushed the starter on my scooter. "Go."

Chapter 20
Search

I jetted off, pushing my sea scooter well over the island's legal maximum speed of five miles per hour. I wanted to make Dane aware of Lauren's presence on the island as quickly as possible. My adrenaline was sky high, and my hands were shaking from the encounter with her. And I was terrified for Benjamin, alone in the ocean with a dangerous killer—and not the marine kind, most of whom were nowhere near as deliberately malicious as I knew Lauren to be.

I was relieved when I saw the familiar cove at RIO, and I pushed my scooter hard. Cutting the engine just before it ran aground, I coasted up onto the shore. I jumped off into the gentle wavelets, shouting for Stewie, and I ran barefoot toward the open dive shop door.

I was surprised when Noah Gibb came out instead of Stewie, but he rushed over to me. "What do you need? How can I help?"

"I need a phone. It's urgent." I could hear the stress in my own voice, and I cursed myself for leaving my phone on the desk in my office.

Noah reached into a pocket of his shorts and handed me his phone. "Here. Use mine." He pressed his index finger against the fingerprint reader and walked away to give me some privacy.

I couldn't remember Dane's direct number, so I dialed 911. When the dispatcher answered, I identified myself. "I'm working with DS Scott on a case, and I need to get in touch with him right away. Can you please ask him to call me as soon as possible? It's urgent." I started race walking toward the back door.

"This isn't an answering service," the dispatcher said. "If you were really working together, you'd have his direct number."

"I do have it. I just don't have my phone…Oh the heck with it." By now I was inside and only a few feet away from my office and my own phone. I strode across the remaining distance. Then I put Noah's phone on the table and yanked mine out of the top drawer of my desk. I'd programmed Dane's number into speed dial last year when we worked together on the kidnapping case, so I only had to hit the designated key.

He answered on the first ring. "Fin, what's up? The dispatcher just called and said you were looking for me urgently. Are you okay? … Is Maddy okay?"

"We're both fine. I just saw Lauren Forster. I rushed back to RIO to call you, but I left Benjamin behind. I'm afraid she'll go after him in her submarine, and he's out there all alone…" I bit back a sob.

"Where is he?" Dane's voice was calm.

"Out on the deep wall in front of Cobalt Coast Resort. We were freediving off sea scooters. He stayed behind to retrieve the anchor." I slapped my forehead. "We should have just left it. I wasn't thinking clearly after holding my breath for so long underwater."

"Okay, don't worry. I'll send a team out to look for him. Take a deep breath. I'll be right there." He disconnected.

I followed his advice and inhaled slowly and deeply. Then again. As my body's oxygen balance returned to normal, I felt calmer. I took a spare pair of flip flops out of my bottom drawer and put them on, then I went outside to return Noah's phone. He'd gone back to work removing the valves from all the empty scuba tanks so Stewie could do the visual inspections faster.

"Thanks for the use of your phone, Noah. I'm sorry I was in such a panic." I handed him his phone.

"No problem, Miss Fleming. You can borrow it any time." He slipped the phone back in his pocket and smiled at me.

"Where is Stewie, by the way?" I asked.

"He went to the hardware store. We needed some more supplies before we could start working on rebuilding the docks. He should be back any minute."

I was surprised Stewie felt ready to start rebuilding the dock this quickly, but when I looked around the dive shop, I marveled at the progress he'd already made in repairing the storm damage. The walls and roof were patched—not finished—but patched well enough to be secure from the weather and casual break-ins.

The inventory had all been put away, and anything that had been damaged by the storm had been cleaned and placed on a sale rack or in the rental gear cabinet. Enough of the tanks had been through visual inspections that we had plenty to last us through a day or two of typical dives, and since right now our walk-in tourist volume was way down anyway, we didn't need many rental tanks. We were ready to open for business, at least for classes, retail sales, and shore dives, which were three of our four cornerstone moneymakers from dive operations. Stewie must have worked around the clock to accomplish all this in such a short time.

I turned to leave and nearly bumped into my friend Chaun who came in carrying three large cups of icy lemonade from the café. "Oh, Fin. I didn't know you were here, or I'd have brought you one." He held out one of the cups. "Here. You can have mine."

"No thanks, Chaun. I'm good. What are you doing here?"

"Just helping out my pal Stewie. And you, of course." He smiled at me, then quickly looked away. His cheeks flamed red.

Chaun was intensely shy, and I knew he had a slight crush on me, so I ignored his blush. "That's very nice of you, Chaun. Make sure Stewie puts in the paperwork so we can pay you for your time."

He raised his eyebrows, and I realized how silly that sounded. Chaun was a tech genius, and owned several companies, including ChaunID, the company that had helped us solve our problem with missing tanks a while back. He was wealthy enough not to need or want the minimum wage payment we'd have given him for his time.

"Consider any time I spend to be part of my annual donation," he said.

"Thank you," I said. The wail of police sirens and tires squealing came from the front parking lot. I quickly said goodbye and rushed out to greet DS Scott.

I met him halfway across the area that used to be the lawn. "Have you found Benjamin?"

"No. I sent a team out there, but he wasn't on the surface. The sea scooter was there though, right about where they expected to find it. They're diving now to look for him, and we're getting a copter to search by air. They'll let me know as soon as they find him." He patted my shoulder. "Don't worry. He's a strong swimmer. He might have decided to swim to shore, or even all the way back here."

I noticed Chaun and Noah standing behind me, talking and gawking. "Let's go inside where we can have some privacy," I said. I did not want to discuss Lauren Forster in front of Noah. After all, she'd murdered his brother Dylan.

Dane nodded, and we walked across RIO's dusty backyard to the rear entrance. I was glad I'd propped it open with that piece of shell when Benjamin and I left, because now I wouldn't have to walk around through the front lobby to get to my office. It wasn't the walk

I objected to but the thought of people watching me when I heard about Benjamin's fate.

Dane frowned when he saw me pick up the piece of shell I'd wedged into the door. 'I see you've taken all my discussions about security to heart," he said.

I blushed. "It was early morning when I left, and Stewie was out here. And very few tourists are on the island now because of the storm. I thought it would be okay."

"Hmm, okay? You just had a woman murdered in your back yard. You saw someone inside RIO the night of the storm. Someone cracked Benjamin on the head and left him for dead. Your crazy ex-husband and his even crazier girlfriend—who may I remind you, tried to kill you several times—are on the island, and you just called me to tell me Lauren Forster, notorious drug dealer and ruthless murderer, is also on the island. So, yes. This seems like exactly the right time to leave your doors unlocked—NOT." He glowered at me.

"When you put it like that, it was pretty stupid, I guess." I hung my head. How could I have been so careless? Not just careless about my own safety, but also potentially putting Eugene, Stanley, Stewie, Austin Gibb, Genevra, and the entire cleanup crew in peril. All to save a minute walking around to the front door. I had to admit, it was not a smart tradeoff. "I'm sorry. I'll think twice before I do something like that again."

His phone rang, and he answered it quickly. "Uhuh. Where? I see. Any sign of a submarine? Okay. Thanks, Roland." He disconnected the call.

I looked down at my feet so he wouldn't see the tears in my eyes. It didn't take a genius to figure out the unheard side of his phone conversation. I started to shake, and despite my best efforts to hold it back, a sob escaped.

He put a finger under my chin and lifted my face so he could see me, and I could see him. "I know you've figured out what Roland just told me. There's no sign of Benjamin or the sea scooter anywhere near where you were diving. But that doesn't mean anything. He could be anywhere, and we're not giving up."

I shook my head and snuffled. "Lauren got him. She tried to clip me with her stupid sub, but I got away. Obviously, she tried to do the same to Benjamin and he wasn't that lucky."

"You don't know that. I've got the Coast Guard, our chopper, and our best dive team looking for him. We'll find him." He put his arm across my shoulders and walked me down the hall to my office. Once there, he pulled a chair away from the little table in the corner and helped me to sit. He took my blue RIO hoodie off the back of the desk chair and draped it over my shoulders. I pushed my arms into the sleeves and zipped it up, hoping the added warmth would stop my shivering.

I was still wiping my eyes on the sleeves when he dialed from my desk phone. "This is DS Scott of the Royal Cayman Islands Police Service. Please bring a large black coffee and a couple of cookies to Fin's office. Thank you." Then he replaced the desk phone and went back to using his own phone again. "Fin needs you. We're in her office at RIO." He disconnected.

Within a minute, one of the kitchen workers came in with the coffee and cookies. She seemed unsure what to do with them until Dane gestured toward me. "Thank you, and please, shut the door on your way out."

Head down, she placed the steaming coffee and plate of fragrant cookies on the table in front of me and turned to go back to the café.

"Thank you," I rasped. She nodded and left.

My throat felt so swollen with grief and terror I didn't think I could eat or drink anything, but Dane wrapped my hands around the cup. "Just a sip. You'll feel better."

My hand shook as I lifted the cup to my lips, and even that one sip made me feel a tiny bit better. Before I knew it, I'd finished the coffee and eaten the cookies.

"Feel better?" he said.

I nodded.

The door to my office burst open and Newton and Maddy rushed in. She folded me into her arms. "My poor baby," she crooned into my ear. "Don't worry. Everything will be all right." She rubbed my back the way she had when I'd been a toddler, and even now, all these years later, her touch had the ability to make me feel better.

Newton stood off to the side, looking helpless. "Thanks, Dane," he said. "I appreciate you taking care of her."

Dane's voice was low and sad. "No problem. We all love her."

The two men left my office, but from the quiet murmurs that reached me from the hall, I knew they hadn't gone far. Dane's phone rang, and there was a change in the tone of his voice after the first few seconds of the call.

He popped back into my office. "The Coast Guard found the water scooter. It was adrift pretty far away from where you told us he'd be. The anchor line had been cut. We're doing a helicopter sweep of the area to see if we can catch sight of him. There's still hope. If his scooter drifted that far from where it started, maybe Benjamin did too. We'll find him."

Although he'd tried to inject a soothing tone into his voice, Dane's face looked grim. I wasn't fooled. The situation did not look good for Benjamin.

Chapter 21
Rebuilding

I could see Dane was trying to keep me from panicking. I nodded to show I understood. "I'll be in the dive shop if you hear anything. You can use my office if you want." I stepped through the door, trudged down the hall, and went out through the back exit.

I was surprised to see Stewie, Noah, Eugene, and a team of temporary workers hired from town were busily working on rebuilding the dock. They'd already erected several of the support posts. The work was going quickly because the former dock's cement footings were all still in good condition. Instead of going into the dive shop, I walked over to where Stewie was cutting a board using an electric table saw attached to a long extension cord. He pulled off the ear protection he'd been using while working with the loud machinery.

"You're really hustling here, Stewie. I appreciate it," I tried to smile.

Stewie nodded. "Thanks. Any word yet? Chaun is pretty upset about Benjamin being missing."

"They've been friends since college, and I don't think Chaun has many friends except Benjamin. And you, of course." I looked around, realizing I hadn't seen Chaun in the group working on rebuilding the dock. "Where is he anyway?"

"He's in the dive shop. He said he was going to work on resetting the RFID readers, but I think he just needed to be alone." Stewie looked over my shoulder toward the open door. "He could really use some good news."

"So could I, Stewie. So could I." I tried to keep my voice steady. "They found his scooter drifting out to sea. The anchor line had been cut. No sign of Benjamin yet, but they're doing a grid search with the helicopter."

"They'll find him."

I nodded. I don't think either of us actually believed he'd escaped from Lauren's clutches.

"I want to get a closer look at how the work's going. We'll talk later." I walked down to the shoreline, but I didn't look at the work in process on the dock. I could only stare out to sea, willing Benjamin to appear.

If I'd had the *Tranquility* back from drydock, I'd have gone out searching for him myself. I probably wouldn't have had any more luck than the Coast Guard, but at least I'd have been doing something. I hated feeling useless.

I turned back to Stewie. "The *Omega*'s tender. I thought I saw it in the boathouse before the storm. Is it still there?"

"Yeah, it is. What'd you have in mind?"

"I can't stand around being useless. I want to take it out and search for Benjamin."

"But Fin, the police and the Coast Guard are doing all they can..."

"And I want to do all I can as well. Will you help me get it into the water please? Then call your friend Alan at the boat storage place and get his team to bring the *Tranquility*, Gus and Theresa's *Sunshine*

146

Girl, and Maddy's *Sea Princess* into their slips. It's time we brought them home."

"Sure thing." He whistled to get the team's attention. "Noah, Brian, Stanley. I need your help in the boathouse for a few minutes. Let's go." Stewie trotted off toward the boathouse, and the three men he'd named followed him. Within a few minutes, they reappeared. Stewie was driving the all-terrain vehicle we used to move the small boats around. The tender—a smaller version of the Zodiacs we used as rental boats—was on a trailer behind the ATV.

Stewie turned the ATV in a wide circle, so the rear end of the trailer was near the water, then he backed toward the ocean until the tender was afloat in the shallows. Brian, one of the *Omega's* crew who was on loan to help out with the repairs, jumped in the small boat and started the engine. He backed it up until it floated free of the trailer, then he held it steady and waited for me to wade out and get aboard.

He hopped out of the boat. "Thank you all," I said with a wave. I put the boat in reverse, but before I could depart, Chaun came running out of the dive shop.

"Wait for me. Wait for me," he shouted, waving his baseball cap in the air. "I need to go too."

I understood Chaun's inability to do nothing while his dearest friend was missing and possibly in danger, but it wasn't a good idea to bring him along. This trip could be dangerous.

"Better if you stay here, Chaun. Benjamin might need you if he comes back."

"I'm coming with you." Chaun waded the few feet to the boat. "He might need me out there when we find him." He climbed into the boat.

I shrugged. Truth be told, I was happy for his company. "Okay, let's go. Stewie, we have our phones if anyone needs us."

Then I revved the motor and left RIO's cove.

Chapter 22
Recovery Mission

I raised my voice to allow Chaun to hear me over the roar of the engine. "I plan to stay close to shore to start out. Benjamin may have been swimming along in the shallows, staying mostly underwater, hoping Lauren's sub couldn't come after him close to the shoreline."

"Good idea," said Chaun. "My thoughts exactly."

We putted along, following the curve of the coastline. I stayed at a very slow speed to be sure we wouldn't miss anything. Chaun used the binoculars we keep in the dry box in the bow of each one of RIO's boats. Every boat is equipped for emergencies, with oxygen, water, blankets, and more in those dry boxes.

Chaun swept his gaze in all directions, hoping to catch a glimpse of Benjamin either walking along the shore or swimming toward us.

Because we were going slowly and weaving in and out as we followed the contours of the island, it seemed to take forever to cover the distance from RIO to Cobalt Coast Resort. We didn't see any sign of Benjamin.

I steered the boat out to deeper water until we were directly over the spot where Benjamin and I had been free diving. I put the engine in neutral to test the direction of the current. The wind was blowing to the east, and it pushed the little boat out to sea.

But I wondered if the current underwater was headed in the same direction. "Hold her steady, Chaun. I'm going in."

Chaun looked startled.

I pulled my hoodie off and tied the sleeves to one of the boat's benches to keep it from blowing away. Kicking off my flip flops, I took a few deep breaths, and rolled off the side of the boat. I dove down, testing the current at about fifteen feet of depth. As I'd suspected, thanks to the remnants of the storm the current was running in a different direction at depth than at the surface. I shot up and grabbed the boat's edge.

"I think the Coast Guard has been searching in the wrong direction. They don't know how Benjamin thinks, and what a strong freediver he is. I think Benjamin's been staying underwater as much as possible, and he's probably headed north, or northeast. He wouldn't want Lauren following him. I think he chose to buck the current and swim underwater in an unexpected direction."

Chaun looked at me like I was an idiot. "He can hold his breath longer than anyone I know, but it's been hours. Even he can't hold his breath that long."

"I agree. I still think he's swimming underwater as much as possible to stay out of sight of Lauren and her goons. But he has to come up for air every few minutes. We'll have to look carefully, but I think we'll find him somewhere between here and West Bay."

Chaun's face broke into a grin. "Let's go,"

We had to travel even more slowly than we had been, because we didn't want to miss seeing Benjamin when he surfaced to breathe. But by now, he must be getting tired, and maybe even lightheaded from the intermittent breath-holding. I was hopeful we'd spot him before his lungs gave out. "Chaun, make sure you look aft of us too. There's no guarantee he won't come up behind us if we've somehow passed his location."

Chaun squared his shoulders and raised the binoculars to his eyes. He scanned in every direction while I held the boat steady. We'd only progressed a few hundred feet when Chaun dropped the binoculars and stood up to point. "I see him. He's over there. Hurry, Fin. He looks tired." Chaun was so agitated he was jumping around making it hard to keep the boat steady.

"Benjamin," I shouted. "Hold up. We're coming for you."

He must not have heard me, because he sank back under. I moved the boat a little way in the direction where we'd seen him dive. "Keep looking, Chaun. He may not know it's us, but either way, he'll have to surface soon."

It felt like hours, but it was less than a minute when Chaun shouted again. "Over there. There he is."

We both yelled out his name. Finally, he heard us and turned to face the boat. He raised his arm overhead and waved, but his wave was distinctly lacking in energy. I knew we'd found him with only a few minutes to spare. Any longer in the water and he'd have succumbed to hypothermia, shallow water blackout due to air hunger, sheer exhaustion, or the aftereffects of the injuries he'd sustained during the storm.

When we were close enough, I shut off the motor and let the boat coast the last few feet to him so he wouldn't be in danger from the engine's blades. Chaun and I leaned over the pontoon and we each grabbed one of Benjamin's arms to heave him into the boat.

The tiny boat rocked wildly with all our weight on one side, but it was sturdy and stable enough that it didn't overturn during the few seconds it took to haul Benjamin aboard and to the center of the boat.

I grabbed the emergency oxygen and water from the dry box. "One sip only. Then the oxygen."

Benjamin nodded. I handed him the open water bottle, and he took a sip. Then I opened the valve on the oxygen canister and swapped it for the bottle in his hand. He took a deep breath of air. "You guys certainly took your time." Then he breathed from the oxygen tank while Chaun and I whooped with joy.

When we'd finished congratulating ourselves for having found Benjamin, I pulled my phone out of a pocket of my cargo shorts.

Dane answered before the first ring finished. "Where are you? We've been worried sick."

Even the anger in Dane's voice couldn't stifle my joy—especially because I knew his anger came from concern. "We're on our way back. We found him. I think we're all fine, but Doc should be ready check Benjamin out. We'll be there in just a few minutes."

There was a moment of silence. "Good work. I'll call off the Coast Guard. But don't ever—and I mean this—ever take off like that again. You could have been killed."

"But I wasn't, and everything is good. Now we just have to find Lauren and then we can prove she killed Cara."

"There's no 'we' involved in the search for Lauren. She's dangerous, and you should leave it to the police."

'Sure thing," I said. "You can count on me." We both knew I was lying. Lauren had tried to kill me again, almost got to Benjamin, and Oliver's freedom was at stake. There's no way I would ever stand down.

Chapter 23
An Afternoon of Meetings

As I approached RIO's small cove, I could see my parents, Dane, and the entire crew who'd been working on rebuilding the dock all standing on the shore, each of them with their arms folded, making it clear they were not happy I'd gone off to rescue Benjamin without letting them know.

Even though Stewie, Noah, Brian, and Stanley had been complicit by helping me launch the boat. I guess they hadn't actually known what I was about to do. But at least the dock was almost ready. I could soon have my own boat back.

Doc was on shore, standing next to a rolling gurney. Benjamin groaned when he saw her. "She'll never let me out again," he said.

He was probably right, but I didn't tell him so.

As soon as I got close enough to shore, I cut the engines and the small boat coasted in. Stewie waded over and held it steady. Brian and Noah helped Benjamin out of the boat and over to the waiting gurney. Once he was strapped in, they helped Doc push the gurney to the infirmary.

Chaun and I got out of the boat and waded to shore while Stewie pulled the Zodiac back onto its waiting trailer. As soon as my feet hit the shore, my parents rushed over and folded me in their arms.

Maddy was openly crying. "I was so scared. Don't ever do that again," she said.

I shrugged out of their embrace. "I love you guys, but I'm a grown woman. I can take care of myself, and I knew I could find Benjamin. If I'd been even a few minutes later, I don't think he'd have made it. I'm sorry you were worried, but I did the right thing."

Newton nodded slowly. "You did at that. And I admire you for it. But please, next time, just tell us what you have in mind. That's all we ask."

He held his arms open, and I walked into his hug.

He kissed the top of my head. "I couldn't bear to lose you. But right now, since you and Benjamin are both safe, I'm going to the jail to visit Oliver. Will you be okay here?"

"Of course. I have a ton of work to do. Justin is coming by later for a meeting about the repair costs, and Genevra will be here settling into her new office."

Maddy joined in on hearing Genevra would be at RIO later. "Congratulations on the new hire, by the way. I really like her, and I believe she'll be a great help to you. Why don't you put her in June's old office? I'll be heading back to Woods Hole as soon as we resolve Oliver's situation, and June and I will be away for months. That office has the best access to all the files and info you two will need to run RIO."

I was disheartened to hear that Maddy and June would be gone for several more months. I wondered what was so compelling about this particular research project with Woods Hole that it took precedence over seeing to RIO's reconstruction. I'd hoped they'd be back soon so I could focus on diving, photography, and marketing, which were my real loves. But her project with Woods Hole was clearly more important to her than RIO. I smiled bravely and said nothing about her plans. "Good idea. I'll let her know."

"And you could move into my old office if you wanted to," she said. "It's the best office in the building, and you should have it while you're running RIO." She looked at Newton. "I won't be here much, if at all."

I felt a chill at her words. She was planning to come back someday, wasn't she? After all, RIO was her life's work—not mine. Despite my PhD in marine biology, my ambitions lay in photography and videography, not science. "Thanks, but nope. That office belongs to you. In my mind, running RIO is a temporary gig, and I really love the office I have now. The light is better for my photography, and I can see the ocean from my desk. I don't want to move."

"Suit yourself. Oh, and Vincent is coming in later to talk about this year's documentary. I'll leave those decisions up to you as well." She looked away and then reached out for Newton's hand.

Dane and I watched them walk away together. From the look on his face, I could see he was as puzzled as I was about her seeming disinterest in RIO, and the surprise of her reaching for Newton's hand.

Dane inhaled sharply once they were out of sight. "I'm going back to HQ to follow up on the investigation into Cara's murder. Don't do anything crazy while I'm gone."

I went into my office, but I wasn't alone for long. Within a few minutes, Justin Nash knocked on my office door. "You ready for me?" he asked.

"How did you get down here without an escort?" I asked him. "I thought I made it clear this area is for employees or escorted visitors only."

He shrugged. "Nobody was at that stupid guard station. I just came in."

I picked up my desk phone and called the lobby guard station. The phone rang, but nobody answered. I ground my teeth. Where was Ralph? Something else to look into.

I called HR. "Where's Ralph?" I asked.

"He asked if he could leave early today. His wife is in labor. I said he could go. I hope that was okay."

"It's fine," I said before hanging up. I'd have let him go to be with his wife no matter what, but it galled me that his absence happened at a time when Justin was due here for a meeting.

I gestured toward the small table in the corner of my office. "You just missed Newton. We could have all gone over this together if you'd arrived a few minutes earlier. But no matter. Let's get to work."

We sat down, and Justin pulled a sheaf of papers out of his leather portfolio. "I marked where you need to sign."

There was a stack of about fifty pages, with small pink paper arrows sticking out at intervals to mark the places where he needed my signature. I sighed. "You might want to go get some coffee or something. It'll take me a while to read all this."

"No worries. Our procedures are pretty complex at Fleming Environmental. We have multiple paper copies of everything. Just read the top set. After that, they're all the same."

I was elated to hear I didn't have to plow through all that paper, although I made a mental note to talk to Newton about streamlining his processes. I read the first set of five pages while Justin watched, then I signed the page on the dotted line. I flipped that set over and scanned the next set. It was the same form, so I didn't read all the text. I just checked the amount and the transfer's purpose, which was identical to the first set. I signed. I did the same on the other eight copies. I put all ten sets of documents in a neat pile and handed the whole stack back to Justin. "All set. That was a lot easier than I expected."

"Good. Then maybe you'll have time for dinner with me tonight?" he said.

"No. I'm sorry, Justin. I am totally swamped. In fact, here's my next meeting now." I smiled at Genevra and waved her in. "Justin was just leaving," I said, "so your timing is perfect."

"You sure? I can come back in a few minutes if you need more time," she said.

"Nope, Justin and I are all set, and if you and I start late, I'll be late for my meeting with Vincent. By the way, you should probably stay for that anyway if you have the time," I said.

"I have time," she said.

"So do I," said Justin.

"Thanks, Justin, but we won't need your input until it's time to put budget numbers in place. Besides, I already have ballpark approvals from Newton. We're good to go. I know you're busy and I really want you to process that funds transfer today if at all possible."

He stood and gathered his papers, sliding the top batch off the stack across the table and over to me. "Here's your copy. I'll see you later."

Genevra and I talked for an hour, planning how we would work together and what her duties would be. I suggested she move into June's office around the corner and down the hall. I was surprised when she asked if she could have the tiny office—it was more like a large closet—next to mine.

"Much more convenient for you," she said, "and I don't mind walking down the hall if I need something from June's office."

I thanked my lucky stars Genevra wanted to work at RIO, and I gave her my blessing to use the small office next to mine.

We had just settled that issue when Vincent Pollilo, the *Omega*'s captain, walked in for our next meeting. I introduced him to

Genevra, and then we started planning for RIO's next documentary.

Vincent cleared his throat. "I hesitate to suggest this idea…"

"There's no such thing as a bad idea," I said. I was puzzled. Vincent wasn't usually shy about sharing his opinions.

"OK," he said. "But stop me whenever you've heard enough."

I smiled at him. "You know I will."

"RIO has only missed doing an annual documentary one time. That was the year Ray died during his freedive," he said to Genevra, bringing her up to speed. "But the overall theme —Save our Seas—was a good one. The idea was to show the effects of pollution and global warming on the oceans and the creatures who live in them. Ray's freedive was to have been largely symbolic, and it would have added a lot of drama."

I was having trouble breathing because I was reliving the terror of that day in my head, but I nodded to Vincent to go on.

"Budgets are going to be tighter than usual this year because of all the storm repairs, and that's not only going to limit how much we can spend on the documentary, but it will also compress the time we have to plan and do the filming."

"But if we go back to that idea, we already have the storyboard, and a lot of the footage we'd need for the documentary. We'd really only need to film the deep dive, maybe make a few updates, and we'd have a finished product. I think it would make for a great show, and it would also be a fitting tribute to Ray if you personally did the freedive he had planned. The viewers will go wild for the idea. We can film it right here in Grand Cayman, and by reusing the footage we already have and eliminating the usual lengthy sea voyage, we can take out a lot of the cost. It'll certainly help to balance the budget. We're known for being champions of the environment, and environmental themes are hot right now with all the climate changes we're experiencing. It works on every level. What do you think?"

I could barely speak. I was focused on one thing only. Ray's death.

For a long, horrible moment I was frozen in that awful time, but when I came back to the present, I said, "I don't freedive."

"Yes, you do," he said. "You just don't do it competitively the way Ray used to. And Benjamin is a super freediver. You could do the dive together if you wanted."

I swallowed the massive lump in my throat. "I can't do it."

"Yes, you can," said Genevra. "I have faith you can do whatever you put your mind to. And Vincent's right. It's a quick and inexpensive solution to a difficult problem. You should at least consider it."

"Okay. I'll consider it," I said. "But meanwhile, try to think of some other ideas. And don't hold your breath waiting for me to agree."

They both groaned at my unintended joke, and after a second, I joined in their laughter. But I still wouldn't freedive for the next documentary. No way.

The meeting adjourned, and since it was late in the day, I decided to stop by the jail to visit Oliver on my way home.

Chapter 24
Steroids

M addy and Newton were already gone by the time I arrived to see Oliver at the jail.

He was pacing around in his cell. "I'm glad you came tonight. I've had a really scary thought. I don't know what to do about it." He was practically panting he was so frightened by whatever the idea was. "I didn't want to say anything to Maddy and Newton. They'd go ballistic. But maybe you can help me make sense of it."

He turned away from me before he spoke. "I think my sister had been giving me drugs," he said. "I can't believe she'd do that to me, but it's the only explanation."

I paused a moment to think about his statement and what it meant. "You've been seeing Lily? You knew she was on the island?"

Oliver blushed. "She's my twin sister, Fin. She needed me. I couldn't say no."

"You do recall she watched while Lauren fed you drugs and threw you in the ocean, leaving you for dead, right? Do you remember she tried to kill me on several occasions? That she managed to kill Ray? What were you thinking?"

"We're twins. She said she needed a place to stay." He seemed embarrassed rather than defiant.

"Oh my God, did you let her stay in Maddy's condo with you? Does Maddy know?"

Now he was so embarrassed he couldn't even look up. "Yes, she and Alec stayed there until Alec's boat arrived a couple of days ago. Maddy didn't know. She never would have agreed to let them stay in her home."

"And knowing Maddy would never have agreed to let them live in her place didn't function as some kind of clue it wasn't a smart thing for you to do?" I was having trouble processing his colossal stupidity, but then, until Oliver's adoption, I'd never had a sibling, never mind a twin. Maybe it was normal behavior. "What makes you think she's been drugging you?"

"When she arrived, she said I didn't look healthy—like I'd been working too hard. She started making these green smoothies and making me drink them. They tasted awful, but after I'd had a few, I really did start to feel better. Healthy. Strong."

He looked down. "But then the mood swings. The rages. Acne. I suspected she was feeding me something, but she swore she wasn't."

"Sounds like roid rage," I said. "She must have been giving you steroids. Those mood swings and all that anger and yelling. It was all so unlike you I knew something was wrong. I thought you were having trouble in school or maybe with Genevra."

"I finished school, and I did okay. Genevra's been a saint about my moodiness. She wanted me to tell you how out of control I was feeling, but I was ashamed. And I couldn't make myself stop drinking those smoothies. I felt strong and powerful."

I nodded. "Who knows what else was in there. Why did you decide to tell me now?"

"Now that I've been in here a few days, I feel like my old self again, and I knew for sure she'd been doping me. I don't know what to do now though."

"The first thing you should do is tell Dane. And don't worry. I'm going to ask Doc to come down and give you some tests, make sure there's been no permanent damage." I paused a moment. "You didn't have any blackouts, did you? Could you have killed Cara in a rage and not remember doing it?"

"Nope. No blackouts, thank God." He looked miserable.

"Thanks for telling me. I'm going to clear Doc's visit with Dane. As soon as I get the okay from him, I'll ask Doc to make checking you out a priority. And meanwhile, don't eat or drink anything that isn't provided by the jail, or by Newton, Maddy, or me. We need you safe and healthy."

He nodded. "Thanks, Fin."

I patted his hand through the cell bars. "I have to go now, but I'll be back tomorrow."

Chapter 25
Evening at Home

I left the police station and got in my car to head home to Rum Point. It had been a long day, although all my days were long. Pretty much everybody in the dive industry worked from sunrise until long after sundown. I was one of the lucky ones, because I could set my own schedule, but still—I was tired. I stopped at the gas station convenience store on the way and picked up a turkey sandwich for dinner. Then I called Doc to check on Benjamin.

"He's fine," she said. "Exhausted, but nothing a good night's rest won't cure. In fact, he's snoring away even as we speak."

I laughed and thanked her for her care and expertise. We were lucky to have Doc at RIO. She was so quietly competent it was easy to forget she was there—until a patient needed her. Then she was like a bear protecting its cub.

I parked my car in the garage and went inside. Despite the long day, I was feeling at loose ends. I don't watch television, and I didn't was too antsy to focus on a book, even one of Ray's old logs. I decided to do what I always do when I'm too stressed to concentrate on anything. I go diving.

I loaded up the trunk of my Prius with a full tank of air, then I packed a lightweight Lycra dive skin in my gear bag. Within a few minutes of my arrival at home, I was back on the road, headed to the ocean.

My favorite dive site is the reef just off Rum Point. I like it because it's close to home, it has easy access from shore, and tons of interesting sea creatures frequent the area. The reef wall here is spectacular—a straight vertical drop that goes down for a mile or more.

I geared up quickly and waded into the warm water. I swam on the surface until I reached the guide ropes that marked out the swimming area and ducked underneath. Then I put my regulator in my mouth and sank beneath the waves. The visibility had improved a lot since I'd been here with Liam right after the storm. It was practically back to normal—around one hundred fifty feet instead of the usual two hundred.

There's a sand chute here that leads right to the wall. It looks like a path created by nature especially to lead divers to the best parts of the site. Stunning fan corals, a few majestic elkhorn corals, and several barrel sponges formed the edges of the path. A thick stand of seagrass swayed with the ocean's movement. The gentle movement felt as though the ocean itself were trying to sooth the ragged edges of my soul.

I kicked along the path, looking in all directions for my favorite Southern Stingray, Suzie Q. I caught site of her gliding up over the edge of the drop-off onto the flat part of the reef. She must have been exploring the wall. She swam in along the reef top until she found her favorite spot—a patch of sand sheltered behind a large orange brain coral. I watched as she landed gently and then used her wings to stir up the sand until it covered her completely. Only her dark hooded eyes and the faint outline of her wings were visible when she'd finished her camouflage efforts.

As always, I pretended not to see her as I swam by, watching her but without turning my head to look at her or, worse yet, swimming directly toward her. Either would send her flying away in a panic.

Killer Storm

Just as I always watched Suzie Q, she always watched me, but I believe we had different reasons. I admired her grace and beauty. She liked to keep me at a distance, as shown by the fact that she invariably left the area if I came too close.

Her eyes followed me as I moved along the sand chute. When I reached the edge of the reef, where the coral dropped off into the lush vertical wall, I turned to face back along the path and hovered for a moment before dropping.

The first thing I did was swim to the tiny grotto where I knew a juvenile drum fish spent his days and nights, swimming back and forth across the open space. His ribbon-like fins fluttered in the current, and his tiny face seemed to be perpetually smiling. I knew he would soon mature and venture out of his haven, but invariably within a few days or weeks a new baby drum would move into the same spot. The thought gave me comfort partly because it was evidence of the continuing cycle of life, but also because I loved to see these graceful babies. They were great favorites of mine.

I descended a few more feet to watch a large Nassau Grouper tootling along near the wall. The Nassau Grouper had once been nearly extinct in the area due to overfishing, but the species was on the comeback trail now. This one had grown quite large. I estimated this grouper was nearly full grown and weighed in at around thirty to thirty-five pounds. I silently thanked the conservationists—people like Maddy and Newton—who had fought so hard to save this magnificent species.

No dive in the Caymans is complete without spotting at least one Green Sea Turtle, thanks to the diligent efforts of the Cayman Turtle Centre. One specific turtle came out to greet me on almost every dive. This turtle and I were old friends. Friends or not, he never came close enough for me to touch him. He had no way of knowing my policy was never to touch the wildlife under any circumstances. It was just too dangerous and scary for them.

A small hammerhead shark swam up along the wall and over the lip of the reef. He was off in the distance, and unlikely to bother me

Sharon Ward

anyway, but I crossed my fingers Suzie Q stayed snug in her little sand pile.

I checked my pressure gauge and saw it was time to head back. I ascended slowly along the wall and back along the sand chute. As I swam, the water gradually became shallower, until it was barely twelve feet deep when I reached the guide ropes at the beach. Once I'd passed under them, I headed straight to shore, letting the ocean do all the work. When the water was waist deep, I stood up and waded out.

I crossed the sandy beach to my car and put my gear away. Taking a moment to admire the setting sun before driving home, I was feeling better and more relaxed than I had all day.

Back at my house, I dumped my gear in the large rinse tank in my backyard and filled the tank with fresh water from the hose. After shutting off the flow, I went in the house through the slider on my patio and pulled my turkey sandwich out of the refrigerator where I'd tossed it when I got home from work.

I tore off a paper towel to use as a napkin and pulled a can of iced tea from my refrigerator. I set my food on a small table next to the armchair where I liked to sit and read. Once settled, I opened a volume of Ray's ship's logs. I'd read all the volumes of Ray's logs several times over, but I loved to go back and read them again. It made me feel close to Ray, who had been more of a father to me while I was growing up than Newton had been.

My late stepfather had been an excellent storyteller, witty and suspenseful, and I often spent evenings lost in one of the volumes. He chronicled all the voyages and adventures he, Stewie, and Gus had on his boat, the *Maddy*. He'd named the boat *Maddy* after my mother, but with her agreement, I'd changed the name to *Tranquility* when I inherited it.

I absent mindedly ate my sandwich while I read. After the last bite, I closed the book and put it on the table beside me. I loved having

Killer Storm

Newton in my life. He was trying to be a great father to me, but Ray had left him some pretty big shoes to fill.

I was drowsily remembering some of the good times Ray and I had had while I was growing up, so I think it was a while before I heard the scratching at my patio door.

Drat. I must have left the gate open when I brought my dive gear through, and here was Chico, my neighbor's rooster, looking for another handout.

I rose, grabbed a handful of seeds, and went out to send him on his way. "Here you go, Chico," I said, dropping the seeds in front of him. "But don't make a habit of this." I reached out to rub his bright red comb, but he ducked away and growled at me, making a deep, angry caaaw sound.

What an ingrate. I laughed and went back inside to get ready for bed.

It was barely eight PM, but I was half asleep when my phone buzzed. Chaun wanted me to take him to Stingray City in the morning. I'd been promising to take him there since we met, and apparently, he was tired of waiting.

"*6 AM pickup*" I texted back.

He sent me a smiley face. I guess that meant we were on.

Chapter 26
Stingray City

S tingray City is one of the most famous dive sites in the world. It's not a tricky or technical dive, because it's only about ten feet deep. The bottom is mostly sand, so there's not much in the way of interesting corals, and not a lot of marine life—except the stingrays.

The story of Stingray City is an interesting one. Years ago, after returning from the day's work, fishing boats would often anchor here in the calm shallow water to clean the day's catch. Many of them threw the scraps overboard, and clever stingrays learned to come to the area for a free meal.

Word spread among the stingray population, and soon there were about one hundred stingrays in the area. Divers, snorkelers, and even swimmers began to interact with the stingrays, feeding them bits of fish and squid by hand.

Although I hated seeing how the handfeeding had changed the lives of most stingrays, I had to admit the site's fame had brought many tourists to Grand Cayman, and it was exhilarating to see all the stingrays swirling around you looking for a snack.

Chaun was waiting near his front gate when I pulled up. We stowed his gear in the back of my car and drove to RIO to board the *Tranquility*. It took only a few minutes to load our gear bags on board, and then we were off.

The trip from RIO's marina to the North Sound took about forty-five minutes. I dropped a sand anchor overboard and looked into the clear water below. Already, about twenty stingrays were gathered below the boat, looking for an early breakfast.

I handed Chaun an extra two pound weight to slide into his buoyancy control device, otherwise known as a BCD. Because the water here is so shallow, it could be hard to stay kneeling on the sand to feed the stingrays. Even steady shallow breathing could cause a diver to float up and down in the water without some extra weight.

Then I gave him a small container of cut fish to feed to the stingrays. "Always use the same hand to get the fish out and to feed the stingrays. Don't touch any part of your body or your gear with the fish or the hand that's been holding the fish. The stingrays will smell it and swarm the spot. Their suction is powerful enough to leave a hickey, so be careful. And keep the container covered or they'll suck you dry in seconds."

He nodded, eyes as big as though I'd bestowed the wisdom of the ages on him.

We stepped off the *Tranquility*'s dive platform and swam a few feet away to give ourselves a little bit of space. It was early enough that we were the only boat on site so far, but that could change. Once I decided we were in a good spot, I signaled Chaun to kneel on the bottom here.

I pulled a small piece of fish out of my own container and palmed it. I waved my hand slowly through the water, and immediately three large and two small stingrays came rushing over. The big ones swooped across my head and shoulders, while the littler ones bumped against my knees. After a few minutes of this, I gave the bit of fish to one of the smaller stingrays, a male. The larger stingrays were mostly females.

I nodded to Chaun to go next. He fumbled at his container, but eventually retrieved a piece of fish. The stingrays swarmed all over him, and I heard him squeal through his regulator in mingled terror and delight. He gave his fish up to a large stingray who had spread her wings across his head and shoulders.

We took turns feeding the stingrays for about ten or fifteen minutes when I noticed that one stingray had accidentally knocked Chaun's mask askew. Without thinking, he raised the hand that had been holding the bits of fish and resettled his mask on his face, touching his cheek in the process.

Almost immediately, a very large stingray settled herself on his face, looking for the fish she could sense. Her wings blocked Chaun's vision, and he dropped his container of fish. I sensed his panic, so I swam over and grabbed his free hand and his container of fish. I towed him to the *Tranquility*'s dive platform and put his hands on the bottom rung of the ladder. Then I reached down and pulled off his fins so he could climb aboard.

The large stingray swam away as soon as Chaun's face and hands left the water, but a large group of them still swirled below us. When Chaun was off the platform, I followed him back aboard the boat. Once I had removed my gear, I popped the covers off both our nearly empty containers and dumped the few remaining fish bits into the water.

I could hear Chaun breathing heavily on the other side of the boat. I thought he was still terrified, until I saw the big smile on his face. He was gasping with the joy and awe of his experience.

I figured that would probably only last until he saw the gigantic red welt that was forming on his face. The stingray, not realizing that in this case, there was no fish where the fish scent lingered, had sucked hard on his skin. He had the mother of all hickeys on his right cheek.

Suppressing a chuckle, I started the engines, and the few remaining stingrays swam away looking for their next handout. Before I could put the engine in gear, my phone rang. Newton's number showed in the caller ID window.

"Hey, Newton, you're awake early. What's up?"

"I was going over some of the accounts at Fleming Environmental, and I saw several large transfers out. They are all for the same amount." He named the exact amount of the donation he'd made to help RIO repair the storm damage. The one I'd signed off on. "There are also several similar transactions from my personal accounts. What's up, honey? If you needed more money, you could have just asked."

"I don't understand," I said. "I only signed off on a single transfer. Maybe there's a glitch in the system. I'll stop over at FEI later and talk to Justin. Don't worry. I'll straighten it out."

"Want me to come too?" he asked.

"No thanks. Since I screwed it up, I'll fix it." I disconnected, feeling uneasy.

I motored back to RIO's marina and eased the *Tranquility* into my slip. After tying her to the cleat on the dock, Chaun and I each grabbed a tank and our gear bags and headed to the dive shop.

We dumped our gear in the rinse tank and left our used tanks on the cement pad with the dust caps off so Stewie would know they needed to be refilled.

I wanted to get right to work. I left Stewie and Chaun chatting and hurried across the yard to RIO's pool house. I took a shower in the locker room, dressed in my usual bathing suit, tee shirt, and cargo shorts from my locker, and hurried back to the dive shop to put my gear in the drying area now that it had been soaking long enough to get the salt out.

As I bent over the trough to retrieve my BCD, I saw a flash of green on the bottom of the tank. It was the Fleming Environmental ID card I'd found after the storm. It must have fallen out of my BCD pocket, and I realized I'd forgotten all about it.

I wiped it dry on my shorts and quickly moved my gear into the drying area. I hung up my dive suit, but I put my BCD and regulator into one of the large wooden lockers we assigned to the staff for gear storage. I secured the door and race walked to my car.

I screeched to a halt at the police station and hurried inside. I needed to see Oliver, to find out if this was his keycard. Since Oliver was the only one in the jail and Dane had given orders to let me in whenever I wanted, the sergeant waved me past. I walked slowly down the hall to Oliver's cell. Now that I was here, I found myself reluctant to confront my brother.

He was sitting on his cot with his back against the wall, doing something on his tablet. When he heard me approach, he looked up and smiled. "You're here early." He paused his game and put the tablet aside.

"What are you playing?" I asked.

"You know that game Liam invented? The one that earned him all those millions. 'Oh! Possum?' It's pretty good, and since it has levels that take place all over the world, it helps me not to feel so confined in here."

I nodded. "Sounds fun. How do you feel this morning?"

He smiled. "I feel more like my real self with every hour that passes. No more rages. No more brain fog. Even the acne is clearing up." He looked away. "The longer I'm away from her, the more obvious it seems that my sister was feeding me drugs. I should have known."

"Don't beat yourself up. It's hard to recognize when people you love don't have your best interests at heart." I knew exactly how that felt from my marriage to Alec. I fingered the green card in my pocket, uneasy about confronting Oliver with this bit of evidence that could be damning.

He eyed me. "What's wrong? There's something on your mind. Spit it out."

I pulled the green card out of my pocket. "Is this yours?"

"Why does it matter?" His shrewd look said he'd guessed his answer was important. "I doubt it's mine. Last time I saw mine it was on the dresser in my room at Maddy's. That was before the storm. You can go check on it if you like."

I breathed a sigh of relief. Oliver wouldn't have been this forth-coming if he'd lost his card in the course of murdering his mother. "Not necessary. I believe you."

Actually, I was lying to him. I believed him, but I fully intended to check before I went to Fleming Environmental Investments to confront Justin. Now I had two issues he'd need to explain.

I slipped the card back in my pocket. "I'm sorry but I have to go. Busy day ahead. I'll come back on the way home if I can."

He nodded. "Catch you later."

Chapter 27
DNA Results

As I was walking out of the jail area, I saw Dane through the open door of his office, his head resting on his hands in a posture that screamed despair and frustration. I debated stopping in to say hi, but I wasn't sure if he would welcome an interruption. He must have sensed my presence though because he looked up. He smiled when he saw me, but the smile didn't erase the fatigue from his face.

"Fin, come in. I didn't realize you were here. I was just about to call you. We got the DNA results from Oliver's raingear back. I wanted to discuss them with you." He waved the folder he'd been staring at in my direction. "The results are puzzling, and maybe you can shed some light on them for me."

"I'll do my best," I said. I sat in one of the visitor's chairs in front of his desk.

Dane stood and pulled his chair around until we were sitting side-by-side. Now we would both be able to see the report. He opened the folder and spread out the pages. "Have you ever read one of these?" he asked.

"Nope. But give me a minute and I'll see what I can do." I bent my head and studied the pages spread before me.

After a few fruitless minutes, I sighed. "I have no idea what all this stuff means, but it seems like there are three individuals—all male—besides Oliver who left DNA on the inside of the oilskins. None of them match any known DNA in the database. Is that right?"

He smiled. "Exactly right. The rest of it is scientific jargon, but you went right to the important point. I'm impressed."

"It wasn't that hard. It says so right here." I laughed and pointed to the summary on the bottom of the last page of the report.

He laughed too. "You're right. I forgot about that." His smile disappeared. "That's why I need your help. I can't just test every male who's ever been on Grand Cayman hoping to get a match. I need to narrow the field. Who else could it be?"

I thought hard for a minute. "Okay, he got the raingear before we left on the treasure expedition. Anyone in the *Omega*'s crew might have worn them during the big rainstorm we had then. I know Oliver didn't have his own stuff with him because he was with me on the *Tranquility*, and I remember I was below decks looking for a set of raingear for him to wear when Newton was swept overboard." I rubbed my chin. "Did you get samples from the *Omega*'s entire crew?"

He nodded. "Everyone who's still in the area. But a lot of sailors are transients, and a few of the researchers finished their projects and went home. We may have missed some people, but they probably aren't suspects in Cara's murder anyway, since they're no longer around."

"Okay. Who else could we have missed?" I thought hard. "One of Lauren's henchmen? Someone was lurking on the dock and in RIO's halls the night of the hurricane."

"Sure, that's possible. But I can't exactly put up a notice in the post office or tack it onto a pole. Missing henchman—please leave a

DNA sample at police headquarters. Somehow, I doubt we'd find our man that way."

He sounded frustrated, and I couldn't blame him. I felt the same way. We both knew Oliver was innocent. We just needed a way to prove it.

We sat there, staring at each other in hopeless frustration until Dane's phone rang. He answered and listened for a minute, and a look of incredulity and happiness spread across his face. "I'll be right there," he said

He put down the phone and turned to me. "They've spotted Lauren's sub on sonar. They're trying to follow it, so she doesn't get away. Sooner or later, she'll have to surface, and then we'll have her." He smiled. "This could be the break we've been looking for. I'm headed out to join them now. I'll let you know when we nab her."

He grabbed his phone and politely hurried me out of his office.

I put my hand on his arm to slow him down. "Wait. Can I go too?"

He shook his head. "No. It's too dangerous. But I promise to call you as soon as we have her in custody." He took two steps away before turning back. "On second thought, we may need your diving expertise, but stay out of the way unless I ask for your advice. The Cayman Coast Guard won't like being second guessed, but if you promise to stay back and do what I tell you, you can come."

I made the childish 'cross-my-heart' gesture and smiled as I hurried along behind him.

Chapter 28
Submarine Sighting

We took Dane's car to the nearby marina, where a Coast Guard cutter was waiting for him. Because the Cayman Islands Coast Guard was a fairly new organization, some of their people were from off-island. The captain of the cutter was new to the Caymans and a stranger to both Dane and me. We introduced ourselves. Introductions over, we scurried aboard. The cutter took off without a moment's delay.

The captain asked me to go below and stay out of the way unless he requested my presence on deck. I didn't want to take the chance he'd put me ashore, so I did as I was told. I would stay below—at least until we were far enough from shore they wouldn't want to turn back.

We were quickly nearing the area where Benjamin and I had been diving the other day, and Dane poked his head into the cabin. "Looks like we lost track of the sub. Would you mind coming up on deck for a moment please? I want to get your impressions about anything you see. Anything that seems out of place. Anything at all."

One of the sailors on deck handed me a pair of powerful binoculars, and I held them to my eyes. I scanned the shore and the surface of the water, slowly and carefully, checking everything I saw against my memories of what this stretch of coastline should look like.

The captain started the boat moving slowly parallel to the shore. I kept my gaze trained shoreward and scanned the water's surface too, but I didn't see anything that seemed out of the ordinary. After a few minutes, the eyestrain I'd been suffering from lately kicked in, and I lowered the binoculars. My eyes were watering, and I brushed away the excess moisture. Then I turned away from shore to look at the horizon for a minute to give my eyes a quick break.

That's when I saw it.

Far off, nearly hidden in the glare from the sun, was a tiny gleam of white. I whipped the binoculars back to my eyes.

Yes. A mega-yacht.

I pointed. "She'll be heading that way."

Dane took the binoculars from my hand and held them to his own eyes. It was hard to see against the dazzling sun, but after a moment, he nodded grimly. "You're right. But it's so far out I think that boat is in international waters. We'll need to apprehend Lauren before she gets there."

"She's not there yet, or the yacht would probably be moving away from us. We'll want to go slowly and keep watching for the sub, so she doesn't slip by us." I said.

"We're using sonar, and we have a lookout on the cutter's bridge. If she doesn't go too deep, we'll spot her," the captain said in a condescending tone.

I thought for a second. "We have to keep her from going deep and getting around us. If she's in front of our boat, there's nothing to stop her from passing into international waters and approaching the yacht from the other side. We'd never even see her. It's what I'd do. That sub she's in can go down below 1600 feet and it can stay down for ten hours. But it only travels at three knots per hour, top speed. We should be able to overtake her in a race, but we have to find her first."

Dane smiled at me. "I knew if we were talking about anything to do with the sea, you'd have all the details at your fingertips. Knowing the specs on that sub is a big help—I didn't realize it had capabilities that advanced. Now we just have to figure out how to stop her from beating us to the yacht."

He and the captain put their heads together and began to confer in whispers as to the best course of action.

I watched and listened for a moment before I broke in. "You need more boats. It's the only way. Otherwise, she'll go around us."

The captain stared without saying anything for a second, and I bit my lip in annoyance. People often underestimated me and tried to push me aside, and usually I ignored it and just went ahead and did whatever I knew needed to be done.

But this time, the smug attitude was going to let a killer get away. I said it again. "You need more boats. She'll go around us, and we won't even know it."

Dane looked at the captain. "As usual, she's right. When it comes to anything in, on, or around the water, she knows her stuff."

I felt a momentary satisfaction that Dane recognized my value.

The captain broke in. "That may or may not be true, but this is the only boat we have. We'll have to figure out a way to stop her with the equipment we've got."

"Okay," I said. "You can try. But I have a lot of boats, so I'm going to do it my way." I pulled my cellphone out of my pocket and called Stewie. "Can you get the *Tranquility* and the *Sea Princess* fueled up, please. And I'm sure Gus won't mind if we borrow the *Sunshine Girl* while he and Theresa are away. It's for a good cause. I need all the boats here super-fast, so use your magic. We've got a bead on Lauren. I'll text you the coordinates."

"Right. Will do. But who's gonna pilot all those boats?" Stewie asked.

"You can take *Sunshine Girl*, since you and Gus are tight." Stewie and Gus had been friends for more than thirty years, and Stewie had been instrumental in saving the lives of Gus and Theresa a while ago when they had been kidnapped. Their bond ran deep enough that borrowing a boat without asking shouldn't be a problem—especially for a good cause.

"I'll track down Maddy. She's probably either with Oliver or at home. Naturally she'll take the *Sea Princess* since it's her own boat. I'll find someone to pilot *Tranquility* and let you know who. You concentrate on getting the boats back in the water."

Stewie hesitated a second. "Doc is on her way over. We were going to grab some dinner, but I'm sure she'd like to help. She can handle *Tranquility* if you're okay with her captaining your baby."

"No problem. I'd trust Doc with my life," I said. In fact, Doc had saved my life several times, so this was no exaggeration.

"But since Doc will be with us, we'll have four captains. We can work even better with four boats. See if you can tow one of the rental Zodiacs behind the *Tranquility*. If you can get it set up fast, bring it along. That way we can surround the target from all sides. But if it's going to slow you down, don't bother. Speed is the key here. The sub has a maximum speed of three knots an hour. It's not superfast. But she has a head start on us, so you'll need to step on it." I knew Stewie would know I meant to pull out all the stops and ignore the Cayman speed limit of five miles per hour. Our boats all had a typical cruising speed of fifty to seventy knots. She wouldn't get much further before the RIO flotilla arrived.

"Got it," he said. "See you in a few."

I disconnected the call with Stewie to call Maddy. When I told her the situation, she said she was at home, but she would be right along to meet up with Stewie at RIO's marina since she was only a half mile from RIO.

Killer Storm

I thought about calling in a few more boats but decided adding any more to the mix would only increase the danger, especially if I couldn't quickly round up an experienced captain. Oliver was in jail and Liam was in Switzerland. Vincent, the *Omega*'s captain, was out at sea somewhere. Benjamin could captain a boat, but he wasn't as skilled as the rest of the team I'd called together, plus I was sure Doc still had him in the infirmary. Best to leave him out.

As it was now, we had pretty good coverage with a boat to monitor each side of the three hundred fifty foot long mega yacht. Coverage would still be thin, but at least we had a fighting chance of connecting with the sub.

The captain had been watching and listening in amazement as I arranged for my small fleet to come to his assistance. "Sorry," he said. "Who are you again? I'm not sure I caught your name when you came aboard."

Dane answered for me. "She's Fin Fleming, the world famous diver and current head of the RIO Oceanographic Institute on Grand Cayman." He was clearly annoyed with the captain on my behalf. "You're in the presence of the queen of the ocean herself."

The captain snorted and went into the cabin, while Dane and I stayed on deck. We took turns using the binoculars to scan the surface for any sign of the sub. When Stewie, Maddy, and Doc pulled up beside the cutter, we still hadn't seen any sign of the sub on our sonar.

Stewie quickly jumped from boat to boat, connecting them by wrapping a line around a hull cleat and hanging fenders between the boats to keep them from bumping into each other. Then he tied the *Sunshine Girl* to the cutter despite the captain's sour look. Maddy, Doc, Stewie, Dane, and I all made our way to the *Tranquility*, which was second in line from the cutter.

We huddled on the *Tranquility*'s deck while I briefed the team on what was going on and outlined my plan. "The sub can only go three knots an hour, but she's had several hours to travel, so we pretty much have no idea where she is. Because she may have gotten ahead of us, we'll each take one quadrant of the search area. We surmise she's headed for that yacht." I pointed to the horizon where the yacht floated just on the edge of visibility.

"The sub can go pretty deep. We won't be able to see it from the surface. We'll need to use sonar, or in the case of the rental Zodiac, the fish finder. If you see anything, let Dane and the captain know, but don't engage on your own. Just follow along and keep tabs on her location. The Coast Guard will handle the rest."

I assigned everyone to a search quadrant, and we all went back to our respective boats. Dane went back to the cutter. Stewie was on Sunshine Girl while I took the *Tranquility*. Doc had the Zodiac. Maddy was on *Sea Princess*. We all sped off to begin a search pattern of the four quadrants surrounding the yacht. Even with sonar, it was a long shot any of us would stumble across the sub in the huge ocean, especially with the head start Lauren had, but we had to assume she would try to head for the mega-yacht.

We moved into position slowly to minimize the possibility we'd miss the sub on the way to beginning our search pattern. I took the area at the yacht's aft, and Stewie in the *Sunshine Girl* took the bow position. Maddy and *Sea Princess* were to the north and Doc in the Zodiac took the south. The Coast Guard cutter stayed just inside Cayman waters, between the yacht and the island. As I passed by the mega-yacht to my assigned area I could see the yacht's name —*Golden Kelp*—painted on her side. Under the ship's name was the same golden logo I'd noticed on the sub when I'd spotted Lauren piloting it.

We all began executing a search pattern—moving in straight lines from one end of our assigned area to the other, then turning and repeating the maneuver a few feet closer to the yacht. It was a boring and exacting process. We had to move at a snail's pace, but we were basically going nowhere and doing nothing except staring at a screen. We had to be careful to stay away from each other and the yacht, while simultaneously keeping an eye on our sonar so we didn't miss the sub.

From time to time, I glanced up and noticed the yacht's captain and crew members watching us as we went through our search patterns. There was nothing illegal about what we were doing, but still, it was a very aggressive tactic. I didn't blame them for keeping watch on us, especially if they were unaware of what Lauren had been doing with the sub. Which, however unlikely, was a possibility.

Since the Coast Guard captain had no jurisdiction in international waters, so he hadn't communicated with the yacht. It more than likely didn't matter. If the submarine belonged to the yacht, the ship's crew must know we were searching for it, and they probably had a pretty good idea of why. If my assumptions were wrong, they'd be puzzled for sure and they'd start to ask questions soon.

Chapter 29
The Golden Kelp

I knew the sub could only stay down for ten hours before running out of air power, but without knowing how long Lauren had been under before we started our surveillance, I couldn't be sure how much longer she could hold out.

The sea is a big place, and four boats couldn't monitor the whole wide-open ocean. For all we knew, the mega-yacht had communicated with Lauren, telling her to turn away, rise to the surface, and stand by somewhere else for a more clandestine rendezvous.

I was trying to decide whether or not to continue our surveillance when a man who must have been the captain of the yacht came to the stern of his ship. He held an electronic megaphone that squealed when he lifted it to his lips.

"Ahoy. Fin Fleming. We'd like to invite you aboard the *Golden Kelp* for a cold drink and a tour."

Immediately, my cellphone rang. Dane's number showed in the caller ID. "Do NOT go aboard," he said when I answered. "You have no idea what you'll be facing."

"They won't harm me with you right out there. And I might learn something," I said.

"If they didn't have bad intentions, they'd have contacted us right away to ask what we were doing. And they'd have invited everyone aboard. And they probably wouldn't have known who you are. I have a bad feeling about this. Please, Fin. Please. I beg of you. Do not go aboard that yacht." Dane sounded on the edge of panic.

I looked around. The Coast Guard cutter was on the other side of the yacht where Dane couldn't see me. He'd only heard the invitation because it'd been amplified by the electronic megaphone. I decided to risk it.

I pulled the *Tranquility* close to the mega-yacht. There was a platform designed to allow a tender to tie up to the ship, and for the tender's passengers to easily get aboard. Two of the *Golden Kelp*'s crew stood on the platform waiting to help me tie up. I threw them my bowline. At thirty-six feet, the *Tranquility* was too large for them to pull it up on the platform, but they quickly made it fast to a cleat. I dropped a couple of fenders over the side to keep my boat from getting damaged by contact with the yacht. Both members of the crew pulled on the line, and the *Tranquility* came right up to the platform. One of the crew held out a helping hand to steady me, and I stepped off the gunwale and onto the *Golden Kelp*.

"This way please, Miss Fleming," he said. "They're waiting for you on the pool deck. May I bring you something to drink?"

Maddy and Ray had drilled into me that I should never accept food or drink from strangers—after all, I was a celebrity child with a wealthy father. But I was thirsty. And Dane was only a few hundred yards away. He'd never let the yacht leave with me still on it. I decided to chance it. "Yes, please. A bottle of spring water."

"Certainly, Miss. Would you like ice and a glass with that?"

"No, thank you. And if you don't mind, I'd prefer to open the bottle myself."

He smiled knowingly. "Of course. As you wish."

I followed him up a flight of stairs past three decks. I glanced in the windows as we passed and saw sumptuous staterooms, a lovely library or gathering room, a dining room with seating for twenty, and what looked like a ballroom that could easily accommodate more than one hundred couples.

Each room was beautifully decorated, and even from a distance I could see the materials and finishes were top shelf. Marble and teak floors. High-end linens in the staterooms. Leather upholstered furniture. Crystal chandeliers in the ballroom. This yacht was huge, and beyond luxurious. Despite myself, I was impressed.

We finally reached the pool deck. A hot tub was bubbling away against the distant railing, surrounded by stacks of fluffy, pure white towels. Half of the open deck area was covered by sail-shaped awnings that cast welcome shade on the forty or so empty padded lounge chairs that ringed the immense swimming pool. A lone man in a cerise speedo-style bathing suit swam laps along its length.

I'd lived in relative luxury my whole life, but this lavishly appointed mega-yacht made me gawk like a bumpkin. I was still staring at the sparkling pool when the sound of footsteps approaching from behind made me jump.

"I'm sorry, Miss Fleming. I didn't mean to startle you. I am Sebastian Lukin, and the *Golden Kelp* is my ship. Welcome aboard."

I extended my hand. "Pleased to meet you, Mr. Lukin. Your ship is amazing. I'd love a tour."

He politely shook my hand. "No need to be formal. Call me Seb. And may I call you Finola?"

"Fin is better."

He laughed. "Fin it is. Ready for that tour?"

I nodded and we took off to explore the wonders of the *Golden Kelp*. It took forever to see the endless staterooms, the large meeting rooms, and the sumptuous dining areas. We passed several members of the crew during the tour, and although it was hard to be sure I wasn't double counting anyone, I tried to keep track of how large the crew actually was. I'd counted twelve—and possibly fifteen different people—by the time we reached the lowest level.

Seb pressed a button and a nearly invisible door slid open in front of us. We stepped into the tiny compartment ahead, and the door behind us slid shut. There was no hiss of air, but my ears registered the pressure inside the compartment increasing. I swallowed to equalize the pressure just as the door in front of us opened.

Interesting. Seb had an airlock on the *Golden Kelp*. I wondered why.

We stepped out of the airlock into an immense room. It must have taken up the entire width and a third of the length of the ship. The floors here were stainless steel, covered with a wire grid that let water drain back into a large square opening that led down to the ocean below. That must be the reason for the pressurization—the enhanced pressure kept the water from flooding the chamber through the hole in the floor.

A Triton submarine identical to the one we had spent the day searching for was suspended above the hole. The same soft blue and green paintjob. The same logo on the side. I had no way of knowing for sure it was the same sub, but I thought it unlikely two identical $35 million subs were within a mile of each other in the open ocean, unless they were part of an exploration expedition.

Seb saw the recognition on my face and smiled. "Would you like to try it out?" he said. "You can see amazing things through the glass. My pilot would be happy to accompany you."

A man in a crew uniform had been sitting unobtrusively in the far corner of the room. He stood at attention when Seb offered to let me try out the sub.

I was chagrinned that we had obviously missed Lauren's return to the yacht. Whether she'd been here all along or whether she'd snuck by our search line, there was no doubt in my mind this was the same sub I'd seen her piloting.

She must have come up under the ship and docked through this airlock without ever breaching the surface. It had never occurred to me she wouldn't have to surface at some point to dock on the rear platform. But why invite me aboard just to rub my nose in my failure to apprehend Lauren? What game was Seb playing here?

And where was Lauren? If the sub was here, she must be aboard the *Golden Kelp*. But I hadn't seen anyone who looked even remotely like her during the tour.

I smiled politely at him when I refused his offer of a ride in the sub. "No thank you. Not today. I have work to do, and my friends are waiting for me."

He nodded. "Of course. And I'm sure you've been in subs like this a thousand times because of your work at RIO. But please, whenever you want to try it out or even borrow it, all you have to do is call me." He handed me an embossed card with nothing but a phone number printed on it. "My direct line," he said. "Come, let's go back to the pool deck. Surely you can stay long enough to join me for a drink." He held out his arm to point the way to an elevator tucked away in a far corner of the room.

The elevator moved smoothly and soundlessly up, and the door slid open with a nearly silent whisper. I stepped out onto the pool deck, squinting against the dying sun's glare.

The man who had been swimming laps when Seb and I had left was out of the pool now. He was standing with his back to us, and he'd donned a gaudily patterned Hawaiian shirt whose main color matched the skimpy cerise bathing suit. He was still dripping from his swim, and he was drying his hair with one of the snowy white towels.

"Ah, Jameson. Come and meet our guest."

The man jumped at the sound of Seb's words and turned to face us, still rubbing his wet hair with the towel. I took in the chunky gold chain he wore around his neck, and the matching heavy gold bracelet on his right wrist. A gold Rolex Cosmograph watch with a green face was on the left, and his feet were encased in a pair of bright green shearling Prada sandals. I suppressed a giggle at the pretentious getup he wore, but the giggle turned to a gasp when he lowered his towel and I saw his face. It was Liam.

He paled when he saw me and flipped his head as though to clear the wet hair from his eyes, but the head flip was enough like a shake of the head that meant 'no' that I caught on.

He meant it as a warning to me not to let on that I'd recognized him. I quickly turned my gasp into a cough. I looked away from Liam and faced Seb, clutching my throat. "I'm sorry. I really need that water."

He studied me for a minute. "Of course. I'm a terrible host. What was I thinking?" he snapped his fingers, and a crewmember pulled a bottle of spring water from a nearby ice chest. He placed it on a silver tray and brought it to me.

"Your water, Miss Fleming."

"Thank you," I said. I twisted the cap off, reassured to hear the hiss of compressed bubbles escaping so I knew the bottle had been sealed. I took a hearty swig. "Much better."

"Liam—Jameson—had stood politely by while I took my drink.

I placed the half-empty bottle on a small table nearby and turned to him. "Pleased to meet you, Jameson. I'm Fin Fleming."

"I know," he said, taking both my hands in his. "I'd recognize you anywhere from your TV show. I'm a big fan. When I heard you were coming aboard, I was hoping I'd get a chance to meet you. This is such a treat."

"The pleasure is all mine," I said. "I hope we have a chance to talk soon, but right now, I have to get back to my friends. Seb, thank you for your hospitality and for the tour of your ship. The *Golden Kelp* is spectacular." I picked up my half-full bottle of water and turned toward the stairs that led to the lower decks and walked away, my head spinning.

What on earth was Liam doing aboard the *Golden Kelp*? Why was he calling himself Jameson? And most important of all, why wasn't he in Switzerland where he'd said he'd be?

Back on the *Tranquility*, I took several deep breaths to regain my composure. The only reason I could imagine Liam would be among the drug dealers on the *Golden Kelp* would be if he were one of them. Otherwise, Lauren would surely have recognized him and told Seb about his real identity.

And speaking of his real identity, why on earth would Liam need to have multiple identities, and why would he lie to me about his travel plans? Just as I was beginning to trust him again, he'd proven once again I couldn't rely on him. It hurt just as much this time as it had when he'd gone back to Australia, supposedly to finalize a divorce from his first wife. For more than a year, I'd waited for word from him, but there'd been no phone calls, no emails—not even a text message.

I finished my water and started the *Tranquility*'s engine. As soon as I'd backed far enough away from the *Golden Kelp*, I spun hard to the south and headed to the Coast Guard cutter. Stewie steered the *Sunshine Girl* over, and Maddy followed in *Sea Princess*. Doc was last in the procession in the jet-black rental Zodiac.

Before I reached the Coast Guard cutter, my cellphone rang. When I answered, I heard Liam whispering. "Don't tell anyone you saw me here. My life depends on them not knowing who I am. I'll explain later. I promise." He disconnected.

I was annoyed as I slipped my phone back in my pocket, and I wasn't sure I wanted to keep Liam's presence on the yacht a secret. What if it turned out he was one of the bad guys and I hadn't told Dane? I'd never forgive myself.

Chapter 30
A Daring Proposal

I pulled alongside the cutter and held her steady so Dane could join me on my boat. I told Dane and the captain, who was leaning on his cutter's gunwales, we'd missed the sub, which was now in its berth inside the *Golden Kelp*. Dane shrugged and waved goodbye to the captain, and we all headed back to RIO to debrief.

Once again, I was amazed at the progress the crew had made on repairing the dock. The full marina hadn't been built out yet, but the length of the main dock was finished, and several slips had been completed. A few more had been roughed out, and flags had been placed on the dock where the rest of the slip separators would be placed.

Chaun was kneeling on the dock, attaching one of his RFID readers to a post at the head of one of the completed slips. Benjamin was standing behind him, wearing a heavy sweatshirt, telling me his body temperature hadn't returned to normal yet after his long immersion.

I was still pretty far out when I recognized Eugene on shore supervising Stanley, Noah, and Austin as they worked together building ladders for the shore dive exits. These would be temporary ladders made of untreated wood because we were still waiting for the metal needed to create permanent ladders.

The wooden ladders wouldn't last more than a week or two in the ocean, but their presence meant we could reopen to shore dives. And the completed dock and partially built marina meant we could soon resume boat rentals and dive training. RIO was just about back to business as usual, even after that debilitating storm. I was impressed at how much progress we'd made in such a short time.

I pulled the *Tranquility* into the slip at the end where I'd always parked my boat. Maddy brought the *Sea Princess* into her usual spot next to me, and Stewie floated *Sunshine Girl* into a slip across from us. I watched as Doc expertly piloted the black Zodiac to shore, where Stanley waded in to pull the boat out of the water. Stewie would chain it up with the other rental boats once we'd all disembarked.

Dane jumped out of the *Tranquility* and wrapped a line around the newly installed cleat at the end of the slip. He carefully wrapped the excess line in a neat circle, then walked the few paces to the next slip where he did the same for Maddy. He offered her his hand for balance, and she gracefully stepped up on the gunwale and off onto the dock. The way they looked at each other, you'd have thought they were the only two people left in the world, and I realized they'd never stopped caring for each other. It seemed likely Newton was in for renewed heartbreak.

I'd no sooner shut the *Tranquility*'s engines down when the back door of the RIO building burst open and Newton came running out, crossing the barren backyard at a good clip. Maddy and I both hurried across the wooden dock to greet him, and he swept us both into his arms. "Don't ever do something like that again," he whispered in my ear.

"I won't," I said, and all three of us laughed. It wasn't the first time he'd said that to me and we all knew it wouldn't be the last time. Dane stood off to the side, with the entire RIO work crew watching us.

Killer Storm

I stepped out of Newton's embrace. "We need to debrief. Let's use the table in Maddy's office," I said. Benjamin walked along beside me. He hadn't been part of the search team, but he had a vested interest in catching Lauren. Nobody objected to him joining us.

We all trudged across what used to be our back lawn to reach the door. Maddy used her keycard to open the electronic lock, and we went inside. We were still getting settled at the big round table in front of the window when the café staff came in with trays of drinks and sandwiches.

"I hope you guys are hungry. I ordered enough food to feed half the island." Newton put a large icy glass of lemonade in front of me, and another one in front of Maddy. He handed her a plate with half a turkey club sandwich on whole wheat toast, and a small bowl of cut fruit and berries.

Everyone else, including me, helped themselves, and for several minutes there was nothing but the sound of famished, thirsty people taking care of those problems. When Doc, always the last to finish eating because she ate so slowly, pushed her plate away, Newton put a large tray of cookies in the center of the table.

Once we'd all taken a few cookies, he called the kitchen staff and asked them to take the remainder of the feast to the café and to let the employees know the food was there for them if they were hungry. They came quickly and cleared everything away. We were ready to begin our debrief.

"Okay," Dane said. "What did you see on the *Golden Kelp*? Anything that can help us find Lauren? And any idea how she got past us? Fin, you have the floor."

I swallowed the bite of cookie I'd been chewing and looked around the room. "I think Lauren and the sub were back on the yacht the whole time we were doing our search patterns. Either that, or she snuck by us by going deep and staying close to the edge of the reef. But she was there. That's why they wanted me to come aboard. It was almost like they were taunting me."

Dane asked the first question. "None of us saw the sub on the yacht's tender platform, and it wasn't tied up nearby. What makes you think Lauren got it back there?"

"Because I saw it. Sebastian Lukin is the owner of the *Golden Kelp*, and he took me on a tour. Showed me practically every nook and cranny. And the very last thing he showed me is the pressurized room where the Triton submarine was docked in all her steely glory. They have a water-lock cut into the bottom hull. The sub approaches from beneath the ship and ascends through the lock. Then they lift it out of the way with a crane and plug it into a charger to get ready for the next voyage. The sub never has to surface to get back to home base."

"Wait a minute," Benjamin broke in. "Isn't the USS Triton sub a nuclear vessel? Are you saying they have a nuclear sub on that yacht? And anyway, wasn't the Triton huge? Bigger than that mega-yacht for sure."

I was glad Benjamin had asked the question because I figured Newton and Dane were probably wondering about the same thing. "Your facts are correct, but we're dealing with two different things that just happen to have the same name. The USS Triton was indeed a 447-foot long nuclear sub, but it was decommissioned in 1969. The Triton sub we're discussing now is a totally different thing. It's made by a commercial manufacturer that caters to ultra-wealthy mega-yacht owners and underwater exploration crews. Their subs are battery powered and come in a variety of configurations."

"Thanks for clarifying," Benjamin said. "I was getting worried about Lauren having access to nuclear power."

We all laughed, but it was a nervous laugh. Lauren was dangerous even without nuclear materials.

"So, the yacht is unbelievably luxurious and has a substantial crew. I saw at least fifteen different crewmembers, and I have no way of knowing if that was everyone. I don't know where Lauren was hiding out during my tour. She could have been in a room I didn't see, or she could have been ahead or behind us at any point. I didn't see any sign of drugs, and no weapons."

"Any guests aboard? Did you recognize anyone?" Newton asked.

I looked him straight in the eye and lied. "I didn't see anyone besides Seb and the crew."

Dane stood up. "If Lauren can pilot that sub without us being able to track her, how can we keep tabs on her? She could land wherever she likes, distribute her drugs anywhere on the island, and be back on the *Golden Kelp* in international waters before we even know it. We need a better plan if we're going to stop her."

"I agree," I said. "But I have a plan that I think will work."

Everybody sat up straight, waiting to hear my plan. I was pretty sure they'd all try to shoot it down when they heard it—but it was a good plan and the only one that would work.

I took a deep breath. "Seb offered to let me pilot the sub anytime I wanted. He gave me a card with his direct number on it. I'll call him, ask if the offer's still good, and make a date to get aboard the sub.

Newton and Dane had both crossed their arms in front of their chests. It didn't take an expert to read their body language.

"No," they both shouted, more or less in unison.

I kept talking anyway. "While I'm piloting the sub, I'll find a way to slip an undetectable tracking device on it. We can monitor the sub's location from shore, and whenever Lauren comes to the island, we've got her. It's foolproof."

"It is NOT foolproof," said Newton. "First, where are you going to get this undetectable tracking device? And how do we know it's really undetectable? You have no idea what kind of tracking equipment they have on the *Golden Kelp*. You said yourself it had state-of-the-art everything, everywhere you looked. Second, you can't go back on that ship alone. It was crazy the first time you did it, but it's downright foolhardy to put yourself in that man's hands again. Those people are dangerous."

"I'm well aware of that, but we are a group of very smart people. And we have a secret weapon they have no idea about."

"What would that secret weapon be, Fin?" said Maddy, looking interested.

"We have one of the foremost electronics and radio communications experts in the world on our team, and he operates completely under the radar. Remember, we have Chaunsey. I'm sure he can figure this out."

They all sat back and stayed silent for a minute.

Then Newton spoke. "Underwater communication is tricky because water absorbs radio and acoustic waves. And what assurance do you have they won't be monitoring whatever frequency we use?"

"Let's ask the expert before we shut the idea down, shall we?' I pulled out my phone and called Chaun.

Chapter 31
Chaun Has an Idea

Luckily, Chaun was still on site at RIO, working on repairing the RFID sensors and readers he'd designed for us to track our rental tanks. He joined us within a few minutes. When he sat at the big round table, I briefed him on what we were looking for.

He nodded repeatedly but didn't take any notes while I spoke. When I finished, he said. "Optical. It's the only way. But it won't be easy. How great of a distance do we need to track?"

"At least several miles, and we're not even sure which direction she'll be traveling in.

He nodded again and held up his hand, curled as though he were holding a pencil. Without a word, I handed him my electronic pencil and tablet. He started sketching.

Everyone in the room stayed silent while he worked. After a few minutes, I heard the printer in my office start to whir.

Again. Again. Chaun's fingers were like a blur as he created multiple system and component design diagrams. At last, he put the tablet down. I rose to get the pages he'd printed, but he waved me back to my seat and stood in front of Maddy's whiteboard. He drew a diagram of the monitoring system idea he'd come up with.

"Fiber optics would be easy, but I'm assuming we can't string a bunch of cables…"

I nodded. "That's a no on the cables."

He erased what he'd drawn and drew a new diagram. "We'll need to find a way to get the optical transmitter onto the sub, and then we'll have to surround the yacht with receiving modules. The transmitter will have to be outside the sub—otherwise, the light won't transmit. It can't get through the walls of the sub. We can deploy the receivers in whatever locations we think best, but it'll be hard to get enough here on the island as fast as you want to move."

"How many can you get in the next twenty-four hours?" I asked.

"Eight. Maybe ten." He thought a minute. "Even that will be tough."

"How hard would it be to reposition them?" I asked.

"Easy," he said.

"What if we did this?" I rose and took the whiteboard marker he'd been using and drew four circles—one on each side of the transmitter he'd drawn. Then I made four more circles a little further away positioned midway between the original circles. "When the sub moves, we'll know it's direction, and we can move the receivers on the opposite side into the direction of movement. We can keep doing that until she surfaces. At that point, we've got her."

"How will we stay ahead of her?" Chaun asked.

"Her maximum speed is only three knots. We can go at least five knots without violating the Cayman speed laws. We'll just need to have enough boats to keep things moving."

"Good, good," he said, pushing his hair back with one hand. "Now, how are we going to get the transmitter aboard?" He drew another diagram. "It's a small square, about three and a half inches per side and a little over an inch thick."

"Can you start the transmitting remotely?" Newton said.

"Yes, but you still have to be pretty close for it to work. Whoever's on the sub will have to start it, probably just before they get off."

"I assume they'll be expecting me to try to plant a tracking device of some kind when I pilot the sub. I'll need a decoy device to throw them off."

"Done," Newton said. "I can get you two, because they'll expect you to have a backup."

Everyone in the room looked at Newton with wide eyes. We all wondered why he would have access to tracking devices, but nobody dared to ask.

"We'll need at least a dozen boats, because we can't make it obvious any one boat is following the sub's path, and none of the boats can be recognizable. That means we can't use the *Tranquility* or the *Sea Princess*. In fact, none of the boats we used today will work." I looked at Maddy. "That even rules out our rental Zodiacs."

She smiled. "I'll arrange for the boats. They'll all be very nondescript."

I stood. "We have a great plan, and we just need to finalize a few details. Many thanks to Chaun for thinking outside the box. Let's end the meeting here. We can all work on our own part of the plan overnight and see what progress we've made when we reconvene first thing in the morning."

Chapter 32
Sneak Attack

I needed some time to think about everything that had happened today, so I went back to my office. Since all I was doing was staring at my computer and tapping my pencil against the desk, I decided I could brood at home just as well as I could in the office.

But first I wanted to see Stewie and tell him how impressed I was with the way he'd pulled the team together to get the dive and boat rental operations back up and running, while still managing to rebuild the dock so quickly. It had been a great effort.

I walked down the hall past Maddy's office, but her lights were off, and the room was empty. She and Newton must have gone home too. I went out the back exit and crossed the still-bare yard to the dive shop.

I was happy to see the safety lights blazing in the gathering dusk, and I knew the security cameras were there too. We'd put them in last year after a series of thefts. Having both the lights and the cameras made me feel much better about being alone back here with both Lauren and a killer on the loose.

The lights were on in the dive shack, so I went in, calling out to Stewie as I entered. I stopped dead in my tracks at what I saw. The counter was littered with an assortment of drugs and booze. Syringes lay next to pills lying next to capsules. Lines of white powder. Cans of several varieties of beer stuck out of the top of a cooler filled with ice. Bottles of high end gin, whiskey, tequila, and scotch were lined up near the cash register and six packs of multiple mixers had been placed nearby.

The most shocking sight was Stewie. He was plastered against the wall near the compressor, as far from this pile of temptation as he could get. His skin was pale and sweaty, and his hands were shaking. His tongue darted out and he licked his lips. "It was like this when I got back from the meeting. I swear. Help me," he said. "Make it all go away," He looked at me, his eyes wide with terror and temptation. "Please."

"Relax, Stewie. I know who did this, and I know it wasn't you. I'll take care of it. Why don't you go out and sit on that beautiful new dock you built while I get this cleaned up. I'm going to call Dane, but meanwhile, you don't need to see this." I went to him, took his arm, and walked him outside. He sat down halfway along the dock and put his head in his hands. "Everything will be fine. You did good. I'll be right back."

I went back into the dive shop and called Dane. "Please come to RIO. You have to see this. I think Lauren's been here. Come directly to the dive shop. And maybe bring Roland and his forensic kit." Then I called Doc. "Stewie needs you. Lauren stocked the dive shop with drugs and booze. Stewie didn't touch anything, but it has him shaken. He's sitting on the dock, trembling like he'd seen a ghost. Can you come?"

Within a few minutes I heard police sirens approaching, and then shortly after that Dane and Roland, his trusted associate, came in, both already wearing paper booties and latex gloves.

Roland whistled. "What a nasty, seductive smorgasbord. I guess she really wanted to hurt him." He placed the case that contained his forensic search equipment on the cement slab outside the shop's door and pulled out his cellphone. He shot picture after picture— closeups and wide-angle shots from every direction. When he finished, he uploaded them to the Cayman Police Department cloud account. The he took samples of the powders, bagged up the pills, and began testing everything else for prints.

We watched him work for a minute, then Dane asked, "Anything missing? Did they touch anything? Move anything?"

I shrugged. "Not that I can tell, but you should probably check with Stewie. He spends a lot more time in here than I do nowadays."

"Okay. Let's go talk to him and give Roland some room to work. But first, let's check on the security cameras."

"No video," I said. I was chagrinned. "The cameras were destroyed in the storm. We haven't replaced them yet."

Dane nodded grimly. "I suspected that would be the case. Let's go talk to Stewie. I'll bring him back inside once Roland has had a chance to clear the junk out."

Stewie and Doc were sitting on the end of the pier, holding hands, and letting their feet dangle in the ocean. Stewie rose when he heard the boards creaking under our feet. "It's not my stuff and I don't know where it came from. I gave all that up. I would never do anything to jeopardize the life I have now." He looked down at Doc, still seated on the pier. "You believe me, don't you?"

She smiled softly at him. "I believe you, and I'm sure Dane does too —especially since you were with him when all the drugs materialized in the dive shop. Don't worry. We all know who put it there, and we know it wasn't you."

Stewie took a deep breath and seemed to relax with the exhale.

Dane turned to me. "I'd like to use your office if I may? It's comfortable and quiet."

"Go for it," I said. "I just want to get to the bottom of this. We'll be here when you're done." I sat down next to Doc.

"Why does she hate him so much?" she asked me.

I knew she was talking about Lauren, and why she seemed to target Stewie. "You know she singled him out, even while we were planning the treasure expedition. I can't figure it out either unless she saw him as the weak link that would enable her to get her drugs into RIO."

Doc nodded sadly. "He's not a weak man you know. There's been a lot of pain in his life."

I'd known Stewie since I'd been a toddler, and I wasn't aware of any episodes of pain. But on the other hand, I'd been a kid for most of our relationship. He was thirty years older than me. While I was growing up, he could have gone through many experiences I wouldn't have noticed or been equipped to understand even if I had noticed.

"Pain?" I said. "What happened to him?"

"His wife died during a dive. He blamed himself," she said.

"Stewie had a wife?

She nodded. "My younger sister." She looked out over the ocean. "It wasn't his fault. She was a real daredevil, always pushing the envelope. They had a fight. She took his boat and went diving alone. She went too deep, stayed too long. Came up too fast. Lung embolism. By the time Stewie could borrow a boat and go after her, it was too late. He found her lying on the deck of his boat. Nobody's fault but her own. You couldn't make him believe that though. He sold his boat and started drinking."

In addition to not knowing Stewie had been married, I hadn't known Doc had once had a sister. These were two of the people I was closest to in the world, and we saw each other nearly every day. Both of them had saved my life on more than one occasion. I felt bad I knew so little about their heartaches, and I realized I often got so wrapped up in relatively trivial aspects of life I missed seeing some of the most important things about the people around me. I resolved to do better in the future.

I put my arm across Doc's shoulder. "I'm sorry," I said. "I didn't know."

Her smile was sad as she said, "It's okay, Fin. You were just a little kid when it happened. I'm not surprised you don't remember."

"But...you and Stewie?"

She smiled again, a soft and dreamy smile. "Yeah. Me and Stewie. I always had a thing for him, even before he and my sister got together. When I saw how gaga she was over him, I backed down. They got together, and the rest is history."

We sat together quietly, dangling our feet in the warm water, until Stewie returned. "Ready, Doc?" Stewie said.

Chapter 33
Aboard the Mega-Yacht

The next morning, we had our meeting to discuss the plan to bug the *Golden Kelp's* submarine. Chaun had come through with a tiny optical transmitter and more than a dozen receivers. I was astonished to see that as far as I could tell, the optical transmitter had been painted the exact same blue green shade as the sub's exterior.

"How did you manage that?" I asked.

"I have contacts," Newton said. "Some of them owe me favors." There was a twinkle in his eye, but the rest of his face told me not to probe any deeper.

Maddy had asked trusted members of the *Omega's* crew to be ready with their boats, and Vincent, the *Omega's* captain, was organizing the retrieval of their boats from drydock.

Newton placed two tiny electronic devices in the center of the table, both traditional radio transmitters. "The silver one can go in your water bottle. It'll be practically invisible, but of course, they'll find it. Don't forget it's in there and accidentally drink it. The black one you'll keep in your pocket. They'll find that one too. I think they'll

213

figure they got everything if they find two devices, so the important transmitter—the optical one— should get through."

He continued. "We'll put the optical transmitter in your bra. It'll show up if they wand you. Just say 'underwires' and try to blush if you can. Don't worry if they do find it, just shrug.

You're famous, and they'll know the police know you're aboard their ship. We'll be there, watching, and they'll know we're watching. They won't hurt you. You should be fine. They'll either put you off the ship or let you ride the sub. Doesn't matter either way. Worst case, we'll have to come up with a different plan." He tried to smile, but I could see the uneasiness in his eyes.

"Okay. No time like the present." I picked up the card Seb had given me and dialed the number.

"Yes?' said the voice that answered.

"This is Fin Fleming. I'd like to speak to Seb please."

"Speaking. What can I do for you, Fin?"

"I thought it over and I'd like to take you up on your offer to let me take the sub out for a jaunt. Is that still on the table?"

"Certainly. When would you like to try it out?"

"Does today work?" I asked.

"Come over anytime. You know where we are."

He disconnected, and everyone in the room with me cheered. We were on.

Maddy called Vincent to confirm he and his team were good to go. They were ready, and the boats were holding in position until I finished my jaunt on the sub. Newton and Chaun were set up to monitor transmissions from the optical unit I was going to attach to the sub, so we could be sure our plan would work. When I reboarded the *Tranquility*, Maddy and Stewie would follow me back to RIO, and the "friends and family" fleet would take up their positions to watch for the sub to set off.

We had decided Seb would assume my friends and family would be watching me, so they could be very visible in their boats while I was aboard the *Golden Kelp* or piloting the sub. We'd have one anonymous looking fishing boat nearby to monitor transmissions and alert the others to take their places after I left in the *Tranquility*. We didn't want the other boats to look suspicious. They'd wait to deploy until we'd left the area.

We all headed out to the dock to begin the voyage to meet up with the *Golden Kelp*. Just before we boarded our respective boats, Maddy pulled me into a hug. "Be careful, Fin. I love you too much to lose you."

I stepped back and smiled at her. "I love you too, Maddy. But remember, I'm the luckiest person in the world."

She nodded. "Luck is great, and as we've always said, luck can make up for a lot of stupid. And remember, there's an infinite amount of stupid in the universe, but only so much luck to go around. Don't waste yours." She smiled and kissed my forehead. Then she hopped gracefully onto the gunwales of the *Sea Princess* and began prepping for departure.

Stewie had been in touch with Gus, who was traveling on business in Europe with Theresa, his wife and Angel, their daughter. Gus confirmed it was okay for us to use his *Sunshine Girl*, so Stewie and Doc were on that boat. Maddy took Benjamin, Chaun, Newton, and Dane on the *Sea Princess*. I was alone on the *Tranquility*. We set off, one after the other, in a line.

When we neared the *Golden Kelp*, I broke off from the others and headed to the docking platform in the aft of the mega-yacht. Maddy and Stewie positioned themselves one on each side. I drew a deep breath as I approached the *Golden Kelp*. I set the *Tranquility*'s engines to idle and went below to get my electronic megaphone.

Before I'd gone more than a few steps, the *Golden Kelp* hailed me. "Welcome, Fin Fleming and the *Tranquility*. You may pull up to the docking platform."

A crew member waited on the massive platform, and he secured the *Tranquility* to it. I dropped a few fenders over my boat's sides and stepped up onto the gunwales to disembark. The crew member offered me a hand, and I stepped down on to the massive mega-yacht, carrying a bright red **RIO** branded canvas tote containing a tube of lip balm, some sunscreen, a comb, a clean t-shirt, a couple of tampons, and my water bottle with the first dummy transmitter inside.

Chapter 34
Submarine Voyage

S eb and a few of his people came down the stairs to the docking platform. He walked slowly over to greet me, air kissing me on both sides of my face. I smiled and made kissy noises, but I wanted to retch. "Welcome back, Fin. I am excited to hear what you think of my latest toy."

"Thank you. And I can't wait to try it out." I hoped my voice didn't sound as phony to him as it did to me. He snapped his fingers at one of the men standing behind him. The man looked like a thug, but he was dressed in impeccable seaman's whites. He reached over to take the tote bag from my hand.

I played my part to the hilt, jerking the tote away. "Hey! That's private."

He paused and looked at Seb for instructions.

"Sorry, Fin. Nobody comes aboard without a search. I'm sure you understand." Seb smiled an evil-looking smile, making doubly sure I understood.

"You didn't search me last time," I pointed out.

"That was then. You didn't know you'd be invited to come aboard that time." He smiled, a thin, tight-lipped smile that held no warmth.

I was wearing a bathing suit with a built in under-wire bra for the first time ever as a way to disguise the optical transmitter that was tucked down low between my breasts. The underwires were digging into me, and it was wildly uncomfortable. But I smiled through the pain.

The man who'd grabbed my tote bag moved over to a small shelf that folded down near the back of the docking platform. One by one, he removed items from my bag. He and I both blushed as red as the bag when he removed the tampons.

Including those items among my belongings was sheer genius on Newton's part. He'd thought this initial embarrassment might make the crew member more reluctant to push me if he wanded me later and got a ping from my bra area.

The crewman took a deep breath and kept removing items from the bag. He held each item up to the light, and he tested the lip balm and sunscreen to make sure they were real. The last thing he took out was the water bottle. It was clear plastic, with a blue top that had an integrated drinking straw. Like many of my belongings, it had the RIO logo on the clear bottle.

He held it up to the sky and looked at it carefully. He swirled the bottle. Once. Twice.

Still playing my part, I bit my lip and furrowed my brow as though concerned about what he'd find.

The sailor looked up at Seb.

Seb nodded for the crew man to proceed.

The crew member unscrewed the top and began to pour the water through a small sieve he'd removed from a drawer in the shelf.

"Hey," I shouted, still acting. "That's my water. I need to stay hydrated."

Seb's thin lips approximated a gracious smile. "Not to worry. We'll provide you with all the fluids you need."

The crew man had finished pouring out the water. He lifted the tiny silver transmitter, no bigger than my smallest fingernail, from the sieve, and held it out for Seb to see.

Seb took it from him, dropped it to the deck, and crushed it with his foot. "Oops," he said. "I'm sorry, Fin. But I can see we'll have to take precautions before letting you aboard again." He nodded to the crew man, who pulled a wand—like security people use to scan people in airports—from the drawer.

I scowled as he walked toward me. "I assume you know the drill," he said.

I kicked off my flip flops, lifted my arms to the side, and put my feet shoulder-width apart. He started by scanning each shoe, and as he finished, he held it for me to slide my foot back into. Then he scanned the parts of my body covered by my cargo shorts. As expected, the wand chirped when it came near my right front pocket. "Empty your pockets please," he said.

I tried to look chagrined as I put my hand in my pocket and withdrew the second transmitter and a handful of Cayman coins. I handed it all to him, and he passed the transmitter to Seb, who casually tossed it overboard.

The man with the wand went back over my shorts, but nothing chirped. He gave me back my change. Then he passed his instrument around my torso, and as expected, his wand beeped in my bra area.

As Newton had instructed, I tried to look embarrassed. "Underwires," I said, looking down at my feet and biting my lip.

Once again, the poor man holding the wand blushed. He looked over at Seb, who shrugged. With a look of relief, the crew member nodded. "She's clean."

"Excellent." Seb held out a hand. "I'm sure you understand why these precautions are necessary."

I looked him in the eye. "It wasn't necessary yesterday."

"We change our procedures every day. It keeps our enemies on their toes. This way please." He smiled, but he still looked like a snake to me.

We took a different route to the submarine chamber today. It took several minutes before we arrived. I didn't know whether he was deliberately trying to confuse me about the yacht's layout, or if there was just no easy way to get there. Seb pushed a button and there was the hiss of pneumatic doors opening. We stepped into a tiny chamber. The door slid shut behind us, and I felt the pressure in the tiny compartment increase. The door in front of us slid open, and we were in the room with the sub.

I couldn't help but admire such a beautiful piece of equipment. I stepped closer to the sub, and walked around it, partly appreciating her sleek lines and state-of-the-art propulsion and buoyancy control systems, but also looking for the best place to attach the optical transmitter. The transmitter needed a spot with a clear line of sight in at least one direction, in a location where it wasn't likely to be bumped and dislodged during maintenance or operation, and where the pilot and mechanic were unlikely to notice it.

It was a tall order, and I knew that even though the transmitter had been painted to match the sub, it was bound to be noticed sooner or later. I could only hope it stayed hidden long enough for us to find Lauren.

The pilot, whose name was Davy Jones—seriously— joined me as I walked around the sub, helpfully pointing out some of its more advanced features. I listened carefully, my eyes scanning the sub for just the right spot. I was acutely aware that Seb's eyes were on me the whole time, assessing me as intently as I was assessing his submarine.

I decided on a location. The sub had a narrow space between the lower runner and the upper extension for seating the small steering propeller. The space backed up to the viewing dome, but it was behind the pilot's and passenger's backs, making it hard to see while operating the sub. The space was open to the sea from the sub's rear, with nothing to block the optical transmissions. Yet the area was shadowed and difficult to reach by hand, so now my only problem was to get the device in place.

One side of the transmitter was a powerful magnet, All I had to do was get it near the sub and it would cling. But I had to be careful, because the magnet was so strong that I might not be able to easily reposition the transmitter if I missed the right spot on my first try. I began to sweat with nerves.

Davy went to the control panel on the side wall and began checking the sub's parameters, making sure there was enough air and juice to keep it running. He held a clipboard and a pencil to record his readings, and his back was turned toward me while he checked.

Good. One down, but I knew Seb had been watching me like a hawk as I examined the sub.

I was saved when the airlock door whisked open, and one of the boat's stewards came in with a message for Seb.

He stepped away and turned his back to read the message, and I quickly fumbled the transmitter out of my bra and flicked it on. With the device in my hand, I leaned across the sub's runners trying to reach the right location. It was a long stretch, even for a tall woman like me, and I lost my balance.

I was teetering on the edge of the open hatch when Davy noticed my predicament. He hurried across the room and swept me away from the edge of the hole with one arm. As he twirled me to safety, my outstretched arm bumped against the sub.

I heard a faint snicking sound as the magnet mated with the sub's steel runner. It wasn't in the cozy nook I had hoped to reach, but it was nearby. It had a clear line of sight behind the sub, so we should be able to track the sub from its beacon. The only problem was that in this position, it was slightly more visible than I would have liked. It was a jarring element to the sub's graceful symmetry.

"Steady there," said Davy as he placed me carefully on the deck. "You don't want to fall in."

"Thank you. I just got a little dizzy in this light, but I'm okay now."

"Good. Ready for your lesson then?" he asked.

I nodded, and he showed me how to climb in through the hatch and seal it behind me. We sat side by side in the ultra-comfortable leather seats while he explained how to use the sub's single control.

The control looked like a gaming joystick, and it coordinated the direction and depth of the sub. I practiced moving it around a little, but it seemed simple enough.

Then Davy showed me how to override the system's buoyancy, directional, atmosphere, and temperature systems. Those systems were all controlled by on-board computers, but the pilot could manually override the computer in an emergency.

"Got it?" he said when he'd finished explaining the last safety aspect.

"Got it," I said.

"Want me to come with you on this voyage? I'm not technically supposed to allow anyone to go out alone until they've had a hundred hours of experience, but you're Fin Fleming, for Pete's sake. I know you'll be fine. You probably could have explained all this stuff to me."

I smiled at him. "I appreciate your training, and maybe another time we can take the sub out together. But I'm considering buying one for RIO, and I'd like to test it out on my own."

"No problem," he said. "Don't tell Seb I suggested this, but if you do get one and you need a pilot…"

"You'll be the first person I call," I said. "I promise."

He grinned and climbed out of the hatch. I sealed it behind him.

He and Seb stood side by side on the nearby control platform. I gave them a thumbs up sign, and Davy began lowering the sub through the hole in the deck into the open water.

I let the sub drift downward until I was sure I'd cleared the yacht's hull, then I gently twitched the joystick to move the sub down and to the south of the *Golden Kelp*. The sub was incredibly responsive, quick to react but smooth as silk as it glided through the water.

I flicked the switch to turn on the external lights and went deeper still. The *Golden Kelp* was anchored on the top of a reef that was about 200 feet down. On the side toward Grand Cayman, the reef sloped up gradually until it leveled off near the shore. In the other direction, it dropped off to who knows how deep—at least a couple of miles. It was an amazing location. And while I'd been diving on the reef and the upper portions of the wall many times before, I'd never had the opportunity to go this deep and stay down this long without worrying about decompression sickness or running out of air.

I kept the sub close to the wall, checking out the sea life and the beautiful corals. When I'd seen enough of the wall, I rose in the water and reached the top of the reef. I floated across the sandy bottom, avoiding the tall rocks and large coral clusters until I reached the spot where I'd seen Lauren the other day. I turned the sub in a complete circle, peering out through the clear acrylic dome to see if I could find anything of interest.

There was plenty to see, but it was all ocean related. Nothing to do with drug trafficking or murder, so I headed back over the wall. I dropped swiftly down to 500 feet and marveled at the speed of my descent and the fact that the pressure inside the sub stayed exactly the same, thanks to the well programmed onboard computers.

I needed to convince Seb and Davy Jones I really was interested in buying a similar sub for RIO, so I had to spend enough time to really put the sub through its paces. Believe me, it was no hardship, although I half expected some form of sabotage to erupt. But I guess in at least this respect, Seb was an honorable man.

I spent an hour at 500 feet, then turned around to head slowly back to the *Golden Kelp*. There was a homing beacon on the *Golden Kelp*. The sub's dashboard displayed exactly where I was in relation to the yacht, making navigation easy. When I was under the hole in the yacht's hull, I ascended slowly and ended up back in the control room in the exact center of the docking hole.

I was practically giddy with excitement when I climbed out of the hatch. Between my nerves about being here undercover and the fabulous sub and its practically unbelievable capabilities, I had trouble catching my breath.

This machine was amazing. I'd have given a lot to be able to buy one for RIO, but even with Newton's generous patronage, it was an extravagance we probably could never afford. We already had an older model ROV—a remote operated vehicle—plus a small, cramped one person submersible, and we'd just have to make do with those.

Davy Jones offered his hand to help me down from the sub's hatch. My feet had just touched the deck when Seb walked in through the airlock doors.

"What did you think?" he asked. He smiled the smile that gave me chills.

I swallowed back my nerves before I answered. "It's amazing. I can't thank you enough for letting me try it out. I only wish I had one like it."

"You could have one, you know," he said. "You could come to work for me. Your skills would be invaluable."

Killer Storm

Over Seb's shoulder, I saw Davy Jones' startled look. We both thought Seb was thinking of replacing him.

"Thank you, but I already have more jobs than I can handle, between my family businesses and my column at *Ecosphere*. And really, I'm more of a marketing person and underwater photographer than a marine biologist. I'm not sure what I'd be bringing to the table as a pilot."

He laughed. "I'm not asking you to be a pilot. Mr. Jones here is more than adequate. And I know you have a PhD in marine biology, so don't sell yourself short as a scientist. But the things I really would like you to bring to the team are your contacts around the world and the legitimacy your name would bring to my little operation." He smiled again, making my skin crawl. "Would you like to hear more about what I have in mind?"

I shook my head. "No thank you. I'm very flattered, but as I said, I'm over-extended with the family businesses and following my own passions. I'll have to pass. Sorry."

He stared at me for a minute before he responded. "You have my card if you ever change your mind. Come. I'll walk you back to your boat."

He held out his arm and ushered me into the airlock. We quickly exited on the other side and walked around the corner to the boat docking platform where the *Tranquility* waited.

"Goodbye, Seb," I said from the *Tranquility*'s deck. "Thank you again for letting me pilot the sub. It was such a treat."

I couldn't see his eyes through the mirrored lenses of the sunglasses he'd donned as soon as we'd left the yacht's interior, but I knew his eyes were cold and hard because they always were.

"You have no idea," he said. "The pleasure was all mine."

I quickly backed the *Tranquility* away from his yacht and headed away as fast as I safely could.

As I came around the side of the *Golden Kelp*, the *Sea Princess* and the *Sunshine Girl* fell into line behind me, and we all headed back to RIO.

The nondescript fishing boat anchored nearby stayed exactly where it had been all day. Vincent, its captain, played his part perfectly. He didn't even look up when we passed him, just took a sip from his empty beer can and turned the page in the book he wasn't reading. Hidden behind his mirrored sunglasses, his gaze never left the *Golden Kelp*.

Chapter 35
Debrief

W e gathered in Maddy's office to debrief. I told everyone about the new information I had gathered on the layout of the *Golden Kelp*. "I saw a few more members of the crew I don't remember from yesterday. It's likely his crew is larger than my first estimate," I said. "Still no sign of Lauren. They have another sub pilot on board. Said his name was Davy Jones."

Newton snorted. "And you bought that?"

"I had no reason to question him," I said. "Plus, I didn't want to antagonize him. I wanted him to like me enough to stick up for me taking the sub out alone."

"Did you see anything suspicious either on the ship or on the dive?" Dane asked.

"No, not a thing." I could feel my pulse quicken. "But that sub is amazing. It's so responsive, and you can take it pretty much anywhere. No worries about decompression sickness, no matter how deep you go or how long you stay down. It was thrilling." I tamped down my excitement a bit. "But sooo expensive."

Everybody laughed.

Maddy broke in. "Let's call Vincent. See if he's noticed any activity from the sub." We had agreed all communication between us and our small fleet of volunteers would be through cellphones to be sure we weren't being overheard.

Dane said, "Good idea. Fin, would you mind going back to your office and taking a look at some mug shots while they're calling Vincent? See if you recognize this Davy Jones. If you do, just click on the photos and the software will save them in a sub-group. Roland can check them out when you're done."

He handed me his police tablet, open to a series of mug shots. I walked down the hall to my office and sat at my desk. I spent more than an hour scrolling through the mug shots without seeing anyone that looked even a little like Davy Jones.

I was relieved when Dane came into my office.

"Any luck?" he said.

I shook my head. "Not a soul. These guys all look like thugs. The Davy Jones I met looked like a 'next door neighbor' kind of guy. Wholesome. He was polite and soft-spoken."

Dane thought a minute. "Okay. I'll see if we can put together a new array with polite, soft-spoken, neighborhood guys." He laughed. "Anyway, you did your best. Thanks for trying.

"Then you're all set with me?" I asked. "It's been a really long day and I'd like to go home."

"Sure," he said. "I think you should stay at your father's place tonight though. Who knows what surprises Lauren has in store for you."

"Sure thing," I said, although I had no intention of staying at Newton's. I still had to talk to Justin, and before I did that, I needed to check Oliver's story about his keycard. I planned to drop by the building where both Newton and Maddy had their residences on my way to Fleming Environmental, but then I was going home. I wanted the peace and serenity of my own house and my own bed. It had been a difficult few days since the storm had hit, and all I wanted was to put my feet up and take a few moments to gather my thoughts.

I grabbed the canvas tote I used as a purse and stuffed my computer in it. Then I slid my feet into the flip flops I'd kicked under my desk while I worked. "Are Maddy and Newton still around?" I asked him.

"No, I think they went out to the *Omega* to bring dinner to the people piloting the other boats we had on standby. Did you need something?"

"Nope. All set. I'll see you tomorrow." I walked past him and down the hall to the main entrance. I drove straight to the building where both Newton and Maddy maintained their separate residences— both luxury penthouse condos, each taking up half the top floor of the high-rise building overlooking the ocean.

I parked my car in Newton's space in the garage and rode the elevator up to the top level. Before I entered the code that opened Maddy's smart lock, I first rang the bell and then knocked on the door. As expected, there was no response to either sound. I punched in the code and the door clicked open.

Maddy's condo was spectacular—all beautiful blues and sandy beiges, with artifacts from her global travels perched on tables and used as book ends to keep her extensive library neat. Rich deep rugs over the gleaming hardwood floors delineated intimate conversational groupings. The artwork was a combination of watercolor seascapes and underwater photographs, several of which she'd taken herself.

Although most of the photos had been taken by Maddy, there were also some I'd taken—which was nice because it meant she thought highly enough of my work to display it in her home. Despite the beauty of each item she had chosen, the most striking feature of Maddy's home was the floor to ceiling window that faced the ocean. Through these windows, she could see for miles, with nothing to interrupt her view.

Today I didn't have time to enjoy the vista, regardless of how mesmerizing it was. I scurried down the hall toward the bedrooms and quietly opened the door to the room Oliver used when he stayed here.

The curtains had been drawn, so the room was dim. I flipped on the overhead light and looked around. I hadn't been in this room since Oliver had claimed it as his own, shortly after my parents adopted him. It hadn't changed much, except for the artwork.

One new addition was a framed poster of my late stepfather, Ray Russo, on a free dive. I remember the day I'd taken that shot, and how happy he and Maddy had been.

I smiled when I saw the large, framed photo he'd hung over his bed. It was my famous shot of Maddy facing down a Great White shark. She and the shark just stared at each other, and she didn't show an ounce of fear. I, on the other hand, threw up with terror for her even while I was enclosed in the safety of the nearby shark cage— but I'd at least waited to vomit until after I'd taken the picture.

I walked over to the dresser on the far side of the room and scanned its surface. On the right hand side was a small dish where Oliver must empty his pockets at night. In the dish there was a pile of coins, a Seiko dive watch, and a green Fleming Environmental Investments employee key card, just as Oliver had said there'd be.

I blew out a breath. The card I'd found didn't belong to my brother. If Dane was able to link it to Cara's murder, Oliver would be in the clear. I snapped a picture of the card. I was just about to send it to Dane when I realized I'd forgotten yet again to tell him about finding the keycard in the ocean right after the storm. I decided to save the picture until he and I had a chance to discuss it.

I shut off the lights and left Maddy's condo, locking the door behind me. My next stop was supposed to be Fleming Environmental Investments to discuss the funds discrepancies with Justin, but I decided to stop by the jail to let Oliver know I'd found his keycard before I went to the FEI building.

The two buildings I needed to visit were only a few blocks away from each other. I parked in the Fleming Environmental lot and walked to the nearby police station. The sergeant was reading from a Michael Connolly paperback. He glanced over the top of his book and waved me into the cell area before immediately dropping his eyes back to his book. I couldn't blame him. Connolly's books are enthralling, and Oliver was still the only prisoner in the jail.

As I approached the cell where Oliver was housed, I saw him studying a sheaf of papers in his hand. The papers were bound in a blue paper cover, the kind often used for legal documents. He was smiling as he read. I guessed it wasn't bad news.

"What'cha got there, Bro?" I asked from the hall outside his cell.

Oliver dropped the papers on his cot and looked up at me, a big smile on his face. "You can call me Mister Fleming from now on," he said. "Or more accurately, Mister Fleming-Russo."

"Huh?" This made no sense. Just a short time ago Oliver had changed his name from Flores, his birth name, to Russo, when his mother had lied to him, saying Ray Russo was his father. Oliver had admired Ray since he'd been a child, so he'd been thrilled to be able to take the name. Since Russo was also the surname Maddy used, he'd kept it after the adoption.

Oliver picked up the papers and handed them to me through the bars. "Newton's been so good to me. He paid for my education and gave me a great job at his company. I was overwhelmed by the adoption, I guess I wasn't thinking clearly. I should have made Fleming-Russo my name right from the start. Now I've fixed the oversight." His grin was contagious.

"Good news indeed. I'm sure Newton will be pleased when he finds out." I said.

"I hope you're right. By the way, what are you doing here again so soon?" he asked.

"I wanted to let you know I checked your room at Maddy's, and your FEI keycard is there, just like you said. That's good."

He blew out a breath. "That's one worry off my mind. Thanks, Fin."

"Hey," I said. "I have a question for you. Why do I have to sign multiple copies of financial transfers when we do donations to RIO?"

He frowned. "Most of the time you don't have to sign anything on paper. We do everything electronically, even signatures. But Newton might want to be absolutely sure he has a complete paper trail. Maybe he treats RIO a little differently because the two companies are so close. Otherwise, I can't imagine why you'd ever do anything on paper."

Now I was really concerned. I knew I'd need to confront Justin about the withdrawal errors and get him to walk me through his process. I had to straighten this out.

I always read all the paperwork, every single page, and I questioned anything that didn't look right. Actually, I realized, that was what I'd always done until this latest round of authorizations covering the cash transfers for the storm damage. I'd been focused on getting RIO back up and distracted by all the tasks that needed my attention—not to mention Benjamin's accident and Cara's murder—that I'd just skimmed the pages to make sure the transfer amount was right.

Oliver was watching me closely as these thoughts flew through my brain. "Can you stick around a while? It's pretty lonely here sometimes," he said.

"Sorry. I can't stay. I have to get over to Fleming Environmental before they shut down for the day. There are a few things I need to take care of right away."

I saw him swallow his disappointment. "Okay. See you tomorrow then."

I nodded and left the police station.

Chapter 36
Confrontation At Fleming Environmental

The Fleming Environmental Investments building was located in an area known as Camana Bay. It was home to expensive condos, world-class shopping, and 'class A' business space. FEI's main entrance opened into a three story atrium filled with elegant but understated furnishings, eclectic art, and modernist sculpture. The lobby whispered of enormous wealth, confident enough it didn't need to draw attention to itself.

Although I was officially an employee of Fleming Environmental, I didn't have an employee keycard. I rarely needed to go into any of the secure areas beyond my office, and while I was here, I rarely went anywhere by myself. Consequently, I'd never picked up my green all-access keycard from the human resources team. I'd never actually needed one since I seldom worked from this building, and even when I did come in, I still didn't need a keycard because my office was right off the lobby.

But Dane and the goings-on at RIO had made me more security conscious, so I resolved to stop by HR on my way out. But right now, I wanted to see Justin and straighten out the mess with the duplicate transfers.

There was a turnstile that allowed people to pass into the inner sanctum and the lobby elevators. Visitors used a phone on the stone counter to request their passes because you needed an employee badge or a visitor's pass to operate the gate. I picked up the phone, identified myself, and told HR I needed entrance. They could also operate the gate remotely, which they usually did for me since they didn't need to see any ID.

The gate buzzed, and I passed through. It was only a few steps to my posh office with its original paintings and contemporary executive-style ergonomic desk and chair. It was a far cry from RIO, where we put most of our money into research rather than staff amenities. But I knew people expected an investment firm to look affluent. I understood the psychology behind the differences in decorating styles. But actually, I liked my office at RIO a lot better. It suited me. And at RIO, I could see the ocean from my windows. Here, I just saw traffic.

I picked up the phone on my desk and called Justin. "Got a minute?" I said.

"Be right there."

True to his word, Justin was at my door within a few seconds. He lounged in one of the visitor's chairs in front of my desk, sipping from a water bottle. "What's up, Boss?" he smiled his most winning smile. "Ready to take me up on that dinner invitation?"

I swallowed back my annoyance at his persistence, and the inappropriateness of his invitation during what was clearly a business meeting. "No. No dinner. I'd like to review all the donation transfers for the last eighteen months," I said. "Can we do that?"

Justin paused a moment. "It might take me a while to gather up all the paperwork."

"Hmm, that's another thing. Why are the charitable donations the only transaction types done on paper? All the other kinds of transactions are approved electronically, aren't they?"

236

He twitched a little—almost imperceptibly—but answered smoothly enough. "It's so we have extra documentation in case we get audited by the government. They're sticklers for that sort of thing."

"We have the ability to print them out of the government requests paper documentation, don't we?" I asked.

"Yes, but it has to do with electronic signatures. They like to be able to see a paper trail because of the tax implications."

I'm no accountant, but I can tell when someone is covering their tracks. I slid my keyboard across the desk to him and swung the large flat screen monitor on my desk around at an angle where we could both see it. "Can you walk me through some of the transactions please? I'd really like to follow the process."

He nodded and put his water bottle on the corner of my desk. Then he logged in and brought up a view of several operational transactions—purchases of supplies and the like. He yammered on for a few minutes.

I interrupted. "Can you print one of these out please."

He nodded, and the printer in the corner of my office whirred to life.

I took a moment to examine the printout and noticed it had been electronically signed and there was verification of the signature, including date, time, the person's login info, and the IP address where the transaction occurred.

"This seems pretty complete to me. Now would you please print out a donation transaction. I want to understand what's different about them."

"That's what I've been trying to tell you, Fin. Those are paper transactions. We'll have to go down to the basement archives to see those, and it's pretty unpleasant down there. Are you sure you want to do that?"

My alarm senses were tingling. I could almost—but not quite—buy the idea that we did paper signatures on charitable donations. But there'd have to be a record in the computer systems somewhere, or we wouldn't be able to balance our accounts on our computerized business systems. I looked Justin in the eye. "Let's go."

We left my office and walked through several hallways and down two flights of stairs. We'd left the luxurious visitor areas, executive offices, and public conference rooms far behind. We were in a dark rear hallway, underground. There were no windows since it was below street level, and only a single dim lightbulb hanging over the door. Justin pulled out his Fleming Environmental keycard and waved it in front of the electronic lock. The system made a loud bleat and refused to unlock.

He tried again. Same result.

"We'll have to use your card," he said. "Mine doesn't seem to be working today."

I looked at the keycard in his hand and noticed it was blue, like a visitor card, not green like an employee card. "I don't have a card with me," I said. "Let's go to human resources and get you a new one."

He shook his head. "Let me see if I can open this door another way," he said. He shoved the door with his shoulder. I heard the wood creak, but the lock held. Still, it didn't seem like the door would withstand his onslaught for long, and I couldn't imagine why he thought it would be okay to batter down the door anyway.

"Justin, forget about it. We'll go another time. In fact, you can gather all the records you need over the next couple of days, and when you're ready we can review them in my office where the light is better."

"No," he said. "It's obvious you don't trust me. I want to clear this up now." He rammed the door again.

Now I was truly alarmed. We were far away from any people and heading into an even more secluded basement. It looked like hardly anybody came this way, and I was frightened by Justin's actions. "I'm going back to my office. Get yourself a new key, gather the records you need, and make an appointment to discuss them with me." I turned and started to walk away.

Justin grabbed my arm and pulled me back around, holding me across his body with one arm. "No!" he said. "You wanted to see the records, and we're going down there to see the records. Now give me your keycard."

"I told you I don't have one," I said, trying hard to keep my voice steady. "Now let me go right now."

A soft voice from behind us said "If you need a keycard, we can use mine." Genevra, my new assistant was here. "Hi, Fin," she said. "I'm sorry I'm late for the meeting."

Smart girl. We didn't have a meeting planned, but I thanked whatever corner of the universe had sent her here to this secluded hallway in the nick of time.

There's no way I could have fought back against whatever Justin had in mind, and it was obvious he had bad things planned. He was taller and stronger than me. I'd have been unlikely to prevail in a fight. Although Genevra was tiny, barely five feet tall, her presence evened the odds at least a little.

I reached up and removed Justin's arm from across my throat. I took a deep breath. "Let's go, Genevra. Our meeting can't wait."

We walked away from Justin, but I could hear him panting behind us. I didn't relax until we got back to the public areas of the Fleming Environmental offices. "Thanks for coming, Genevra. I don't know what got into him."

She shrugged. "You were coming here, and I thought maybe I could help since I'm your new assistant. It looks like I got here just in time."

"For sure," I said, as we entered my office. I picked up the phone and called Newton. He didn't answer, but I left a voice mail telling him what Justin had done. "I think I figured out the problem with those extra transactions. It seems like Justin may have been embezzling. I'm worried about him," I said. "I think he's gone over the edge." I disconnected.

I was just about to call Dane when I noticed Genevra about to pick up the water bottle Justin had been drinking from. "Stop," I shouted. "Don't touch that. I have an idea. Can you find a plastic bag for me while I call Dane please?"

She nodded and left my office.

I hit the speed dial button assigned to Dane, but I got his voicemail too. "Justin Nash just tried to forcibly pull me into the sub-basement at Fleming Environmental. I think he's been embezzling from Newton's company, and I have a hunch he was the mysterious person I saw lurking at RIO the night of the storm. I'm leaving here now, but there's a bottle in the bottom drawer of my desk he was drinking from. I think you should arrest him. You might want to test the DNA on the bottle against the unidentified DNA you found in Oliver's raingear." Then I called HR and told them to discreetly evacuate the building and wait outside for the police.

Genevra came back in with a sealable plastic bag FEI used to package up its marketing literature. We carefully slipped it over the bottle and sealed it without touching the bottle. Then I put the bag in my bottom drawer where I'd told Dane it would be.

I grabbed my canvas tote from the floor under my desk. "I'm going home," I said. "This has already been a long day. Coming?"

"No,' said Genevra. "I'll wait here for DS Scott. He should be along soon."

"Stay here in my office with the door locked until you see Dane or his team arrive. Justin is still somewhere in the building, and I think he's dangerous. And thank you, Genevra. You're literally a lifesaver."

Chapter 37
Chico Pays a Visit

As usual when I'd had a bad day, I stopped at the gas station on my way home and picked up a ham and cheese sandwich for dinner. I just wanted to have some quiet time in my own house, with my nose buried in one of Ray's logbooks, remembering those simpler times when Ray had been around. My beloved stepfather had been gone a few years now, but I still missed him every day. Reading and re-reading his logs always made me feel close to him.

I pulled my car into the driveway and went through the gate into my backyard. I wanted a quick swim in the pool to cool off before I settled in for the night. I dropped my tote bag on one of the nearby chairs and kicked off my flip flops.

After stripping off my T-shirt and cargo shorts, I dove in, but it wasn't as risqué as it sounds. Since I'm in and out of the water so much during the day, I almost always wear a bathing suit under my clothes, and today was no different.

After a few laps, the water had worked its magic. The tension had drained from my shoulders and neck. I was relaxed and ready for a cozy night at home.

After drying off, I slipped into a clean pair of baggy flannel shorts, and an old RIO t-shirt, so threadbare you could practically see through it. I loved the shirt because it had been Liam's and it was soft and cuddly.

I unwrapped my sandwich and popped open a can of lemonade and settled into a corner of my couch with a small, soft blanket over my knees. After taking the first bite of my sandwich, I picked up the logbook I'd been reading. Pure bliss.

The logbook was so engrossing I didn't notice the passing of time until I heard a faint scratching on my glass patio door. I must have left the gate open again, because it sounded like Chico was back looking for a handout. This was a bad habit he'd gotten into, and I didn't want to encourage him. I went back to my reading.

The scratching continued.

I ignored it.

It didn't stop.

Finally, I heard a thump, like maybe Chico had knocked hard or possibly even kicked at the door. This behavior would definitely have to stop. I refused to be at the beck and call of a rooster. I put down my book and stood up.

I stopped in the kitchen to dispose of the wrapper my sandwich had come in, and also to toss the empty lemonade can into the recycle bin. I stood in front of the jar where I'd stored the seeds I gave to Chico, staring at the small handful of seeds I'd picked up. Then I stopped, debating with myself over whether to give him some or not.

If I gave him seeds when he came at night, I would be training him to come every night. But I remembered from one of my psychology classes in college that rats would go crazy trying to get treats by pushing a bar when the treats were dispensed at random intervals instead of on an easily recognized schedule. I'd already given him treats at night several times.

I wondered if Chico would recognize that morning was different than evening, or if the lack of treats at night might confuse him. Then I remembered Chico was a rooster. His job was to crow at dawn, so of course he knew morning was different than night. I dropped the seeds back in the jar and wiped my hands on a paper towel. This whole time, the scratching on my patio doors continued.

I flipped on the outside light on my way to the doors, planning to shoo Chico away in no uncertain terms. My heart stopped when the lights came on. There was a man lying on the ground, scratching at my door. He lifted his head and my heart stopped.

It was Liam.

His face and hands were bloody, and his blackened eyes were barely open. There were massive bruises on his shoulders and arms. A string of bloody drool hung over his split lip. He was wearing only a pair of cargo shorts, and he shivered violently even in the warm Cayman evening.

I opened the doors and fell to my knees to help him. "What happened? Can you stand?" I pulled his arm over my shoulder to hoist him up, and he whimpered in pain, but with my help, he managed to stay on his feet. Haltingly, we went inside.

Together we made the short walk to my bedroom, the closest place where he could stretch out. He fell onto the bed with a groan.

With the arm that wasn't dislocated, he fumbled at one of the pockets of his cargo shorts. "Gun," he whispered.

He kept pawing at the pocket, and eventually he managed to withdraw a small black pistol.

I recoiled. What was Liam doing with a gun?

I took it from him and placed it on the nightstand with the barrel pointed away from us. According to the engraving on the gun, it was a Smith & Wesson Bodyguard .38 special. It had a label proclaiming it was equipped with an integrated Crimson Trace laser focus. In theory, the bullet would hit wherever the red dot appeared on the target.

"Take it. Aim red dot. Center mass," he rasped.

I didn't own a gun, but I knew what Liam was trying to tell me. "Okay, I've got it, but I don't need a gun. I'm calling Dane," I said. "He'll know what to do."

"First Newton. Safe house," he said through his swollen lips. "Then Dane. Nobody else." It obviously hurt him to talk. He was still trying to speak when his eyes rolled back. He passed out without another word.

I had no idea what he'd been talking about, but since he seemed to think it was important, I dialed Newton's number first. "Newton, Liam is here. He's unconscious, but before he passed out, he said to call you and say safe house. I hope you know what that means. Call me when you get this message, please. If it's busy, it's because I'm calling Dane right now. Keep trying. I need you."

I called Dane's direct number, and this call too went straight to voicemail. I groaned in frustration but left a message. "Call me. I'm at my house in Rum Point. Liam is here, and it looks like someone beat him to within an inch of his life. He needs—no, we both need help right now. Please come quickly."

I bit my lip and stared at Liam. He was so badly injured I didn't know where to start. I did a quick assessment. Both of his knees and the palms of his hands were scraped raw, as though he'd been crawling. Good Lord. Had he crawled here all the way from wherever they'd dumped him?

I continued the assessment and realized one of Liam's legs was probably broken, in addition to all his other injuries. It must have taken superhuman determination to make his way to my house.

Seb or someone on his team must have done this, and I was furious. I had no idea what Liam had been doing on Seb's mega-yacht, but whatever he'd done, nobody deserved this.

I didn't have the skill to manage Liam's injuries on my own, and I didn't think I could get him to my car by myself. I was just about to call Doc when I heard the sound of my front door crashing open. There was another crash from the front room, as though someone had knocked over the glass table that stood inside the door. Then someone shouted my name. The voice sounded familiar, but I couldn't quite place it. It might be Seb or one of his team, looking for Liam. Whoever it was, I didn't like what was going on, and I didn't want Liam to be hurt any more than he already had been. Reluctantly, I picked up the gun from the nightstand and left Liam unconscious on the bed. I walked out of the bedroom, shutting the door behind me.

In the dimly lit hall, I checked out the gun. It was very small, and since it was a revolver, it would be simple to handle if I needed it— although my plan was not to need it.

The intruder shouted again. "Fin Fleming, get out here. I know you're home. Your car's in the driveway. You can't hide from me."

I stepped into the front room. "Justin. What brings you here?" The gun was down by my side, hidden by the fabric of my baggy shorts.

Justin had a gun of his own. He raised it and pointed it toward me. "I didn't want it to come to this. I tried. I really tried. If you had agreed to have a relationship with me, we could have been married. A year or two together, then an amicable divorce. I'd have taken my share of your money and been out of your hair. But no. You had to be stubborn. Now it's too late." His hands were shaking. "Shut your eyes," he said.

I raised my own gun and aimed it at Justin. The red dot shone across his mid-section, but my own hands were shaking so badly it danced all over his torso. "It doesn't have to be like this. Newton already knows you've been embezzling, but I'll talk to him. We can work something out." While I was talking, Chico walked in through the open front door and strolled casually across the room.

Justin scoffed at me. "Do you really think I'm that stupid? I know you figured out I've been stealing from Fleming Environmental. Even if you'd let it slide, do you really think I'm stupid enough to believe Newton would? And put that stupid gun down. You don't even know how to hold it right. For one thing, you should be using both hands."

"Like this?" I said, wrapping my left hand around and under my right on the butt of the gun. The red dot stopped dancing quite as much as it had been.

"Shut your eyes," he growled again. "I can't shoot you if you're staring at me. I really did care about you. This hurts me as much as it hurts you."

"I don't think that's true, Justin," I said.

I saw his finger begin to tighten on the trigger, and I did the same. Just before the guns went off, Chico pecked Justin's big toe, vulnerable in his flip flops. Justin jumped in surprise and his shot went wild.

Mine didn't.

Both of us stared at the spreading red stain on the front of Justin's t-shirt. He looked at me in disbelief. "You shot me," he said. His gun clattered to the floor.

The sound of sirens in the distance came clearly over Chico's distressed crowing. Within a minute, Dane and Roland raced into my home, guns drawn. "Down on the floor," Dane said.

I put my gun down, pushed it toward Roland, and knelt on the cold tiles with my hands in the air. Justin simply collapsed. Roland picked up the guns with plastic evidence bags, marked them, and put both bags in his ever present forensics case.

The sound of squealing tires set Chico to crowing again. Doc and Stewie hurried through the front door. Chico made a run for it out the back patio sliders.

"Where's Liam?" Doc asked as soon as she'd cleared the threshold.

"Bedroom. How did you know?" I said.

Stewie pointed Doc toward the bedroom. "Newton called us. Said to get here fast, but he didn't tell us anything else. What's going on?"

Doc had her medical bag in her hand as she ran toward my bedroom, but she was back out within a minute. "Liam's in bad shape, but his injuries will keep until I stabilize this guy. It looks like he needs immediate attention," she said, kneeling beside Justin. She went to work immediately.

Dane walked across the room and held out a hand to help me to my feet. "I thought I told you to spend your nights at Newton's," he said.

I was saved from answering by the arrival of the EMT crew. They shunted Doc aside and took over working on Justin. Doc went back to the bedroom to take care of Liam.

Within a few minutes, the EMT's had stabilized Justin enough that they felt he could travel safely. They strapped him to a gurney and pushed it outside.

Doc came out of the bedroom. "Liam needs to go to the hospital too," she said. "Or I can take him to RIO. The infirmary there has everything I think I'll need."

Dane turned toward me. "What was Liam's part in this?"

"Nothing," I said. "I swear. I found him by my backdoor, all beat up. I'd just gotten him to the bedroom when Justin arrived. Liam was unconscious through the whole thing."

"Okay" he said to Doc. "You can take him to RIO." Then he turned back to me. "Where'd you get the gun?" he asked.

"Liam's pocket. I didn't mean to shoot anyone, honest. When Justin broke in, I thought it was Seb. If I'd known it was Justin, I'd have left the gun in the bedroom."

"Good thing you didn't know then. Luckily Genevra got nervous about what went down earlier at Fleming Environmental and talked to me about it. She said she thought Justin had been planning to kill you when she found you two in the sub-basement at FEI. I went to Newton's to warn you, and when you weren't there, I came straight here."

"Is Newton okay?" I asked.

"He wasn't in his condo. But Maddy's safe at the police station with Oliver. You can join them in a few minutes, just as soon as Roland and I finish up here."

Chapter 38
Confession

My phone rang early the next morning. Dane was calling to let me know that Justin had confessed to killing Cara and to embezzling money from Newton and from Fleming Environmental Investments.

"Why was he stealing money," I asked. "He comes from a wealthy family."

Dane sighed. "Yes, apparently, he does. But his family believes each generation should make it on their own. They set him up with a trust fund to get him started when he graduated from college, with the understanding that would be all he could expect. But he must not have believed it, because he blew through the money pretty fast. Newton took pity on him and offered him a job, but Justin was jealous of your family money."

He cleared his throat. "His plan was to get you to marry him, and then, in a few years, to ask for a divorce. He'd ask for half your trust fund in the settlement, which I understand would be a substantial sum. Lucky you didn't fall for his flattery. He's not a nice man."

I thought about how lucky I truly was. If I had fallen for Justin, who's to say he'd have been happy with half my trust fund. He might have decided he wanted it all.

Dane continued. "He also admitted to whacking Benjamin with that log during the storm. He thought you were in love with Benjamin, so he needed to get him out of the way. Justin thought without Benjamin around, he'd have a clear field with you. After he hit him, he thought Benjamin was dead, or that he soon would be. He didn't count on you finding him and having the skills to take care of his injuries."

Poor Benjamin. He hadn't deserved to be attacked and left for dead. And besides, I realized, Benjamin hadn't ever really been Justin's competition.

Liam was.

Always had been.

I chewed on the story for a minute. If I hadn't been seeing Benjamin—and hung up on Liam—I might actually have gotten involved with Justin. Who could know—I might have ended up like Cara or Benjamin if Justin decided later that I was getting between him and his true love—money.

I shuddered before I asked my next question. "But why did he kill Cara? I didn't even realize they knew each other."

"They didn't," Dane said. "Justin knew he wasn't getting anywhere with you, although that didn't mean he'd given up trying. But he'd always had an alternate plan—to take over from Newton at Fleming Environmental. From what I understand, it's practically a money printing machine."

"It is, but only because Newton's a genius at knowing what to invest in. There's nobody else like him," I said.

"That's probably true," he replied. "But anyway, Justin was jealous of Oliver because your father obviously cared about him. When Justin saw Newton giving Oliver all the important assignments he'd once have had, he knew he needed to find a way to get Oliver out of Fleming Environmental before it was too late. Oliver was in the office when he told Cara she could stay on his boat in the RIO marina if she kept a low profile, and Justin overheard the conversation. Justin thought if he killed Cara on Oliver's boat, we'd arrest Oliver without looking for other suspects. He thought his twisted idea would have been an open and shut case."

A chill ran up my spine. "He didn't realize how well you know Oliver. You knew all along he couldn't have done it."

Dane was quiet for a few seconds, and I pictured him nodding in that thoughtful way he had. "That's true. And the DNA match to the rain gear cinched it. That and the Fleming Environmental employee card you found, which we confirmed was his. By the way, if you'd given that to me sooner this investigation would have gone a lot faster."

He frowned at me before he continued. "When Justin knew we had placed him inside RIO at the time Benjamin was attacked and Cara was murdered, he knew he was caught. He figured it would go better for him if he confessed. It probably will. His parents are sending down an expensive lawyer to help him through this mess."

"But it won't help, will it?" I asked. "He'll be found guilty. I mean, he confessed, right."

"Right," said Dane. "And now, why don't you come down to the police station. Oliver is being discharged, and Maddy is here too. Make it a family thing."

"Be right there," I said.

Chapter 39
Maddy's Place

We managed to get Oliver released from jail with a minimum of paperwork. Since Dane had strongly suspected Oliver was innocent right from the start, he'd never actually processed any arrest forms. Essentially, Oliver had been a guest at the jail. No wonder they were lax about visitors. And now Oliver, Maddy, and I were holed up in her condo.

"I'm grateful for you two, "she said. "I'm lucky to have been blessed with such a wonderful family."

"We're lucky too," I said. "I just wish we knew where Newton went off to."

She bit her lip. "I think it's my fault he's gone," she said. "I told him it was time we divorced again, since we only got married to stream-line the adoption of our wonderful son. But the adoption's been settled for a long time. There's no reason to keep up the pretense."

Oliver looked shocked. "But you two get along so well. You're a great team."

"We are a great team," she said. "We just shouldn't be a married team. Newton did the same thing the first time we divorced. He left for months. Years actually." She looked at me. "It started when you were not quite three years old. When I told him Ray and I were going to get married, he left again. I only saw him at board of director's meetings. I know you never saw him at all."

"Where does he go when he leaves?" I asked.

"I don't know. He never says." She wiped a few tears from her eyes. "But this last year, I was working on the project at Woods Hole only so he and I wouldn't have to be together. That first project ended recently, and they'd offered me an extension. But I was also considering committing to a two-year research project in Antarctica so Newton and I wouldn't be in the same place. Then I realized it wasn't fair to you two. Leaving RIO in your hands on top of everything else you have going on. Your own careers. Your own lives. I'm sorry. I'll be back at my desk full time Monday morning."

I was relieved to hear that, because although I didn't mind managing RIO, especially now that I had Genevra to help out, administrative work was really not my favorite thing to do. But I didn't want to let on to Maddy that her absence had been a burden, since she'd clearly needed to be away.

"We don't mind taking care of RIO while you're off doing things that make you happy," I said. "Do we, Oliver?"

"Nope. If you'd rather be in Antarctica, it's fine with me," he said. "And we'll take care of everything here. No problem."

She smiled. "You're such great kids. But come Monday, I'll be exactly where I want to be, and that's at RIO."

I was about to say more when my phone rang. The caller ID showed Stewie's number. I answered on speaker.

"You'd better get down to the dive shop right away, Fin. You need to take care of this." He sounded like something big was going on.

"Take care of what?" I asked. "What's wrong?"

"Nothing's wrong. You just need to get down here as fast as you can." He disconnected the call.

Chapter 40
The Submarine Returns

W e piled into my Prius for the short drive to RIO. As we walked along the crushed shell paths that meandered across the newly reseeded rear lawn, I caught sight of the blue submarine tied up to our dock, next to the *Tranquility*. I ran the rest of the way to where Stewie, Benjamin, Dane, and Doc were all standing on the shore, staring at it.

"What's going on? Is Lauren in there?" I asked, panting a little from the run.

"No," said Dane. "There's a young man in there. He won't come out. He says his instructions are to talk only to you."

I looked at the sub and recognized Davy Jones in the pilot's seat. He waved when he saw me recognize him.

Maddy and Oliver had caught up to us by now. "Don't go over there," said Maddy. "It could be a trick of some sort."

"Wow" said Oliver. "That thing is crazy amazing. You got to pilot it?" He sounded awestruck and slightly jealous.

"I did. And that's Davy Jones, the pilot. He taught me how to operate it. He won't hurt me." I started walking down the dock.

"I'm going with you," Dane said. "You don't know this guy well enough to be totally sure he won't hurt you." He turned to the group huddled on shore, walking half backwards so he could see them and still keep up with me. "The rest of you stay there. I'll let you know when it's safe to come nearer."

As soon as I reached the sub, Davy opened the hatch and climbed out. He handed me an envelope with my name on it and what looked like a set of legal papers. As soon as I had the papers in hand, a small white Zodiac came racing toward us from where it had been anchored at the edge of our cove. The boat pulled up to the dock in a shower of spray. Dane pulled me down to the dock and used his body to try to shield me from what he clearly expected to be an attack of some sort.

Instead, Davy jumped aboard the Zodiac, and the boat rocketed off.

Just like that, he was gone.

"I don't like that quick disappearing act. Let's get you away from the sub as fast as we can," said Dane. "I still think it could be booby trapped."

"I don't think so," I said. "Look at this." I held out the blue-covered legal document, which was a transfer of title to the submarine from Golden Kelp Incorporated to me.

"I still don't like it," he said. "Let's get everyone inside until I can have someone check out the sub. And if you wouldn't mind, please don't open the envelope, or let anyone handle it until my team has a chance to look it over. You never know." He held out his hand. "In fact, why don't you let me hold on to it. I'll wait out here for my team."

I led Stewie, Benjamin, Doc, Maddy, and Oliver to the infirmary. With no outside windows, it was the safest place in the RIO building. Liam was asleep in one of the cubicles, recuperating from his injuries. We stayed very quiet for over an hour until Dane finally came in, bearing the letter.

"Sorry for the drill. It's perfectly safe. Just a letter." He handed it to me. "I'm sorry. I couldn't help but see what it said while we were dusting it for prints and hazardous substances. It's an amazing read."

I silently read the letter all the way through. Dane was right. It was amazing.

When I lowered the pages, Oliver said, "Well?"

"Apparently, I now own a multi-million dollar submarine. And Chaun will be heartbroken to realize they knew about the optical transmitter all along. In fact, in the letter Seb says "...giving you the submarine, free and clear of all encumbrances. Title transfer includes the modifications you made to the sub the day you test drove it."

"Is it bugged? Sabotaged?" Maddy asked.

"The team is checking it out, along with some experts from the Coast Guard. So far, it doesn't look like there's anything wrong with it." Dane made a face. "I don't understand why he'd give away such an expensive piece of equipment, especially one that was perfect for his drug operation."

"I do," said Liam, who had awakened and was now sitting up on the edge of his hospital bed. "This way he creates an obligation from Fin to him. And he can't use the sub to deliver drugs anymore, because we'll always be on the lookout for it. He won't stop selling drugs, but he'll take a break until he finds another method that works."

"Hey, you're awake. How do you feel?" I asked. The joy in my voice was unmistakable, and I noticed Benjamin wince at my words.

Liam smiled at me. "I feel like I was beaten by thugs, wrapped in chains, and dropped off a mega-yacht. Like I slammed into the yacht on the way down, which is when I broke my leg, and once I was in the water, like I had to dislocate my own shoulder to get out of the chains. I believe I'm missing at least one tooth from the beating. I swam to shore with a broken leg and basically limped and crawled a couple of miles to my girlfriend's house so I could keep her safe. I was afraid the bad guys would come after her next." He smiled again. "But she saved me. At least twice, I believe."

"Chico helped," I said with a laugh.

"Who's Chico?" almost everyone present said.

"The rooster who lives next door," I said. "He came over to get a treat and he pecked Justin on his big toe. Startled him enough to spoil his aim. This story might have had a completely different ending without Chico." I vowed to myself never again to be annoyed at Chico, no matter what time of the day or night he came looking for a handout.

"Thank goodness for Chico," Maddy said. "I might have to bring him a few treats myself." Everyone started cheering, "Hooray for Chico."

Dane broke in, interrupting our high spirits. "In some other news, the *Golden Kelp* has sailed away. I got the word just as we were finishing checking out the letter."

"They'll be back," said Liam. "You can count on it. They just won't be as easy to spot when they return."

"Speaking of easy to spot, did I do something to give your real identity away when I saw you on the yacht? I tried to play it cool, but I was surprised to see you there."

"You were great. Nobody would have guessed we knew each other. I didn't realize Lauren was on board until later. She spotted me that same day after you left, and she told Seb who I am. He put me in the brig until after you came back from your jaunt in the submarine the next day. I was terrified they planned to hurt you to get back at me."

Oliver looked thoughtful for a moment. "I think I understand what's been going on."

Liam interrupted him, "If you have, you should keep the information to yourself."

Oliver continued anyway. "You're not just who we think you are, are you?"

Liam interrupted again. "Is anybody? Can we ever really know someone else?"

Undaunted, Oliver tried again. "When I was in jail, I spent a lot of time playing Oh! Possum, the video game you wrote. And I had to do a lot of research to figure out where in the world he was. Right after the release date of each level, I noticed a lot of drug activity in the same locations…"

Liam interrupted for a third time. "Oliver, I am begging you—for both our sakes—to keep quiet about whatever you think you've figured out. Please."

Just then, Newton strolled in through the main door of the infirmary, looking tanned and healthy, his silver hair gleaming in the overhead lights. "Here's where you all are," he said. "I wondered where you'd got to." He looked at Oliver. "And Liam's right. Idle speculations could prove dangerous to certain people in this room."

Liam looked uncomfortable. "If you could keep all that speculation to yourself, Mate, it would help me—and Newton—a lot. Could save all our lives someday."

"Got it. My lips are sealed," Oliver said, making the traditional locking his lips and throwing away the key gesture.

I looked from Newton to Liam and back, trying to connect the dots. Then I thought better of it. Both Newton and Liam had said we were better off leaving these particular dots unconnected. "Now that we're all caught up, I need to donate the sub to RIO. No way I need a personal sub, but RIO could sure use it. Benjamin, can you help me with the paperwork?"

There was no response, and I realized Benjamin had quietly left the room at some point.

Chapter 41
Fair Weather

I t was a week later, a beautiful Saturday morning, and I was sitting on the bow of the *Tranquility*, my back against the glass windows of the pilot house, enjoying the early morning sunshine and the gentle waves in RIO's sheltered cove. I was still recovering from the storm and its emotional aftermath. I needed the break.

I heard footsteps approaching along the rebuilt dock, and I turned to see Benjamin Brooks headed my way. I jumped to my feet and hopped off my boat onto the wooden pier to greet him. "Morning."

"Good morning, Fin," he said. "I just came from talking with Maddy. I wanted to tell you personally that I've resigned."

"Oh, no. But why are you leaving?" I asked. "And what will you do if you're not working at RIO?"

"I think you know the why," he replied. "And as for the what—I've decided to join up with Chaun. We're starting a new company together, and I'm very excited about it. It's all still pretty hush hush, but we'll be making an announcement soon. You'll be one of the first to know when we're ready." He looked at the sky and bit his lip. "But anyway, today's my last day here."

"I'm sorry you're leaving, but at least you'll still be around. We'll still see each other, maybe dive together, right?'

"Sure thing," he said. "Whatever you want." He didn't sound too happy about any future diving with me. He touched my cheek before giving a little half wave and walking away. He didn't look back.

I was torn between anguish at his departure from my day-to-day life and relief that he was making his leaving easier for me.

As Benjamin walked along the newly refurbished crushed shell path toward the parking lot, RIO's back door slammed open. Liam limped out, with his broken leg in a cast. He was using crutches and Genevra walked beside him, helping to keep him steady. They made their way down the shell path to the dock. The layers of shells were unstable, so he was being super careful and moving slowly. It seemed to take them forever to cross the distance. As they approached, I catalogued the fading bruises on his face, and I knew his whole body was in a similar condition. It had to hurt to move, but there was determination in his face.

I grabbed a folding chair from the cabin and stepped up on the *Tranquility*'s gunwales to unfold it and put it on the dock for him. When he had reached my slip, he sat down on the chair and handed me his crutches.

Genevra stepped down onto the *Tranquility* and sat sideways on the bench, putting both Liam and me in her field of view. "When can we start my dive lessons?" she asked. "Can we dive today?"

"Nope. You need to get some classroom instruction and some pool time before I can take you into open water," I said. "But if you want, we can start the classroom lessons today. I'll give you your assignment and we can squeeze in the lecture part over lunch."

"Told you so," said Liam with a grin.

She looked at him and shrugged. "Whatever." Then she transferred her gaze to me. "Sounds perfect. Thanks for making the time."

Killer Storm

The sound of an approaching boat broke the early morning stillness. I looked up to see Oliver's boat backing into the slip next to mine. His boat had been in the boatyard for repairs and refurbishment, and the fresh white paint practically glowed in the sunshine. Oliver was at the helm, and Newton stood beside him.

Genevra helped Liam out of his chair and retrieved his crutches while I walked over to catch the line Oliver threw me. I caught it easily and wrapped it around the cleat at the end of his slip, coiling the excess line in a neat circle while he dropped a few fenders over the sides and off the bow.

"Permission to come aboard, Captain." I said.

He grinned at me. "Welcome aboard. Anytime. I can't wait for you to see what I've done."

Newton held out his hand to steady me as I stepped down to the boat's deck. Genevra had brought Liam's folding chair along, and she set it up and helped him sit down since the combination of his full leg cast and the rocking of the boat would have made it too hard for him to maneuver onto the boat's deck. Once he was safely settled, Newton offered Genevra his hand.

Genevra and I looked around while Oliver beamed with excitement. His boat was an older forty-five-foot wooden boat, but he had upgraded everything about it to the latest and greatest. The instrumentation and electronics were top-shelf, state-of-the-art models. The cabin was comfy and cozy. The engines had been over-hauled and purred like twin kittens. He'd outfitted the deck area with enough tank racks for twenty-four tanks, and there was a new stainless steel ladder folded up over the transom.

Obligingly, we oohed and aahed over everything he showed us. He really had done a great job of upgrading and retrofitting. The boat seemed ready for anything.

When he'd showed Genevra and me everything—Liam had stayed seated and declined the tour—Oliver stood in the middle of the deck. "But I can't wait to show you the best part," he said. "Follow me."

Liam stood up and hobbled along the slip while Genevra and I followed Oliver along the length of the boat to the stern and stepped down onto the platform.

"Tada" Oliver said, waving his arms like a game show hostess at the boat's name, freshly painted on the transom.

'*Flemingo*' it said.

Genevra put her hand to her mouth. "Oh, no! They made a mistake. It's spelled with an a, not an…"

"No, it's not wrong. It's bloody brilliant." I started laughing.

I'd gotten the joke right away.

Flemingo.

For Fleming.

My name. Newton's name. Now Oliver's name as well.

Within a few seconds, they saw the joke, and Genevra and Liam both joined in the laughter.

I thought about how grateful I was we'd all survived the storm. It was wonderful to be with friends and family.

Acknowledgments

So many people help me with my books that it's hard to remember everyone.

C. Michele Dorsey, my partner in crime and fellow traveler on the self-publishing journey, thank you.

Mary Beth Gale, your detailed critiques and analysis of my drafts make each book better than it otherwise would have been.

Kate Hohl, my North Star, reminding me always why I do this. World's best cheerleader, for sure.

Andrea Clark, I'm still in awe of your talent just as much as I was the first day we met at Yale Writer's Workshop. Jeez, you are good.

Stephanie Scott-Snyder, your writing scares the crap out of me, both because it's scary good and because you are sooo good at writing creepy bad guys.

Molly, thanks for the pokes. I'd be frozen to my chair without you.

And jack, my world. Thank you.

About the Author

Sharon Ward is an avid scuba diver. She was a PADI certified divemaster and has hundreds of dives under her weight belt. Wanting to share the joy and wonder of the underwater world, she wrote In Deep.

She lives on the south coast of Massachusetts with her husband, Jack, and Molly, their long-haired miniature dachshund. Guess who's in charge?

Killer Storm is the fourth book in the Fin Fleming Sea Adventure Series. Hidden Depths is up next.

Also by Sharon Ward

In Deep

Sunken Death

Dark Tide

Killer Storm

Hidden Depths

Or see the entire series Fin Fleming series at this link.

If you enjoyed Killer Storm, you can continue reading about the adventures of Fin and the gang by following the links above.

Also, nothing helps an author more than a positive review, so please give Killer Storm (and me!) a boost by leaving a review at the link above.

And if you'd like to subscribe to my totally random and very rarely published newsletter, you can sign up here.

Writing as S L Ward

Smart Self-Publishing Strategies: A Roadmap for Beginners

CPSIA information can be obtained
at www.ICGtesting.com
Printed in the USA
LVHW040953020723
751361LV00004B/72